Chasing THE Wind

Chasing THE *Wind*

PATRICIA H. RUSHFORD

Guideposts
New York, New York

www.guideposts.com
(800) 932-2145
Guideposts Books & Inspirational Media

Cover design and illustration by Lookout Design, Inc.
Interior design by Lorie Pagnozzi
Typeset by Aptara

Printed and bound in the United States of America
10 9 8 7 6 5 4 3 2 1

To my husband, Ron, and all the years and
tears and joy we've shared together.

Acknowledgments

Thanks to my writer friends for their brainstorming help as well as their constant support. And thank you for the help and support of my fellow Guideposts authors and editors.

Chapter One

OUCH!"

Anabelle Scott glanced over at her friend and quilting buddy, Genna, who stuck her thumb in her mouth. "Are you okay?"

Genevieve Hamilton pulled her thumb out and examined it. "I'm fine. Just another pinprick."

"I'm sorry."

Genna reached into her sewing box for a bandage. "What's a quilt without a little bloodstain?"

Anabelle chuckled and went back to pinning her three quilt layers—the top, batting and back—together. Once she'd finished the pinning, she would do a meandering freestyle stitch on her sewing machine to quilt the layers together. They were working in Anabelle's upstairs studio on charity quilts with two other women: her eldest daughter, Ainslee, and Pricilla Nordberg, their friend and a longtime quilter.

The Deerford Quilting Guild, one of the best guilds in Illinois, donated hundreds of quilts yearly to various service organizations in Bureau County and to soldiers overseas. They had recently received a truckload of fabrics from one of the major fabric companies, many of them designed for children.

This weekend, the women were focusing their efforts on quilts for abused children. Anabelle loved working on the project. Not only did she adore kids, but she also did whatever she could to protect them.

The women had been at it all weekend, stopping only to eat, sleep and go to church. Their efforts had produced four completed quilts, six that needed more work, and forty pre-packed kits to distribute at the guild's monthly meeting.

The kits contained enough material to make various sized quilts. Members of the quilt guild picked up the kits with a promise to return them within six months. Once they finished the top and back, Anabelle or one of the other women machine-sewed various patterns on the quilt. Some of the more traditional quilters sewed their patterns by hand.

Anabelle preferred stitching freehand on her Pfaff Creative Vision. She'd given up hand quilting several years before when she'd developed arthritic pain in her right hand and wrist.

Straightening, Anabelle rubbed her back. "Much as I hate to quit, I think we'd better call it a day."

Genna looked up at the wall clock and sighed. "You're right. I'd best head home. The good doctor will be wanting dinner soon."

"You tell Drew he needs to be patient."

"Ha. He doesn't know the meaning of the word." She sobered. "If he isn't careful he just might *become* a patient."

"What do you mean?" Anabelle frowned. "Is he sick?" Dr. Drew Hamilton worked at Hope Haven as a general surgeon. Anabelle had a special fondness for Doctor Drew. Not only did she like working with him, twelve years ago he'd saved her daughter Kirstie's life. And for that she would be eternally grateful.

"Not sick exactly." Genna went on. "He's been antsy lately and grumpy. I told him he needed to go in for a checkup, but you know doctors—"

"Make the worst patients." Anabelle completed the sentence and added, "Next to nurses." Being a nurse herself, she spoke from experience. "He looked fine when I saw him on Friday."

Genna placed her hand on Anabelle's arm. "Do me a favor and keep an eye on him tomorrow, okay? I'm probably just imagining things, but he's got me worried."

"I will. Maybe I can urge him to see someone."

"Good luck with that." Genna boxed up her sewing accessories and put them into her wheeled craft bag along with her sewing machine. "Want to meet again next Saturday?"

"Sounds good. I'd love to get a few more kits put together before the August meeting. And this coming weekend will be our last chance."

"How about you Pricilla?" Anabelle looked her way.

"I'll try. With school starting, I have my hands full." Pricilla had six children, four still in school. She also had a six-month-old baby girl, who right this minute lay snuggled in Ainslee's arms cooing and smiling at her.

Pricilla often brought the baby, which no one minded at all. Olivia rarely cried or demanded attention. But then with four women around, she probably had more attention than she wanted.

"Keep me in the loop." Pricilla took the baby from Ainslee and set her in her carrier. "I'll come when I can." She picked up one of the kits and stuffed it in the diaper bag. "I might as well take one now in case I have a little downtime."

"Good idea." Genna grabbed a couple of the kits as well.

Pricilla and Genna gave and received hugs, said their good-byes and left.

"How about you, sweetheart?" Anabelle stepped up behind Ainslee, shifted aside her thick mane of mahogany hair, and massaged her slender shoulders. "Do you want to help us out again next week?" Ainslee had been unusually quiet that afternoon.

Ainslee squeezed her mother's hand and continued cleaning up her sewing area. "I don't know. Quilting is a lot harder than I thought. Maybe I should just stick to knitting."

Anabelle laughed. "Knitting wasn't all that easy at first either, remember? You'll get the hang of it."

"Maybe." She heaved a great sigh that seemed to come from the soles of her feet.

"What's going on?"

Ainslee stood up and gave her mother a hug. "I'm fine, Mother. I would like to learn more about quilting. It's just that when I watch you, Genna and Pricilla doing it, I feel like such a dud."

"We all started out as beginners." Anabelle began straightening up the room. "Would you like to have dinner here with your dad and me? You could call Doug and have him join us."

"Thanks, but not tonight. Doug is picking me up and then we're meeting some friends at the new Thai restaurant." She kissed Anabelle's cheek. "See you later."

"Are you leaving right now?"

"Not unless Doug's here. I'm going to say good-bye to Pop."

Anabelle watched the closing door and heaved a heavy sigh of her own. Even though her daughter was grown and married, she couldn't help but be concerned. She felt certain some of Ainslee's moodiness came with the monthly disappointment of not being pregnant.

Anabelle knew what it felt like to try for years to have a child. Her first one, Evan, hadn't come along until she was thirty. Apparently Ainslee had inherited the same genetic makeup. Since Ainslee was only twenty-nine, maybe there was still hope. Anabelle would like nothing better than to have a grandchild. Watching Ainslee interact with Olivia today just about broke her heart.

With the quilters gone, the room seemed sad and forlorn—as though it already missed their creative energy. Anabelle smiled. "They'll be back and so will I." She picked up a basket of quilting kits and set it in the storeroom.

Quilting as much as she did, she was thankful for her studio. After Evan and Ainslee moved out, her husband surprised and delighted her by tearing down the wall between their two bedrooms and making one large room. Cameron had dubbed it *Annie's Studio* and had made a wooden sign for the door.

Cupboards and shelves lined one wall, and it was there she kept her fabrics. More bulky things like batting and supplies went into the roomy storage closet. She had a beautiful oak sewing cabinet plus an oversized table for sandwiching quilt layers. Last Christmas, Cameron and the kids had gone together and bought her a computerized longarm quilter, which allowed her to create king- and queen-sized quilts.

If things were a mess, she could close the door. And things often got messy as a nurse on call 24–7.

While she worked at putting things away and picking up loose threads, she prayed for Dr. Hamilton. "Lord, please keep that precious man safe and well." Genna's concern for her husband worried Anabelle. She knew her friend wouldn't voice her concern if the situation weren't serious. She also knew Dr. Hamilton's propensity for forging ahead.

Anabelle turned down the air conditioner, a godsend with the humid and hot weather they'd been having. She closed the door to her studio and paused when she heard voices coming from Kirstie's room. Or what used to be Kirstie's room before her baby girl moved into her own apartment this summer. Anabelle had turned it into a guestroom, but a lot of Kirstie's things remained. Most of her old toys and stuffed animals along with clothes she hadn't needed for summer were stored in the closet or in the attic.

"We probably should get Pop to carry it down for us." Ainslee's voice drifted into the hallway.

"Don't be silly, Ains." That was definitely Kirstie.

Anabelle tapped on the door before pushing it open. "It's just me."

Kirstie and Ainslee held a supersized plastic bin between them. From what Anabelle could see through the plastic it held Kirstie's winter clothes. Her daughter had that impish caught-with-her-hand-in-the-cookie-jar look.

Not that she was doing anything wrong. The guilt was a residual of Anabelle's overprotectiveness. She had not wanted Kirstie to move out. Now Kirstie felt like she had to walk on eggshells. Anabelle knew perfectly well that Kirstie was hoping to have the container in her car and hidden from sight before her mother saw what was happening.

"Hello, Mother." Kirstie gave her an oversized grin, set the container down, and gave Anabelle a hug. "What's up?"

"I was going to ask you the same thing."

"I'm picking up my fall and winter stuff. School starts soon, and I need to see what has to be pitched and what I need to buy."

Ainslee waved a hand in her sister's direction. "I told her she needs to scrap all of her old clothes and start fresh."

"Yeah, like I can afford to do that." Kirstie rolled her eyes. "I don't have the mucho bucks like you and Doug have. Besides, I have student loans to pay off."

Kirstie had gotten her BA and her teaching certificate mostly on grants and scholarships; but with tuition increases, they'd had to go with a loan the last two years. Anabelle regretted that. She'd hoped their savings would have covered all three children, but the economy had left them short.

"Come on, Ains." Kirstie bent to pick up her end of the bin. "We can make it. No need to bother Pop. He's still into the game."

"Kirstie, you shouldn't be . . ." Anabelle's gaze took in her beautiful daughter's wavy black hair and striking blue eyes, slender figure, white top and shorts, and her prosthetic leg.

"Mother, I'm fine." She spoke with the confidence and authority one would use to speak to a student. Where Kirstie's independence was concerned, Anabelle still had a lot to learn.

"I appreciate your wanting to do this yourself, sweetheart, but your leg . . ."

Kirstie's right leg had been badly damaged in a biking accident, and Dr. Hamilton had been forced to amputate. In the beginning, Kirstie had made it a point to keep her leg covered, especially at school. Some classmates had been cruel at first, but over the years her daughter learned to ignore the teasing.

She had recently been fitted with a new top-of-the-line prosthesis with a curved foot that allowed her to have more movement—to run and participate in sports.

"My leg works just fine." Kirstie bounced up and down to illustrate. "I can handle this."

Anabelle held her breath. As much as she wanted to halt the demonstration, she wouldn't. She'd promised to stop interfering. Sometimes, probably because she was a professional caregiver, the line between caring and being overbearing blurred.

"Kirstie's right, Mother," Ainlsee said. "You should have seen her run into the house and up the stairs."

"All right." Anabelle released a long sigh and moved out of the way. "But if you fall down the stairs and break your neck, don't come running to me."

"That's a really dumb saying." Kirstie threw her mother an I-love-you-anyway look.

"It's a mom thing, smarty. I'll have you know mothers have been saying that for generations."

Both girls laughed. Anabelle, pretending to be hurt, followed them down the stairs.

Kirstie reached the landing and grinned back at her mother like a child who'd accomplished a major goal. "I told you I could make it."

Anabelle grinned. "Yes, you did." Pride almost overrode her concerns.

"Well, what do we have here?" Cameron Scott emerged from the den. "Were you girls planning on leaving without saying hello to your dear old dad?"

"Hi, Pop." Kirstie reached up and gave him a one-armed hug "Of course not. We were just trying to get this thing to the car before Mother Dear caught us. I still think she has eyes in the back of her head."

Anabelle chuckled. "It's a radar, actually. Besides, I heard you two as I was coming out of the studio."

Ainslee hugged her dad as well.

The doorbell rang the same time as it opened. "Wow, a welcome party for me?"

Ainslee turned from her father and embraced the man of her dreams and husband of seven years, Doug Giffen. The family had liked Doug from the moment they met him, when he'd come to pick up Ainslee for their first date. Doug was one of those steady, quiet men who stayed the course. He'd studied engineering and architecture and now had his own firm.

When everyone had hugged everyone else, Doug said, "Are you ready to go, honey? We have reservations in five minutes."

"I am. Just as soon as I help Kirstie carry this bin to her car."

"Here, let me take it." Doug hefted it up on his shoulder and led the way. Anabelle watched all of this with bittersweet thoughts. Her children were all adults now—even her baby. She had definitely entered the empty-nest years so many of her friends talked about. Anabelle had sworn it wouldn't affect her since she was involved in so many activities. Now she was beginning to understand what they meant.

Cameron slid an arm around her waist as if he were having similar thoughts. They walked out to the cars and waved to Doug and Ainslee as they drove off.

"See you later, guys." Kirstie opened the door to her well-used Honda.

"Wait a second, Kirstie." Anabelle took a step forward. "You're not leaving already, are you? You just got here. Don't you want to stay for dinner?"

"Sorry," Kirstie waved and maneuvered herself into the car then closed the door and stuck her head out the window. "I have a date."

Just like that she was gone, leaving her parents to wonder the age-old questions: who, what, where, when and why?

Cameron chuckled. "You want to follow her?" He seemed to be as curious as she was.

Anabelle sighed. "No. Kirstie already thinks I'm overprotective." She leaned up against him. "She's all grown up."

"That she is, lass," he said, using his pet name for her. "That she is."

Chapter Two

EELING A BIT FORLORN, ANABELLE HEADED back to the house and into the welcome coolness. Even those few minutes in the Illinois sun and humidity had heated her to the core. She walked through the tiled entry and into the kitchen/dining area, turning her attention toward making dinner for her one and only love. Forty-five years ago, she and Cameron had met in high school, fallen in love, and never looked back.

"Guess it's just the two of us for dinner tonight." Anabelle sighed.

"Ah, sure it is, me lovely lass. I cannot think of anyone I'd rather be with." He used his mock Scottish burr when he wanted to elicit a smile from her, sounding every bit as Scottish as his Highland ancestors. "Mulligan stew, am I right? I've been smellin' that ambrosia all afternoon."

"You are." She'd learned long ago that a Crock-Pot was a busy woman's best friend. This morning she'd taken the lamb roast out of the freezer and placed it in the slow cooker with spices, veggies and broth. She appreciated knowing dinner would be on time and as delicious as if she'd spent the entire day in the kitchen. Teasing, she added, "What I'd like to know is why you don't have the rest of dinner ready for me." She leaned back against him.

"I've been helping the Cubs win another ball game. Cheering them on, you know."

She chuckled. Anabelle didn't mind being responsible for dinner. In fact she loved cooking as much as she did quilting and nursing. "As soon as I pop the biscuits into the oven and put the salad together we can eat." Anabelle turned, placed her hands on either side of his handsome face and gave him a loud smooch on the lips. His mustache tickled, but she liked it just the same. At sixty-four, Cameron could still turn the ladies' heads.

She wasn't so bad either, if she said so herself. Anabelle had maintained her weight around 125 pounds, except during her three pregnancies. She had a few more worry lines, and her beautiful mop of chestnut hair had turned to salt and red-pepper— mostly salt. For sixty-two, that wasn't bad at all. However too many helpings of her delicious Mulligan stew and she could develop a spread in no time.

After dinner, Anabelle and Cameron played Scrabble while they watched a Miss Marple Mystery on PBS. Cameron won as usual but only because he used the dictionary to find words.

Just before the news came on at ten, Anabelle started getting ready for bed. Minutes later, she padded back out to the living room and snuggled down next to her husband. He wrapped his arm around her and said, "According to our weather girl, it looks like we're in for a series of storms."

"*Hmm.* I was hoping for a bit more summer weather."

He smiled and kissed her forehead. "Oh, we'll still have a bit of summer, just more rain, thunderstorms and high humidity."

A heavy rain started just after midnight waking Anabelle from a sound sleep. As she listened to the drops beating on the awning just outside their bedroom, Anabelle wondered if her flowers would be damaged; wondered if it would be raining tomorrow morning when she left for work; wondered how Dr. Hamilton was feeling and if Jeanine Parsons, a friend from church, had had her twins yet. That got her thinking about Ainslee and her disappointment about not having a baby and Kirstie, who'd had a date.

Kirstie had recently moved into her first apartment, a converted brick house on the corner of Oak Avenue and Kline Street. When they'd helped Kirstie move in, she and Cameron met the attorney who lived right above Kirstie and an accountant on the third floor. They were both in their twenties. Was she dating one of them? Or maybe she was going out with one of her teacher friends. Anabelle remembered the young man, Mark, who'd been sitting at the kitchen table in Kirstie's apartment when she'd popped in for a surprise visit a few weeks ago. He'd seemed entirely too comfortable there.

Anabelle sighed. Kirstie's dating is a good thing, she reminded herself.

She turned onto her right side; and a few minutes later, to her left. Anabelle did not like waking up during the night and ruminating about all the things that created a traffic jam in her brain. She finally turned back to her right side and began the deep breathing exercises she'd learned long ago in stress-relief classes.

She focused on breathing, putting all else out of her mind and finally drifted off.

For some folks, Monday mornings were a drag, having to get up early and trudge to work after a restful or fun-filled weekend. To Anabelle morning was a gift. Though she enjoyed her days off, she loved her job as Nursing Supervisor in the Cardiac Care Unit at Hope Haven Hospital. She also loved new beginnings and mornings were just that: a time to reflect and aim for new opportunities.

Anabelle yawned and did a few stretches before heading for the shower. After drying her short, easy-to-style hair, she dressed in navy slacks and a pastel floral top. Makeup was a matter of dashing a little mascara on her lashes and blush on her cheeks— and, lately, drawing pencil lines on her vanishing eyebrows.

She grabbed one of the half dozen lab coats that hung in her closet, made sure she had her glasses and name badge and headed out of the bedroom.

Cameron was still sleeping and probably would be until seven when he'd have his coffee, read the paper and then go to the gym for a workout. Not that he needed a gym. Their small farm kept him busy enough. The property included two pastures and a small barn, which housed a number of cats and a palomino gelding named Rusty, owned by Heather Jones, their darling twelve-year-old neighbor. The Joneses paid them thirty dollars a month to keep Rusty in their pasture since they had no land other than their small lot.

She smiled, not feeling the least bit jealous of Cam's retirement. With the amount of time he spent puttering around the farm and his shop and helping Evan out with his landscaping business, he was busier now than when he'd worked full-time. But he seemed happy, and that's what counted.

Anabelle poured coffee from the full carafe on the coffeemaker. She enjoyed being able to set the timer the night before and having the coffee perfectly brewed and ready to drink.

How spoiled they were getting. She smiled and set the carafe back, knowing it would stay hot for Cameron. It hadn't been that many years ago when she'd shuffled out to the kitchen first thing in the morning all bleary-eyed to put the coffee on. Back then they'd had few choices and always bought generic coffee. Now she preferred the special roasts and usually got the whole beans to grind herself.

Taking her Kinkade-design cup to one of her two favorite spots in the wide living room, Anabelle set it on the end table and opened the vertical blinds to the sliding patio door. She pulled open the door and breathed in the fresh, damp air. Her plants had weathered the storm just fine.

After closing the door, she sank into the cushioned rocking chair that had once been her mother's. Placing her feet on the ottoman, she paused to enjoy a patch of sunshine as it dappled the trees in the private backyard and turned last night's rain into crystal droplets. Moments later clouds blotted out the patch of blue sky.

Summer was coming to an end. By October the leaves would be turning. She still had some dahlias along with several large hydrangeas blooming. The leggy geraniums would need cutting back soon, and she needed to deadhead the roses. Maybe she'd have time after work today—if the weather cooperated.

Anabelle slipped on her reading glasses and dipped into her basket of books and magazines. This year she'd chosen to use Oswald Chambers's *My Utmost for His Highest* as her daily devotional. Starting the day in thoughtful introspection and prayer always seemed to improve her perspective on life no matter what lay ahead.

Today, Anabelle had a hard time staying focused. Her mind kept going back and forth, from reading about prayer life to thinking about Drew Hamilton. She finally gave up reading and spent the next few moments praying specifically for the good doctor. She prayed, too, for her children, especially Kirstie and her mystery date. Anabelle determined that she would not ask. She would let Kirstie tell her when she was ready.

After fishing a package of salmon out of the freezer for dinner, Anabelle poured an orange juice and ate a quick granola-and-yogurt breakfast. At 6:30 AM, she backed her new silver Ford Fusion out of the garage and headed into the rain.

Wipers swished at the sheets of water but did little good. She smiled at the irony. With all the innovations made on automobiles lately, surely someone could invent a better way of clearing the window in a downpour.

Her new sedan got around forty miles per gallon and could go about seven hundred miles before needing a fill-up. The dashboard with all its buttons and displays looked like the panel of a 747. She still didn't know what half of them were for.

Anabelle maneuvered the car along the familiar road, barely able to see the bulky shapes of cars and trucks. The two and a half miles to Hope Haven took twice as long to navigate as it normally did. Finally the hospital loomed ahead of her. By rote, she eased into her usual spot in the staff parking lot. Retrieving her floral umbrella with a Monet garden scene from the seat-back pocket, Anabelle waited for a few moments in hopes the rain would subside. No such luck. If she waited much longer, she'd be late. And Anabelle Scott was *never* late.

She opened her umbrella and made a dash for the door. She held it open for several other staff members including Elena Rodriguez, her good friend who worked in Intensive Care.

"Thank you!" Elena sounded winded. "I forgot to grab my umbrella this morning. Too much else on my mind, I guess." Elena shook the rain from her long dark hair. "But what's a little rain? I'm certainly not going to melt." She laughed. "Although for a few minutes there, I was afraid I might wash away."

"You're in a good mood." Anabelle closed her umbrella and shook off some of the water.

Elena's dark features brightened even more. "I am. Isabel is turning five, and I am going to throw her a big party."

"That sounds delightful. I must say, I envy you having that darling little girl around." Anabelle pressed the elevator button and the doors swished open.

"I know you do." Elena gave her an empathetic smile. It wasn't the first time Anabelle had brooded over not having a grandchild of her own. Elena didn't seem to mind. "You are always welcome to share Isabel with me—especially when I need a babysitter."

"You are too kind." Anabelle chuckled.

"In fact, Isabel told me to be sure to invite Auntie *Amabelle* first. You are her favorite person since you made her that adorable princess quilt."

"Well, you tell her I'm honored." Having her quilts used and loved by those who received them gave Anabelle as much joy as making them.

The women hurried off the elevator and to their lockers. Anabelle removed her rain jacket and stowed her umbrella. She adjusted the long chain that held her reading glasses and tucked the glasses into the upper pocket of her lab coat. Pausing at Elena's locker, she asked, "Want to plan on lunch around noon?"

"I'll do my best." Elena pulled her hair into a ponytail and twisted it into a scruffy bun. She was wearing her *Finding Nemo* scrubs. Elena, being a talented seamstress, made many of her own clothes. "You know how crazy Intensive Care can get."

"Cardiac Care as well. Let us hope for an uneventful day."

"Right. And what dreamworld are you living in?" She laughed at the idea.

"We can always think positive." Walking away, Anabelle had no illusions of a quiet day in CCU. They had at least one patient going to surgery with more likely to come as patients received diagnoses.

"See you later," Elena called after her.

Anabelle took the stairs down to the second floor and turned right to go into the Cardiac Care Unit. She then crossed the hall to the nurses' station, intending to go straight to her office.

"Morning, Anabelle," Debbie Vaughn, one of the night-shift nurses, called out from the nurses' station.

"Morning." Anabelle paused at her door. "How was your shift?"

Debbie grinned. "Not bad—just the usual chaos that comes with getting a new admission just before shift change. Name's Olga Pederson."

"Ah." Anabelle knew the feeling well. She'd been a nurse at Hope Haven for over thirty years, only taking leave to have her children and to care for Kirstie after the accident. "Did you get her all settled in for us?" Anabelle asked as she punched in the code for the digital lock on her door.

"Of course." Debbie's grin faded. "You might want to talk to Dr. Hildebrand about getting her something for anxiety though."

"Sure." Anabelle stepped inside her office and left the door open to air the small space out. The stacks of files and notes on her desk told her the weekend must have been hectic. As nursing supervisor, she kept tabs on all the patients coming and going in the Cardiac Care Unit.

Anabelle pulled out her glasses and scanned the weekend happenings to bring herself up to date. They'd admitted a couple of patients who were sent home on Sunday. Mr. Blake had been admitted the day before in preparation for his surgery this morning. And Olga Pederson, the woman admitted at five this morning. *Age 83—atrial fibrillation.*

Anabelle jotted a note about Olga's medication on her clipboard. Heart patients often struggled with anxiety, though some had more difficulty than others. She would visit with Olga after report. Sometimes she could calm patients down and alleviate their fears by talking with them and answering their questions.

Anabelle paused to check the schedule for the day's surgeries. Though she worked in cardiac care, she liked to keep up on other areas as well. This morning, however, she had a specific reason. Dr. Hamilton would be doing the open-heart surgery on Mr. Blake at 8:00 AM, which meant he probably wouldn't be out of surgery until around one. She'd try to talk with him then. Working in the hospital required a great deal of flexibility—the staff never knew what their days might bring or when they might be called into a critical situation.

Tucking her concern for him toward the back of her mind, Anabelle took off her glasses, slipped then into her pocket and then grabbed her clipboard and headed to the unit. She checked her watch and inhaled a deep breath. Just in time for report, in which she, the day nurses and the aides would hear details about each patient and formulate care plans for the rest of their shift.

Chapter Three

JAMES BELL'S MORNING WAS NOT GOING WELL. Aside from its being Monday, he'd awakened late. Not a good thing. Dr. Hamilton had called him last night and asked him to assist as his surgical nurse for the open-heart. James usually worked in Med/Surg—the General Medicine and Surgery Units—but for some reason, Hamilton liked having James assist him.

James thought maybe it had to do with the fact that he'd been a medic in the military. Plus, James had more surgical experience than most of the nurses at Hope Haven.

Sitting down to breakfast with his wife and oldest son Gideon, who had just turned fifteen, had been like entering into a war zone. Gideon had recently returned from faith-based military camp for kids in Kentucky, where kids could play soldier and get a true idea of what the military was all about. Which explained why Gideon was up so early on a summer day while his brother was still in the sack and probably would be until noon.

"Tell him, Jim. Tell Gideon he is not going to join the military." With a shaky hand Fern poured a cup of coffee for James and began to carry it from the counter to the dining room table. He moved quickly to take it from her. He'd told her numerous times not to try to carry hot things, but she was determined to try. She refused to let her multiple sclerosis get the upper hand. James wished he could say she was winning the battle.

"Mom, it's not like I'm going to the front line. It's just ROTC." He rolled his eyes. "By joining now, I'll be an officer when I finish college. And I'll get college paid for."

Gideon had been interested in the military and had always enjoyed playing soldier. James thought military camp might give him a dose of reality and possibly swing him in another direction. Apparently it had done just the opposite.

"Do we have to decide this morning?" James took a sip of his coffee. "I need to look into it before I can respond."

He glanced at his watch and caught the imploring look in his son's blue eyes. Looking up at Fern, who had a plate of eggs and toast in her hand, he said. "We can talk later, okay?" He hoped the stress of this touchy situation wouldn't worsen her condition.

Fern had been diagnosed with multiple sclerosis seven years ago. Now at forty-two, her symptoms were still come-and-go, but lately had worsened. She'd offered to cook breakfast, and so far everything had gone all right.

"It's always later with you." She set a plate of eggs and toast in front of him. Her arm jerked back in a spasm. The eggs slid off the plate and onto his last clean pair of jeans.

James pushed back the chair and jumped to his feet.

"I'm sorry." Fern bit her lip and, with tears in her eyes, turned away from him. "I'm going upstairs."

"Do you need help?" He started mopping up the mess with a napkin.

"No. I can do this myself," she said in a tone that indicated she was upset with him. She used the walker to get to the stairs and then turned around, going up one step at a time on her behind.

James sighed and rubbed the back of his neck wondering how long she'd be able to handle the stairs on her own. She'd fallen once, not all that long ago, and from then on he'd insisted she go up and down on her bottom.

She deserves better than this. James had been meaning to get some bids on expanding the first floor and adding a master suite. Trouble was, being a nurse didn't bring in a great salary. And recently, the nurses had taken a cut in pay in order to keep the hospital open during the last financial crunch. Fortunately, Fern's disability check kept them afloat.

"Dad." Gideon placed a folder on the table. "I need you to sign the papers."

James focused his attention back on his son, feeling annoyed that Gideon would ask again. "Not right now. I told you I'd have to look into it."

"You always take her side." Gideon tossed his napkin aside and stormed out the back door.

James swiped a hand through his hair. He did not want to take sides at all. He just wanted breakfast which was now history. After cleaning up the mess, he gulped down his orange juice, rescued half a piece of toast from his plate and headed for the kitchen sink.

With a wet washcloth, he wiped the remaining egg off his jeans. Knowing the toast wouldn't hold him until lunch, he grabbed a granola bar out of the pantry and headed out the door.

In his rush, he forgot to take a jacket, and by the time he arrived at the hospital, the rain was coming down in sheets. In the race from his car to the staff entrance, the rain soaked through everything. A large puddle remained in the elevator as he stepped out onto the third floor where he then slogged to his locker.

Like many of the nurses who wore scrubs, James usually changed at the hospital. He preferred wearing the hospital-provided blue or green, which saved Fern and him from having to do even more laundry than they already had. He removed his shoes and set them in the bottom of his locker while pulling out his white clogs. He hung his damp jeans on a hook to dry and pulled a fresh pair of scrubs off the linen cart.

James barely made it in time for report. Susan Mills, head nurse for the unit, smiled up at him. "Rough morning?"

He grinned and wiped a hand over his wet hair. "I'm good. Dr. Hamilton called me last night to assist with his open-heart surgery this morning."

"He called me too. I'm going to have to talk with the nursing director about bringing someone on to fill in for you when he does that."

James agreed. He appreciated her compliance with Dr. Hamilton's requests. Truth be told, James rather enjoyed serving as the doc's assistant. "So what are we doing today? Do we have enough nurses?"

"Not really. I'll cover your patients until you come back."

"Thanks." He stood. "I suppose I should head right up to the OR."

Susan nodded. "Good plan."

James entered the General Surgery Suite, which was situated next to Day Surgery on the third floor, and went straight to the sinks. He performed the presurgical washing ritual they always did. James stood next to Dr. Hamilton and sensed that something was off. Moisture beaded on the older man's forehead and he looked uncomfortable. "Are you feeling all right, sir?"

"I'm fine." He took in a sharp breath. "A little heartburn is all. I should know better than to eat sausage for breakfast."

The cardiac surgeon, Harriet Hildebrand—Dr. Hildie to her patients and much of the staff—arrived and began talking with Dr. Hamilton about their patient, Dillon Blake. James completed his scrub, shoved his arms into the gown the operating room nurse held out to him and turned so she could tie it behind his back. He donned the sterile gloves and cap and headed into the sterile area.

One nurse was assigned to stand watch and keep the area sterile. Another laid out instruments on the trays; and the anesthesiologist sat at the patient's head, watching the monitor. The patient murmured something unintelligible as a nurse told him he'd be asleep in less than a minute, which he was. The tray holding the heart-lung machine, which would support the patient's circulation during the surgery, sat at the ready. Even though the surgery was commonly done, James couldn't help feeling anxious.

The doctors approached the patient and the procedure began. Within minutes the man's chest had been opened and clamped. James had seen the inside of the chest cavity many times, but seeing someone's heartbeat was nothing short of a miracle. He prayed the surgery would go well and that the heart valve would be repaired perfectly.

James watched intently, handing off instruments as Dr. Hamilton asked for them—anticipating his every move. The heart-lung machine took over the work of the patient's heart so that repairs could be made. Everything was running smoothly.

Then, suddenly, Dr. Hamilton moaned and began to sway. The instrument he was holding clattered to the floor.

"Oh no!" someone shouted.

"He's going down!" James's adrenaline kicked into high gear. He grabbed Dr. Hamilton under the arms and pulled him back away from the patient and toward the door.

In the ensuing chaos, Dr. Hildebrand stepped in and almost seamlessly took her colleague's place. She quickly reordered the room and the OR staff continued on as if nothing had happened.

But something *had* happened. James paid little attention to the surgical team now. He had taken one look at the doctor's ashen face and sweating brow, put his ear to the doctor's chest and began shouting orders.

"Call a code blue."

James immediately started chest compressions as a respiratory therapist tipped Dr. Hamilton's head back to establish an airway and attach the valve mask resuscitator.

"Code blue surgery. Code blue surgery."

The operator's loud steady voice repeated the order again and again over the hospital's PA system. Within seconds the emergency response team appeared. While James continued the compressions, four members of the team lifted Dr. Hamilton onto a stretcher. James rose with the stretcher and ran with them as they moved him from the operating arena to the Day Surgery Unit.

James kept up the compressions, then stepped back when the paddles appeared and one of the nurses yelled, "Clear!"

Someone had already hooked the doctor up to a portable heart monitor. The first jolt with the paddles produced no change in his weak heart rate. A second zap along with the epinephrine got the heart beating on its own. Dr. Hamilton's heart transitioned into a normal sinus rhythm.

James felt like he'd just run a marathon. He sat for a moment while the team took Dr. Hamilton into one of the Day Surgery cubicles and hooked him up to the necessary monitors.

Since Dr. Hildebrand was still in surgery, James took it upon himself to call Dr. Hamilton's wife at their home. After several rings, he heard the voice mail greeting and began to speak. "Mrs. Hamilton, this is James Bell at the hospital. It's your husband, ma'am. We need you to come to the hospital as soon as possible."

Anabelle had been making rounds and looking over charts when she heard the code blue. As always she wondered what was going on, but a code blue in surgery had her heart racing. Her first thought was of Dr. Hamilton and his patient.

As much as she wanted to know the details, Anabelle resisted the urge to rush to the surgical suite. Since she was not on the code team, she'd just be in the way. Besides, their team had excellent training, and she had a job to do. Still, she paused to offer up a prayer for the people involved.

After looking over Olga Pederson's admission informa-tion, Anabelle stepped into the room. "Good morning, Mrs. Pederson." Anabelle introduced herself, assessing the small, perky woman. The chart had indicated a weight of 115 and height of five foot two. "I heard you had some heart trouble last night."

"Oh ya. Felt like my heart was gonna jump right out of my chest." Olga had a definite Scandinavian accent. "Wasn't sure they were gonna let me in here though."

Anabelle frowned. "What do you mean?" She couldn't imag-ine anyone in the ER turning a heart patient away. The triage nurses were well-qualified staff who were the first to examine a patient and determine the level of care and how quickly they needed to be seen.

"My neighbor drove me here, thank the Lord. First I had to tell the girl at the desk why I was there, then we had to tell this fellow named Triage. He says, 'Since you are eighty-three, we need you to sign a paper to let us know whether you want to be resuscitated or not.' I told him if I'd wanted to die, I'd a done so in my living room instead of coming all the way over here and waking up my neighbors to boot."

"I guess you told him." Anabelle grinned. She liked this lady's spunk.

"Ya—it got him moving anyways."

"I'll bet."

"The doc in the ER didn't seem to think whatever I have was such a big deal, but it sure felt like it to me."

"Atrial fibrillation can be scary, but it usually isn't life threat-ening. It is an emergency, though, and can lead to some problems.

I'm glad you came in. It looks like the medications Dr. Weller gave you to slow your heart are working."

"Ya, I think so. I'm still not breathing so good. Is it going to happen again? Was it a heart attack?"

"Not a heart attack." Anabelle glanced up at the monitor. "Your heart seems to be working just fine now. It isn't unusual for people to be frightened or feel stressed when something like this happens. I'll see if the doctor can order something to relax you."

"How long do I need to stay in here?"

"Just until we determine what's going on. Maybe two to three days. I didn't see any family listed on your admission chart."

"I have a daughter in Portland and four grandchildren and seven great-grandchildren. The oldest girl recently had her second baby. I got to go out there this summer to see my newest great grandchild. What a beautiful baby."

"Would you like me to call your daughter?"

"Oh no. You mustn't call Carla. She's so busy; and if you call her, she'll insist on coming. I'd just as soon she not know. The last thing I want is to be a burden to her."

"I can understand that. But what makes you think you'll be a burden?"

Olga sighed and glanced out the window. Her blue eyes had taken on the dim gray of the sky. "Carla has been asking me to come live with her for the last ten years. I would like to be near the children, but I'd go crazy living with them. Besides, I met my husband in Deerford. We raised our children here. I can't give up my home."

Anabelle had met many people like Olga—senior citizens facing the prospect of not being independent anymore. "Sometimes we have to make difficult decisions, but for you it's a little too soon to worry." Anabelle explained that medications usually worked well. "There's no reason to think you won't be back to your usual self soon. Besides, no one can force you to move as long as you are able to care for yourself."

"I am that," Olga said. "Or I was. People tell me all the time to slow down, but I'm not about to quit now."

"Good for you." Anabelle patted her hand. "You might want to tone it down a bit while you're in the hospital. We want to get that heart of yours stabilized and running like it's supposed to."

"Maybe I should have something to make me relax. My daughter complains about my fidgeting—tells me I can't stand to sit around doing nothing."

"I'll do that." Anabelle pulled the business end of her stethoscope out of her pocket and warmed it in her hand. "Do you mind if I take a listen to your chest and lungs?"

"Go ahead. I was alive the last time I checked."

Anabelle laughed and placed the stethoscope in various areas of Olga's chest. "Your lungs sound clear and your heart sounds good as well. I can definitely verify that you're alive."

"Thank you." Olga grasped Anabelle's hand. "I've never been sick—not enough to put me in the hospital. I always prayed that when I went, it would be fast."

"I've prayed that for myself too, but sometimes God has other ideas."

"Ya. He does." She sighed and rested her hands on her abdomen.

Anabelle smiled and gripped Olga's hand. "I have a feeling that whatever happens, you'll be right where God wants you."

When Anabelle stepped out of the room, Becky signaled to her from the nurses' desk. "We're getting a new patient. I've asked the girls to get 206 ready." She blew out a breath, ruffling her dark bangs. "It's not good, Anabelle. It's Dr. Hamilton. He had a heart attack."

Anabelle felt as though she'd been punched in the stomach. She gasped for breath; and though she didn't think her legs would hold her up, she struggled to maintain her composure.

"He's stabilized and should be down here in a few minutes."

Chapter Four

WITH SHAKING HANDS, CANDACE CRENSHAW fumbled in her purse for money to pay the cafeteria attendant for a tall cup of black coffee. Hopefully the brew would calm her shattered nerves.

Tears edged near the surface. She'd thought she was ready to be on the code blue team. Today proved her wrong. She'd barely been able to function. One look at Dr. Hamilton lying on the floor, being stripped, poked and prodded nearly broke her heart. The images yanked her back three years as flashbacks of Dean flooded her mind, making it impossible to focus on her duties. Her husband had died from a brain aneurism, leaving her with two small children to rear.

But she couldn't think about that now. She had to get beyond the grief and move on. Time and again she thought she'd done just that, only to have it surface again.

Heath Carlson from Radiology, also part of the code blue team, had noticed her distress right away. He'd led her to a chair and told her to sit down. "I'll take over for you," he'd said. He'd done that and more. The ordeal was over now; but for Candace, shreds of panic still remained.

Why is it so hard to forget? Why do the flashbacks keep coming back? Candace wished she knew.

With the trauma resolved, Heath had ushered her to the cafeteria. Now, he came up behind her with his coffee and a pastry and offered to pay for her coffee as well.

She started to refuse, then gave in. "Thanks. I'll pay you back later."

"My treat."

Her cheeks warmed at the kind gesture. With all the crazy feelings churning her insides at the sight of Dr. Hamilton, she didn't trust herself to speak. Part of her wanted Heath to leave her alone so she could process the series of events on her own. Candace feared his soft gaze would send her into a full-scale crying jag. Lord knew she'd had enough of those.

Another part of her was thankful for his presence. They had met when she had helped his sister-in-law Chrissy deliver her baby. Candace got to know him briefly when he'd come to see his new nephew.

At five foot ten, Heath was fit and trim with curly golden-blond hair and vivid blue eyes that seemed to read her a bit too easily. His cheeks creased in a smile as they sat down at one of the tables. "Are you sure you don't want anything else?"

"I'm sure." Though she found Heath attractive, nothing could come of it except, maybe, friendship. She was nowhere near ready for a relationship. They sat in silence for several minutes while Candace drank her coffee and Heath attacked his croissant.

"Thank you." She appreciated that he didn't try to make small talk while she gathered her frazzled self together.

"You're welcome." He grinned again. "You're looking better. What happened back there?"

"Flashback." While she had not seen her husband being worked on by the hospital staff, she knew what had happened. Being a nurse made the scenes in her head as real as if she had been there in person.

"Did it have something to do with your husband's death?" He hesitated. "I'm sorry. I shouldn't have asked that."

"It's all right. It did actually have to do with Dean." She took another sip of coffee. "I should probably resign from the code team. I thought I was ready, but apparently not."

He set his plate aside. "I know this isn't any of my business, but Chrissy tells me it's been three years since Dean's death. Have you considered seeing a counselor?"

He talked to Chrissy about me? Not that it mattered, everyone associated with the hospital knew. She bent her head and rubbed her forehead. "My mother and sister have suggested that, but honestly, I don't know if it would help. I know grief inside and out. What is a counselor going to tell me that I don't already know?"

"Sometimes," he said, "we go about the healing all wrong. We try to work things out and figure that if we look good on the outside and are coping, we're doing okay. But true healing happens from the inside out."

Candace raised her head and found herself looking into his empathetic blue eyes. "It sounds good, but how does this kind of healing happen?"

"It just does. You open yourself up to it." He checked at his watch. "I'm sorry. I have to run." He rose and leaned toward her, hands pressed on the table. "Would you like to meet me for coffee after work? We can talk some more."

Candace swallowed hard and couldn't quite meet his eyes. "I can't."

He pursed his lips and nodded in understanding. "You'll be okay?"

"Yes. Thanks." Candace actually didn't feel okay, but she didn't want to concern anyone with her problems. The turmoil she'd suffered off and on since Dean's death threatened to drag her under once again. All she wanted to do was go to bed, pull the covers over her head and sleep for a month.

Thankfully, she had a job; and right now, she needed to get back to the Birthing Unit and her duties there. Candace pushed aside the oppressive thoughts and, after tossing her trash, hurried toward the stairs.

In the lobby, she paused, her gaze taking in the chapel door. Maybe a brief detour there would help her gain perspective. She entered the small room and eased into the back pew. There were six oak pews, all empty at the moment. A plain oak altar drew her attention to the front of the room. Above it, light streamed through the abstract design of a stained-glass window creating colorful images across the room. In the left front corner, a large cross of dark cherry wood stood in the center of a raised platform. At the base, a gentle stream of water circulated over rocks, creating the gentle sound of a babbling brook. Green foliage crowded around the cross and the water's edge.

Candace drew in the beauty and the sound as she prayed once more for strength to carry on. She thought about Heath's comment about healing. "Please, Lord, let me heal from the inside out. I don't want to forget Dean, but I can't go on in this way either."

James stayed with Dr. Hamilton until CCU called saying they had a bed ready. He personally guided the gurney along the hallway into the service elevator to the second floor and into the Cardiac Care Unit.

The nursing supervisor, Anabelle Scott, and Head Nurse Becky Simms left the nurses' station and led them into what would be the doctor's room.

Anabelle had paled when James brought him into the unit. He knew how close she was to Dr. Hamilton.

"I've assigned Becky to him." She pinched her lips together as her gaze shifted from James to Dr. Hamilton.

James nodded his approval. "That's good." Becky was one of their best cardiac nurses. Her experience of ten years in both ER and Coronary Care made her an exceptional choice.

James followed them and helped Anabelle and Becky transfer Dr. Hamilton onto the bed and hook up the monitors.

Doc Hamilton opened his eyes and closed them again. "What's going on?" he murmured.

"Hey, doc. You gave us all quite a scare." James attached another lead. "You went into cardiac arrest during the operation. Dr. Hildebrand was able to take over the surgery for you."

"That's impossible. Are you sure?" The doctor clutched at the bedspread. He started to sit up, groaned and sank back against a pillow.

"I was there, sir. I managed to catch you when you passed out. I called the code blue myself. I did the chest compressions." James blew out a sharp breath. "I saw you flatline. So, yeah, I'm sure."

Dr. Hamilton closed his eyes again. "I thought it was just heartburn."

"I'm afraid not." James wiped the perspiration from his own forehead with the back of his hand.

"I guess I have you to thank for saving my life, then."

James smiled. "I just happened to be at the right place at the right time. The code team brought you back."

"This shouldn't have happened. I'm in great shape. I run twenty miles a week and work out nearly every day." He paused. "You'll forgive my skepticism, James, but I need to see the test results for myself." He glanced up and back at the heart monitor. "Looks pretty good now."

"Let's try to keep it that way." Becky checked his vital signs and jotted them down. "We'll let you rest for a while. And, Dr. Hamilton, please do try to relax."

"*Humph.*" He frowned and placed a hand on his chest right over his heart.

"I'd better be going." James turned toward the door.

"James." Dr. Hamilton's voice sounded scratchy and weak.

"Yeah?" He turned back just before stepping out of the room.

"Thank you."

James nodded and followed Anabelle and Becky back to the nurses' station. He gave the women a detailed report even though the incident and everything that transpired had been written up in his record. "I called his wife, but she didn't answer. Maybe you have a cell phone number or something."

"I'll make sure we reach her." Anabelle scurried to her office across the way.

The adrenaline rush that had gotten him through the ordeal had fizzled under a load of concern and guilt. He leaned against the wall and tipped his head back.

"Are you okay James?" Becky paused before going into the doctor's room again.

"Yeah. I've been through these before, you know, but—"

"It's always harder when the patient is one of our own." She offered an empathic smile.

"You're right about that." James turned and headed toward Anabelle's office. He found her on the phone. She shook her head and set the receiver back in its cradle. "Genna isn't answering."

"Can we talk for a minute?" James rubbed the back of his neck.

"Sure. Close the door and have a seat." Anabelle's eyes belied the businesslike tone of her voice. Like him, she was having trouble holding it together. "What's going on? Is it Fern?"

He and Anabelle had been friends for a long time and went to the same church. He often confided in Anabelle about Fern's MS.

"No, not Fern. I wanted to talk to you about Dr. Hamilton."

Anabelle frowned. "Okay."

"There's a problem." James leaned forward, elbows on his knees. "Dr. Hamilton shouldn't have been in surgery this morning."

"What do you mean?" She met his gaze head-on.

"I had a feeling something was wrong before surgery. The doc didn't look so good. He insisted he was fine, but I should have said something to someone. I shouldn't have let him operate."

Anabelle sighed. "Oh, James. I can understand how you must feel, but you and I know hindsight is always better than foresight. I'm sure you did your best."

"I'm not so sure." He frowned.

"James." Anabelle placed her hand on his arm. "I hate to say this, but if anyone is negligent in all of this, it's Dr. Hamilton. If he wasn't feeling well, he should have stepped down." She paused as if the words she'd spoken were just sinking in. "We both know that Drew would never do anything to harm a patient—which leads me to believe that he sincerely felt he could safely operate when he walked into that room."

James wasn't convinced. He should have followed his instincts. He just hoped everything went well with the patient and with Dr. Hamilton.

Dr. Hamilton was one of the most liked and popular doctors at Hope Haven, and nearly everyone who worked there had come into the unit to check on him.

He also had to be one of the most disgruntled patients Anabelle had ever had in the unit. She knew his grumpiness came out of fear and denial, but that didn't make caring for him any easier.

After at least two dozen visitors, Anabelle called the volunteer desk. Phyllis Getty, the feisty eighty-four-year-old volunteer and member of the Hospital Auxiliary, answered the phone.

"Hi, Phyllis. This is Anabelle. We're getting way too many visitors for Dr. Hamilton."

"I think so too." Her hoarse chuckle followed. "I'll put a stop to it, but we might want to let this next one through."

"Oh?"

"It's Genevieve."

Anabelle blew out a long breath. "Good. Send her back, but no one else."

"Okey-dokey," Phyllis added before hanging up.

Anabelle sent a prayer upward. "Maybe now that Genna is here, he'll settle down a bit."

She hurried toward the unit entrance to greet Genna. "I'm so glad we finally reached you."

"How's Drew?" Genna asked, out of breath and panting. Tears rimmed her eyes. "Is he going to be okay?"

"He's ornery so we are expecting good things."

That brought out a smile and slowed Genna's steps. "Good. I knew something was going on, but I thought it was his stomach—like ulcers or something. So did he."

"You were right to be concerned." Anabelle gave her a brief overview of what had happened. "He has a good strong heartbeat now. Dr. Hildebrand should be in shortly to see him. We need him to rest, but he doesn't seem inclined to do that. Maybe you can help."

"I'll try."

Anabelle escorted Genna to the room. Tears surfaced as she watched the couple embrace. She pulled the curtain slightly to give them privacy and went to answer a call light. She hoped Becky would return from her break soon. She definitely needed one of her own.

Several minutes later, Dr. Hildebrand came into the unit. Her thick blonde hair was pulled back in a tidy bun. She wore oversized green scrubs that washed her out and made her already-overweight figure seem larger. "How is Dr. Hamilton?"

Anabelle brought her up to date. "The results of the lab tests are here."

Dr. Hildebrand called his information up on the computer. "I see that. No surprises here."

"He's not taking this very well. Of course no one does, but he's in denial. He says he won't believe it until he sees the results himself."

"Okay, print them out and we'll let the good doctor diagnose himself." Dr. Hildie was usually good natured with an easy smile. Now she seemed annoyed and out of sorts.

Anabelle highlighted the page, hit the Print button and brought the results with her to the room. Dr. Hildebrand took the results from Anabelle and handed the papers to Dr. Hamilton and crossed her arms. "See for yourself."

He studied the results and handed them back and shrugged, his face showing none of the concern Anabelle felt he should have. "Okay, you win."

"Drew, you need to take this seriously." Dr. Hildie glanced over at Genna and back again. "This may be a onetime thing, or it may be an ongoing problem. We need to do a full workup. I'll order a nuclear scan, echocardiogram and angiogram."

She sighed. "I hate to ask, Genna, but I really need to talk to Drew alone for a moment."

"Oh, sure." Genna rose from the chair, leaned her slender form over the rail and kissed her husband's cheek. "I need a latte anyway. Be back in a few minutes."

Anabelle stepped out of the room as well.

Just prior to the glass door's sliding shut, she heard Dr. Hildie say, "This doesn't look good for either one of us, Drew."

Five minutes later Dr. Hildebrand stepped out of the room and sat in front of one of the computers at the nurses' station.

Seri, one of the nurse's aides, sidled up to Anabelle. "I don't know what Dr. Hildebrand said to Dr. Hamilton, but it did not make him happy."

"She told him the truth about his condition." Anabelle, too, had been stubbornly hoping that Dr. Drew hadn't really had a heart attack.

"Okay, I know about the emotional stuff, but he's just laying there staring out the window."

"That's a good thing right now. He needs to rest." Anabelle appreciated the girl's concern.

Anabelle checked on him again just before her break. The change was palpable. He'd gone from being irascible to sullen. Anabelle knew that when patients experienced a tragic event, part of the grieving process was often denial. With acceptance came sadness and often depression. Something in his countenance told her it might be more complicated than that. She prayed he would recover and come back as strong and energetic as ever. And she prayed that James and Dr. Hildie were wrong and that there would not be any legal implications against Drew for going ahead with the operation when he wasn't feeling well. Doctors had been sued for less.

Chapter Five

B Y NOON ON MONDAY, ELENA RODRIGUEZ WAS more than ready for a break or, even better, a day off. Maybe even a week off. The Intensive Care Unit was usually one of the busiest places in the hospital, and today was no exception. That morning, they had gotten two admits—both in critical condition. The first was a fifty-year-old man who'd fallen from a two-story building at a construction site; the second, a woman who'd been involved in a head-on collision just outside of town. She had been put into a medical coma to rest her body and her brain and to allow both to heal. Her husband sat in the chair beside the bed, holding his head in his hands and occasionally looking up at the monitors.

Her nursing supervisor, Marge Matthews, had assigned both patients to Elena, and she'd been running back and forth between the two of them all morning. The morning had been crazy, and unfortunately, she hadn't been able to meet Anabelle as they had planned. Anabelle hadn't minded of course—flexibility was an important part of the job.

At one, Elena finally took her lunch break. She ate quickly and then pulled out her notebook, efficiently swapping from nursing hat to Grandma hat. Her sweet Isabel would be five soon, and Elena was probably more excited than the birthday girl. Elena pictured her adorable dark-haired princess and smiled.

Isabel and her daddy—Elena's son Rafael—lived with her and her husband Cesar. They would have the party in their backyard, which had recently been beautifully landscaped by Evan Scott, Anabelle's son. He had done the work at cost this past spring. Such a gift. They had thoroughly enjoyed it all summer, especially the pool and hot tub. It was an extravagance; but with both Elena and Cesar using part of their salaries, they were able to manage and invest in their home.

She had already started a guest list for the party. First on the list was Anabelle, then Candace and James. She had jotted down several neighbors and family members, including her own mother and grandmother. Thinking about them brought pleasant memories.

Every year, Elena managed to get a five-generation picture. She hoped this year would be the same. Her grandmother would turn eighty-eight this year. So far, she'd been active and in relatively good health. *Abuela*, the Spanish word for "grandmother" and "old lady," had always told Elena they were blessed with longevity genes.

She and Isabel had put together a list of children from the day care/preschool and Sunday school class. This would be Isabel's first time to invite friends, and that would be a challenge in itself. Elena told her she could invite five children close to her age.

"Hey there." Anabelle took the chair across from her. "I'm surprised you're still here, since this is the earliest I could get away."

"Me too." Elena told her about her admissions and they talked for several minutes about Dr. Hamilton. News had spread quickly among the hospital employees.

Candace took the seat next to Anabelle. "Hi, guys. I'm glad you're still here. You must have had a busy morning too."

"You might say that." Elena smiled.

"What are all these notes for?" Candace asked, nodding toward Elena's papers.

"Isabel's party." Elena told them all about her plans so far. "You and the kids are invited."

"How fun. Howie and Brooke love parties." Her smile turned bittersweet. "Though with Brooke's being eleven-going-on-twenty, she may consider herself too old to play with the *children*."

Anabelle sighed. "Kids grow up way too fast. Enjoy those parties while you can."

"I am fortunate to have a second chance." Elena put a star on Candace's and Anabelle's names indicating they'd been asked and would be coming.

"You are indeed," Anabelle agreed. "I loved planning parties for my three when they were little. I must have made every kind of cake you can imagine. I did a princess cake one time where you bake part of the batter in a bowl to make a dress. I bought a doll to slip into the top. It was gorgeous with pink and white frosting. Loveliest cake I ever made. When I went to cut into the skirt to serve it, the inside wasn't done and batter oozed out all over the place. The kids thought it was a hoot. Called it a lava cake and ate it anyway."

Elena laughed. "Now they make lava cakes on purpose."

Candace set her fork on her plate and reached for her water. "I've had a few fiascoes myself. Mom usually makes the cakes now, or we get ice-cream cakes at the grocery."

For the next few minutes they talked about past birthdays, decorations, the party store and themes. Elena wanted something colorful with a fiesta theme so they could have a piñata.

After a few more minutes of planning, Elena checked her watch. "I have to get back."

"You're leaving already?" James set his tray down. "I was hoping to hear about Dr. Hamilton."

"Not much to report." Anabelle sighed. "He's stable; but you saw him, James. He's not taking this well at all."

"That poor man," Elena said. "He's spent all his life healing people, and now he's on the other side. I think that would be especially hard."

"It's just the heart attack." Anabelle tossed her napkin on her tray. "I think he's feeling guilty about going ahead with the surgery."

Elena nodded. "Of course he'd feel guilty. He's a doctor and didn't recognize the heart attack symptoms."

"Or refused to." James took a bite of his hamburger leaving them all to puzzle over the ramifications of his statement.

As Anabelle stepped off the elevator on the second floor, she almost collided with Genna.

"Anabelle! I was hoping to run into you, though not literally."

Anabelle gave her friend a hug. "I was just coming back from lunch. Is something wrong?"

Genna's grin gave way to desperation. Her eyes closed as she heaved an exasperated sigh. "Oh-h-h. That man!"

"I take it you're referring to the good doctor."

"*Good* is not a word I would use to describe him at the moment."

"Is there something I can do?"

"Talk some sense into him." She pulled a tissue out of her bag to wipe the tears spilling onto her cheeks. "I know he isn't upset with me. He's angry with himself. Says he should have known what was happening but didn't want to admit it. He's upset that his *stupidity*, as he calls it, put a patient's life at risk."

"Come on." Anabelle led her friend to the waiting room and settled her into a chair with a cup of coffee.

"Dr. Hildebrand said the patient came through surgery just fine, but Drew is worried. She reminded him they'd have to write up an incident report." Genna held the cup with both hands. "Anabelle, what if they take away his license? Could that happen?"

"Did he tell you it could?" A hollow ache formed in Anabelle's stomach.

"No. But if they find him negligent . . ."

"That isn't going to happen. Drew is one of the finest doctors around." Anabelle patted her friend's arm. "You stay here and finish your coffee; I'll go in and speak with him."

When she reached Drew's room, Anabelle tapped on the glass. He turned slightly, harrumphed with crossed arms and looked away.

"Well, hello to you too." Anabelle opened the door far enough to get into the room.

"Did Genna send you to cheer me up?" Some of the color had come back to his cheeks, but he still had an unhealthy pallor.

"No. She's the one who needs cheering up. You need a swift kick in the you-know-what."

He chuckled and met her gaze. "Leave it to you to tell it like it is."

"I'm not about to pussyfoot around where you're concerned. We've known each other far too long for that."

He sighed. "Okay. I won't lie to you. I should have realized my symptoms were heart related."

"You are a doctor, yes, but you are not perfect. It's normal for people to dismiss heart attack symptoms for heartburn."

"For some people, but not for me. I did think heart early on, but refused to admit it. That makes me negligent. It also makes me a fool. I should have known better."

"You need to stop beating yourself up and focus on getting well."

"Easier said than done."

"I know this is hard on you. But try to go easy on the nurses and on Genna. This is scary for her too."

"You're right as always." His gray eyes met hers. "I will try to be on my best behavior."

"Good."

"Did Genna tell you that she and Dr. Hildebrand think I should take a month off?"

"No, but I think that's a good idea." Anabelle smiled. "It would do you a world of good."

"I don't think so. I have patients to tend to. There's no way I could take a month off. Sitting around doing nothing would drive me nuts."

"I hear you, but you know what? You have at least a week before you have to make that decision. Right now, you need to think about healing that heart so you *can* make a decision." Anabelle frowned. "We want you around so you can see all those patients who depend on you—now and in the future."

He nodded. "I suppose you're right."

"Okay then." She grinned and headed for the door. "I'll have Genna come back in. Just promise you'll behave yourself."

"Aye, aye, captain."

Anabelle headed for the nurses' desk to check in with her staff for any new orders or pertinent changes before making rounds again. Becky, Olga Pederson's nurse, stepped out of the elderly woman's room and smiled when she saw Anabelle approaching. They started for the nurses' station together.

"Did Dr. Hildebrand ever order the sedative for Mrs. Pederson?" Anabelle asked.

Becky nodded. "I gave it to her a few minutes ago."

"Good. Hopefully she'll be able to relax for a while."

"She has a visitor. Not family, but it's the neighbor who brought her in."

"Oh, good. Maybe she can fill in some blanks about Olga's history."

As Anabelle was doing her rounds, Olga stirred when she came into the room but didn't open her eyes. A young woman sitting in the recliner near the bed rose when Anabelle entered.

She wore jeans and a fitted print top. "I'm Christina Godwin, Olga's neighbor."

"Nice to meet you. I was hoping someone could be with her." They walked out into the hall so as not to disturb Olga.

"I've been trying to find out more about her condition; but since I'm not family, no one can tell me anything." Christina crossed her arms.

"I know. The confidentiality thing can seem frustrating, but it's important. I can tell you that she's stable."

"I understand. The information on the Internet says atrial fibrillation is pretty serious."

"If not treated, yes." Anabelle wrote Christina's name and phone number down as a contact person on her clipboard.

"I called her daughter Carla in Oregon." Christina glanced into the room. "I thought she should know."

"I'm glad you did. Olga asked us not to."

Christina smiled. "I was afraid she'd do something like that. She's so independent. Carla doesn't know if she can get away, but she'll be calling the hospital to get a report."

Anabelle made a note about Carla on her sheet. "I understand Olga lives alone. Does she take care of the house by herself?"

"She does," Christina said. "I swear she has more energy than I do. She gardens and I have never seen anyone over there helping her. Well, except for my husband and me. We've sort of adopted her as grandma. She even came over to help me clean after my baby was born." Christina laughed. "Not only that, Olga is active in church, she knits and crochets. Seems like she's always busy. She knit the cutest sweater for my little guy for Christmas this year."

Anabelle chuckled. "She told me she likes staying busy. Looks like she meant it."

Christina frowned. "It would be really hard on her to have to give up her home."

Anabelle sighed. "Like I told her, there's no reason to think she'll have to leave her home. There are ways to get around that."

"I've told her she should think about moving out to her daughter's place, but she's so stubborn." Christina turned to look at her friend. "The thing is, I think she really wants to be closer to her family. You should see how excited she is when she goes to visit."

"It's hard to have family living so far away." Anabelle was thankful her children lived in town. Her pager vibrated. "That's Carla now. If you'll excuse me."

"Oh, right." Christina grinned. "I need to go anyway. Thanks."

"Thank you for being such a good friend to her." Anabelle ducked into her office to take the call. "Anabelle Scott speaking."

"Oh, thank goodness." The woman sounded agitated.

"You must be Carla." Anabelle settled into her chair. "How can I help you?"

"The operator put me through to Mama's room, but no one answered."

"I'm sorry. The ringer must be off. She's asleep right now, but I'll make sure she gets the message that you called."

"Thank you. When I called back, someone said I should talk to you. Is Mama—I mean do you think I should fly out there?"

Anabelle hesitated. She wanted to say, "Yes, you should. She needs her family right now." But it wasn't her place. Instead she said, "Your mother seems to be stable right now. Her doctor plans to run some tests to determine what the next steps will be."

"What's her prognosis?"

"Carla, I feel really terrible about this, but your mother doesn't want us to release information."

"But I'm her daughter."

"I know." Anabelle sighed. "But we have to respect a patient's wishes. Did Christina tell you what your mother was admitted for?"

"Yes, atrial fibrillation."

"Good. Here's what I'd like you to do. Go online to a reputable site like the Mayo Clinic and read about the condition. That might help you determine what to do."

"Thanks, Anabelle. I will. Tell my mother that we love her and are praying for her."

"I'll do that." Anabelle hung up feeling frustrated. She'd like to call Carla back and encourage her to come.

Anabelle then called the recovery room to get the status on Dillon Blake, the patient who'd had the open-heart surgery that morning. "He's doing great," the recovery nurse reported. "We're sending him up to you in a few minutes."

"Thanks." She whispered a brief prayer for him. Mr. Blake would be in the room across from Dr. Hamilton. Anabelle wondered how Mr. Blake would react when he discovered his doctor had suffered a heart attack—during surgery.

The rest of their patients were doing well. Two would be going home tomorrow. She visited them, answering any questions or concerns they had. Anabelle always made it a point to check on all of the Cardiac Care Unit's patients at least twice a day. She felt they appreciated the extra attention and having a supervisor caring about them made them feel like a priority and well cared for. Plus, it helped her discover staff problems as well as being able to give compliments to nurses and aides who made that little extra effort to comfort their patients.

She stayed through the shift change and report, adding comments as necessary, and then headed back to her office. Ordinarily she'd be going home about now, but she needed to catch up on some extra paperwork from the weekend.

Before tackling her stack of files, she paused to look out the window. Dark, metal-gray clouds covered a distant sky and the darkness swept to the ground. The rain had let up some, softer now than this morning. But a nasty-looking storm appeared to be headed their way.

She pulled her cell phone out of her pocket and called Cameron to tell him about Dr. Hamilton and her workday. "Looks like I'll be staying at the hospital until around five."

"I'll put potatoes in the oven then go to work grilling the salmon," he said. "Be careful. Weather forecast is predicting tornadoes across our area later tonight."

Anabelle looked out the window again as a pang of anxiety struck her. Tornado warnings would put anyone on edge.

She'd just ended the call when she heard a tap on her door. "Come in."

The door opened and Winona Stouffer poked her head in. "Got a minute?"

"For you? Certainly." Winona was one of her favorite nurses. She stood all of four foot ten and usually wore colorful scrubs.

Today, she had on a pink and black set with a Betty Boop theme. In fact, the black-haired cartoon character reminded Anabelle of Winona. Cameron jokingly called Winona an attitude in a small package.

"I like your top."

"Thanks. Got it on clearance for three bucks." Winona perched her hip on Anabelle's desk.

"Did you need something or did you just want to visit?"

Winona grinned. "Would that we had time to just visit. Actually, I have two things on my agenda. First, since school is about ready to start, we need to have a meeting of the Bike Smarts committee to decide who's going to present the programs and when."

Winona and Anabelle both served on the committee geared toward helping kids and adults stay safe when riding their bikes. After Kirstie's accident, Anabelle had been instrumental in beginning a bike safety program called I've Got Bike Smarts. The program was established with a grant from the town council that the entire community contributed to. Thanks to them, the program reached every child in the fourth grade in the district's four elementary schools, and each child received a bike helmet. Anabelle still served as an adviser, program presenter and member of the committee.

Anabelle nodded. "I can't believe summer is almost over."

"Tell me about it. I'm taking the kids out to buy school supplies this weekend." Winona shuddered. "There goes the budget."

Anabelle nodded. "How well I remember." She would need to shop for supplies as well. Her and Cameron's church, Church of the Good Shepherd, had a program for which parishioners either donated supplies or money to help parents and kids who couldn't afford them. "When are you thinking we should meet?"

"How about Wednesday night at your place?"

"I could do that." Anabelle picked up a pen and jotted a reminder on her calendar.

She sighed. "Good, now for the tough one."

Anabelle raised an eyebrow. "Tough one? Uh-oh, something tells me this isn't good."

"It isn't. You know the new aide we hired last month?"

"Seri?"

Winona folded her arms. "That's the one. She seems very sweet and is nice to the patients; but according to Michelle, Seri isn't getting her work done. The girls from evening shift are complaining about the work your day girls are leaving. Personally, I think she's more interested in socializing than working."

Anabelle pinched her lips together. "Thanks for telling me. She's been fine with me."

"Me too, but we're her superiors."

"True, but I'd like to give her a chance." She recalled Seri's comment about Dr. Hamilton and added, "She seems intuitive and caring. I'll keep an eye on her and talk with her in the next few days."

"Okay." She set her hands on her knees and pushed herself away from the desk. She grinned and gave Anabelle a little wave. "I better get back to work before the others decide I'm shirking *my* responsibilities."

When Winona had gone, Anabelle jotted a note about talking to Seri on her to-do list. "Just what I need."

Truth be told, Anabelle had suspected she might have some trouble with Seri, but she saw promise there as well. Maybe the girl just needed a firm hand. After a thoughtful moment or two, Anabelle pulled the top memo from her stack and got to work.

Chapter Six

*J*AMES CLOCKED OUT AT THREE, THANKFUL TO BE leaving. Once he'd come off the adrenaline high, he'd gone into a slump. He wished now he'd said something to Anabelle and Elena about Gideon. They might have been able to offer some sage advice. Unfortunately, he'd taken an even later lunch than they had.

James had reservations about his son's going into the military; especially knowing what combat could do to a soldier. He remembered all too clearly arguing with his parents about the same thing. His dad, a Vietnam War vet, still suffered effects of post-traumatic stress. His mother had cried every time James mentioned joining up.

But James was young and headstrong, not all that different from his son, and signed up anyway. He'd trained as a medic and saw enough action to know he didn't want that kind of life for his son. Neither did he want to argue with Fern. James didn't suffer from debilitating flashbacks like some vets did, but he had the memories. One scene in particular came to mind. He'd been choppered in with another medic to take care of children who were in school when a bomb hit. James closed his mind to what he had seen. No, Gideon should never have to experience the ravages of war.

James noticed the dark clouds moving toward them and hoped it didn't mean another heavy rainstorm. In the locker room, he shed his work shoes and scrubs and donned the still-damp clothes from this morning. Nothing like getting into wet jeans and tennis shoes. One good thing about it, though, was he wouldn't have to worry about getting rained on again.

James headed home, hoping Fern's mood had improved. Gideon's as well. Though he didn't feel responsible for the arguments this morning, he planned to apologize and to patch things up with Fern.

He wished he had an answer for Gideon, but he still needed time to think and pray on the subject. His son deserved to be rewarded for his good grades. So far he'd managed to stay out of trouble and James couldn't have been more grateful.

On the way home, James stopped at the grocery store to pick up some pink roses. While there he shopped for items they might need for dinner like prewashed baby spinach leaves and raspberry sherbet.

Once home, James parked in the garage, collected his purchases and went in via the kitchen door.

"Hey, sweetheart." James set the bag of groceries on the counter.

"I'm in here."

He carried his peace offering into the living room. The walker beside Fern told him she'd had a rough day. On good days, she managed with a cane.

"For me?" Fern's grin lit up her face. "I should be the one bringing *you* flowers."

He placed the bouquet in her arms and bent down to kiss her. While he was bent over, he greeted Sapphire, Fern's four-year-old Maine Coon cat and constant companion. The cat meowed a greeting of her own, stretching up to keep the chin scratches coming.

"I'm sorry I snapped at you this morning. It's just that Gideon is still a boy. He's too young to be thinking about the military." Her speech came slower than it had that morning, but he still managed to understand most of what she said.

"I tend to agree; but he *is* thinking military, and we'll have to address that." He smiled. "But not right now. We'll talk with him as soon as the opportunity presents itself. At the moment, I need to find a vase for the roses and take a shower before I start dinner."

James kissed her again and started for the laundry room off the kitchen. Finding a suitable vase, he removed the plastic wrap around the flowers and filled the vase with water. He sprinkled in the packet of food that was supposed to keep cut flowers fresh and arranged the roses and greenery. He then carried the bouquet in and set it on the coffee table with a flourish.

"You missed your calling." Fern grinned up at him. "You would have made a great florist."

He chuckled. "I don't think so. I barely know the difference between a rose and a carnation."

He sat down on the couch next to her pausing to admire Fern's cute face, framed in a pixielike hairstyle that she kept short so it was easier for her to handle. Her cocoa brown eyes met his. "What are you looking at?"

"You. Just thinking about how beautiful you are."

She closed her eyes for a moment, her smile gone. "Don't you mean were?"

"No." He pulled her into his arms. "I mean *are*."

They snuggled for a few minutes before being interrupted by their thirteen-year-old barreling through the front door.

Nelson dropped his backpack where he stood. "Sheesh, I can't believe my parents are kissing and stuff in the front room. What if I'd brought a friend home?"

"Oh, the horror of it all." James rose from the couch to meet Nelson as he crossed the room. Giving his son a hug, he said, "I'd think you'd be used to us by now."

"Yeah, well I guess it's better than fighting." Nelson maneuvered around the coffee table and gave his mother a kiss on the cheek and endured another hug.

"How was the swimming?" Fern asked. Nelson had spent the afternoon with his Scout group at the community pool.

He straightened. "Good. I'm close to getting my badge." Nelson hadn't taken much interest in sports—preferring books and computers. James often shot hoops with the boys but could tell Nelson wasn't exactly crazy about the game. Still, James insisted his sons get some exercise every day, so hoops and Scouts seemed just the thing.

"Where is your brother?" James asked.

Nelson shrugged. "I have no idea. I didn't want to wait, so Cody's mother brought me home."

"Ah. Listen, why don't you shower and get dressed. Then I will attempt to feed you."

"Then can I play my computer game afterward?"

"We'll see."

Nelson hooked the strap of his backpack over his shoulder and headed for the stairs.

James rested his hands on the sofa arm and leaned over to kiss Fern on her forehead. "Do you need anything before I take a shower?"

She shook her head. "I'm fine."

James took his time in the shower, mentally scrolling through his long list of things to do that evening. With Fern growing weaker and less able to handle household chores, he had to take on more.

He hoped the MS would go into remission again. This summer he'd had the boys pitch in, but with school starting soon, he might need some outside help. Fern had family nearby. Her parents and sister, Beth, were always willing to help out. As much as he hated asking for assistance, he might not have much choice.

Feeling normal again, James dressed in a Miami Beach T-shirt and khaki shorts and hurried downstairs. He paused at the bottom when he saw Fern reading her large-print book. She held it close to her face to compensate for her worsening vision.

"Blurry vision again?"

"I'm not good for anything anymore. I can't even read."

"Honey, don't do this to yourself. Try not to get so down."

"I know, it's just that days like this, I have to work very hard to keep from . . ." Tears gathered in her eyes.

James caught them on his forefinger and kissed her on the nose. "Well, Princess Cries-a-lot. Pity party is over. I need your assistance in the kitchen."

"Oh." She squealed in surprise as James swooped her into his arms. He carried her into the large kitchen/dining room area then set her on a special safety chair at the counter where she was elevated and could coach him while he worked. He made a quick trip back into the living room for the flowers and set them on the counter. Sapphire protested with a chirpy whine and jumped off the couch. Seconds later she had settled in the kitchen near Fern's feet.

"How about a steak and spinach salad for dinner?" James asked.

"Sounds perfect. You'd better make potatoes for the boys."

"I'll roast enough for all of us. I could use some comfort food myself."

For the next few minutes they talked about their day. James told her about Dr. Hamilton's heart attack and the part he had played in it. He still had a hard time believing it had really happened.

"Oh, James, how awful. Is he okay?"

"I sure hope so. He's the best doctor Hope Haven has." He set the opened bag of baby spinach in front of her with a bowl.

"I hope so too."

"Did you make it to the health club today?" Physical therapy was an important factor in her care, but since she could no longer drive, they had to depend on friends and family to take her there.

She nodded. "Beth came over this morning to help. She took me and brought me back." Fern frowned as she picked through the spinach leaves and dumped them into the bowl.

"Is something wrong?"

"It's just that I hate asking Beth and my parents to help me so often. Maybe we need to look into home health care for me." She tipped her head to one side. "Am I bad enough for that?"

He grinned at her as his stomach took a tumble. "You're not bad at all." He didn't want to face that obstacle just yet, though he supposed they would have to sooner rather than later.

On Monday at five, Anabelle was more than ready to go home. She'd caught up on her paperwork, but wanted to check her patients one more time before leaving. She was especially concerned about Olga and Dr. Drew.

Anabelle slipped into Olga's room and crossed over to her bedside. "You're looking better." The elderly woman was awake and looking more relaxed. "How are you feeling?"

"Pretty good. The doctor says she can fix me up as good as new."

"Great. Did you get the message that your daughter called?"

"I got it."

"And did you talk with her?"

"Nope. Why is she calling me? I told you I didn't want her to know."

Anabelle splayed her hands. "Actually we didn't call her. Christina did."

"*Uff-da*. That girl. Always poking her nose into my business." She smiled then. "The girl acts just like my own daughter wanting to help with this and that."

"I'm sure she's trying to be a good neighbor. Would you like me to phone your daughter so you can talk to her? She's worried about you."

"Well she shouldn't be. I can worry enough for the both of us." Olga clasped her hands together and examined her antique garnet ring. "I suppose I should talk to her. Tell her she doesn't have to come."

"At least let her know what happened and what the doctor said." Anabelle couldn't imagine not wanting to have her children with her if she was sick. On the other hand, she could certainly sympathize with Olga. Like her patient, she wouldn't want to be a burden and she certainly wouldn't want to leave her home.

Anabelle punched in the numbers needed for the long-distance call and handed the phone to Olga. "I'm going home now. I'll see you in the morning."

Olga gave her a wave and began talking to whoever had answered. The smile on her face made Anabelle's day.

She made one more stop, detouring into Dr. Hamilton's room. Genna had gone. Anabelle was both surprised and pleased to see Drew resting. His healthy tan had replaced his earlier pallor.

He turned to study her. "You still here?"

"I had some paperwork to catch up on." Anabelle stepped closer to the bed.

"*Humph.*"

"Did Genna go home?"

"I wish she would. She just went to the cafeteria. Maybe you can talk her into going home and getting some rest."

Anabelle smiled. "I don't think so. If you were in her shoes, would you go home?"

"No, but..."

"I rest my case."

He moved his head from side to side. "They'll be shipping me home tonight or tomorrow, if Hildie ever gets back to write my orders."

"So soon?"

"I don't need to be taking up a bed in Cardiac Care. If she doesn't hurry up, I might have to write the orders myself."

"You may be improved, but you don't want to leave here too soon. I'm glad you're feeling better, but you and I both know you need to take it easy."

"You're worse than Genna." His half smile softened his grouchy tone.

He glanced out the window and then let his gaze slide back to Anabelle. She saw worry there, a glimpse of fear. Then it was gone.

"Hi, Anabelle," Genna said as she came in. "Is my husband complaining again?"

They chatted for a few minutes. Dr. Drew was beginning to sound like his old self. Anabelle hoped his improvement was genuine and not just a ruse to get himself released sooner than was wise.

"I'd best be heading home." Glancing out the window, Anabelle shuddered. "Those dark clouds are getting too close for comfort."

Chapter Seven

*L*OOK WHAT I HAVE." CANDACE ENTERED Jeanine Parsons' room with a tiny bundle in each arm. After the excitement of birth and initial examinations, Candace and her aide had taken the Parsons twins into the nursery to clean them up and perform all the other duties required for new babies. The baby girls were tiny, only five pounds five ounces each, but seemed healthy and viable and, of course, absolutely adorable.

"Oh, how sweet." Jeanine held out her arms, more than ready to hold her little ones. Dad's wide smile showed his delight. He snapped several digital photos of Candace handing the babies to his wife, then set the camera down so he could hold one himself.

Candace made certain the couple had everything they needed and checked out with her co-workers.

Even if she was running late, days that ended like this energized her.

The morning had been a disaster with the code blue and her reaction to seeing Dr. Hamilton. Candace felt better after talking with Heath over coffee after he'd stepped in to help her. Fortunately, the afternoon had gone well; and they had delivered the twins just an hour ago.

Now, going out to her car, Candace felt she had enough stamina to be a mother to her two children: Brooke, eleven, and Howie, five. She often felt tired when she came home. It didn't help to have guilt weighing her down.

Candace tried to be a good mom and would like to be with her children more. But someone had to work. Though Candace struggled with the unfairness of it all, truth be told, she loved her job.

A twinge of anger rose up as it occasionally did, anger at Dean for leaving her and anger with God for taking him so early in life. Sometimes she even felt angry with her mom for being with her kids when she couldn't be. Not rational, of course, but there just the same.

After parking her car in the garage of their spacious four-bedroom, split-level home, she hurried inside. As always, Candace appreciated the clean house and the wonderful aroma coming from the kitchen. Some days, coming home was like getting an injection of joy. She loved the way the kids welcomed her and the way her mother had dinner nearly ready.

"Mommy! Mommy!" Brooke and Howie nearly trampled one another as each tried to reach her first.

Candace leaned over the children and wrapped her arms around them. She inhaled the scent of them, sweat, lingering bath bubbles, chocolate-chip cookies. She kissed and hugged her wiggling imps while trying to stay upright.

She could almost feel their unadulterated love soak from their skin into hers. "Come on, Mommy. Come see what we made." Howie pulled at her arm.

She chuckled. "I'm coming. Give me a chance to get up." Listening to their laughter and excitement lifted her spirits even higher. These were the moments she needed to focus on. The children kept her going and made her feel alive.

As quickly as they'd rushed to her side, they scrambled back to their projects—Howie to his Play-Doh and Brooke to her drawings.

Candace looked over their work. "You guys are very good artists."

"Yes, we are." Brooke's grin brought out her cute dimples. She had drawn a girl's face, cartoon style, with large eyes and a tear on her cheek. Candace had noticed her daughter often drew people or animals with very sad expressions. Brooke had taken her father's death terribly hard. As Candace praised the drawing, she gave her daughter's shoulders an extra squeeze.

Her mother, Janet, emerged from the kitchen to give Candace a hug. "How was your day?"

"Horrible and wonderful, but not all at the same time."

"Would you like some tea? I just put on some water to boil." Janet wiped her hands on a dishtowel.

"Tea sounds perfect." She hesitated. "I'd like to change first and shower."

"I'll have the tea and some fresh cookies for you when you come down."

She hurried up the stairs to the upper level and into the master suite. Candace paused to admire the room as she always did. She and Dean had picked out the beautiful queen-sized cherry sleigh bed and matching dresser, end tables and chest of drawers. It had been their first purchase of brand-new furniture. In the early years of her marriage, they'd decorated with hand-me-downs and thrift store bargains.

After Dean's death, Candace often came into their bedroom to sit in the cushioned armchair and hold his pillow or one of his shirts on which his scent still lingered.

His scent was gone now, but she still had his photo on the small table and the adorable stuffed bunny he'd given her when they were dating. Candace still loved the suite—loved the comforting and bittersweet memories it brought back.

The room was a respite of sorts, and she did her best to keep it that way. Every morning she made the bed and straightened the room so it would welcome her home as it did now.

Candace stepped into the walk-in closet and shed her comic frog top and white pants. She liked the colorful designs of her own uniforms, rather than the blue and green scrubs the hospital provided.

She took a longer shower than usual, imagining today's traumatic event and her overall sadness as grime flowing out of her body and down the drain. Some days that's all it took—a shower infused with a little imagination and a lot of willpower.

She stepped out of the shower feeling somewhat restored. Catching sight of herself, she startled. Maybe it was the shadows in her eyes, more hazel now than green. She'd also lost weight again.

"Okay Candace," she met her own eyes in the image. "The flashback today set you back. It's not the end of the world." Candace pulled the blow-dryer out of the drawer and brushed in body as she dried her brown hair until it shone with copper and gold highlights. When it dried, she brushed through it, parting it on the side, shaping it into the bob she always wore. She liked this style, as had Dean.

Minutes later, feeling refreshed and relaxed in a pair of white shorts and pink V-neck, she joined her mother in the kitchen.

Candace told her mother about Dr. Hamilton but didn't mention the flashback that had disabled her during the code blue. Mentioning that would only fuel her mother's case for Candace to see a counselor.

Switching subjects, she said, "The good news is that Jeanine Parsons had twin girls. They're healthy and doing great. Jeanine is too." Ordinarily, because of confidentiality issues, Candace wouldn't have mentioned her patient's name, but she and her mother knew Jeanine personally and had been waiting for the big day.

Janet grinned. "Must be all that heavy praying we've been doing. I'll have to take Brooke and Howie out to buy gifts. The kids will love seeing the babies."

Candace set down her tea, then rose to get the children's drawings from the basket on the counter. Placing them on the table she slid back into the chair to leaf through them. "Look what they drew," she said.

Janet admired the brightly colored pictures. "They're doing very well," she said, then drained the last of her tea and headed for the kitchen to stir whatever was simmering on the back burner.

Candace called after her. "Thanks to you."

After her father died, Brooke would not speak. Candace had sought counseling, and after two months the crisis seemed to pass. The counselor had recommended that Candace provide as much consistency and stability as possible. Janet had done that and more.

Candace followed her mom into the kitchen. "You've really done a great job with them, Mom." Candace took her mother's hand. "I don't know what I would have done without you."

"They're wonderful kids. And I love them to pieces."

"I know and they adore you." In that respect Candace felt extremely fortunate. Many parents had to drag their kids to day care every day and hope they were being properly cared for.

Her mother's smile transitioned into a worried look. "I—um . . ."

"What's wrong?" Candace wrapped her hands around her cup. She had a feeling she wasn't going to like Mom's answer.

"I need to tell you something." She sighed. "I know you're going to be upset with me, but I made an appointment for you with a grief counselor."

Candace nearly dropped the cup. "You didn't."

Janet held up her hands in mock surrender. "Just hear me out. You and I both know you need help. You're still having nightmares. It's been three years now. I know you'll never forget, and no one's asking you to, but honey you need . . ."

"I'm doing just fine." Her initial anger subsided as guilt moved in. *You are not doing fine. This morning made that clear.*

"I'm sorry. I can't sit around and watch you live in such despair. You've been promising to see someone for two years, but you never seem to get around to it." Janet squeezed her daughter's hand. "If not for you, do it for Brooke and Howie. They need more from you."

"More? I'm a good mother." Even as Candace said the words, she had her doubts. As much as she loved her children, she could do better.

"Yes, you are, but sometimes it feels like you are only half here. This is a difficult word to hear, but, honey, you're depressed."

"Depressed sounds so extreme. I'm functioning."

Her mother shot her a skeptical look.

"Besides, what could a counselor do for me that I can't do myself?"

"Candace, please."

Candace felt herself relenting when she looked into her mother's pleading eyes.

"When is the appointment?"

"Tonight—at seven."

"Tonight?" Candace coughed as she set her cup down on the table.

"I was afraid if I made it for later in the week, you'd cancel."

She probably would have. Candace rubbed her forehead. "In case you haven't noticed it's stormy out there and there are tornado warnings."

"Lila said she'd come here. She wants the first session here at the house so she can get a feeling for family dynamics."

"Lila? Why do I know that name?"

"She's in practice with Tony Evans. He's the counselor Brooke was seeing."

"Right, I remember." Candace rose and gripped the back of the chair. "I have a headache. I'm going to take a nap on the sofa."

"I'll call you when dinner's ready."

Candace settled on the comfy sofa, where she could watch her kids play. She'd barely gotten settled when Howie brushed off his hands and climbed up beside her. She wiggled back to give him more room. Brooke set down her pencil and snuggled in as well.

Candace closed her eyes, smiling at the scent of the Play-Doh, as she draped her arm across them both. What she needed, Candace thought, were more moments like this. Maybe after their nap, she'd call Lila and cancel the appointment.

As Anabelle started for home, the wind and rain returned with a vengeance. The radio announcer repeated the message that Cameron had given her earlier. "Tornado warnings have been issued throughout Bureau County."

"I hate tornadoes," she muttered aloud. She'd seen more than her share of disasters. A tornado could touch down in one area, leaving a swath of devastation and even wipe out an entire town and then skip over the next without leaving a tree limb on the ground. Illinois had an average of twenty a year. Deerford had been lucky. The last one to hit their little town was in 1975, leaving one dead and fifty injured. They'd been lucky.

Anabelle prayed that her family and all the people of Deerford and the neighboring areas would be safe from this new threat.

Once again, she could hardly see through the sheets of rain pelting the windshield. She drove by instinct, grateful that she knew the route to her house so well. Even so, the drive seemed to take forever. By the time she reached the house at 6:30 PM, her hands were practically frozen to the wheel from sheer tension.

Cameron stood in the open and welcoming garage as she pulled into the driveway. He motioned for her to pull inside. Once she'd parked, he opened the car door for her.

Anabelle gathered her things and stepped out into his waiting arms. She leaned against him, letting her jangled nerves melt away as she drew in his strength. Cameron pushed the button for the garage door opener and watched to make certain it closed.

As they turned to go inside the house, everything went black.

"I knew that was coming." Cameron chuckled.

"We just lost our electricity and you're laughing?"

"I was just thinking that if I were a much younger man, I'd have taken immediate advantage of the darkness to kiss my sweetheart. Now my first thought is to find the candles and eat dinner."

Anabelle gripped his hand and pulled him back. "I don't know about you, but let's pretend we're young."

He drew her into his arms and kissed her.

"*Hmm*, that was nice." She moved ahead of him. "Now we can eat. I'm famished."

Although the sun wouldn't be setting for another hour, the dark clouds ate up any daylight they had left. Cameron had already set the table. He took the salmon and potatoes out of the oven where he'd been keeping them warm.

Candlelight and the flickering flames in the fireplace made the meal seem like a romantic interlude rather than a nuisance. They feasted on grilled salmon—which, in Anabelle's opinion, was a little dry but still tasty—baked potatoes and a fresh salad.

"We should do this more often." Anabelle took a sip of her drink. "By the way, you did a great job on dinner. Maybe I'll have to work late more often."

"You'd grow tired of my meager menu. I can do grilled chicken, baked potatoes, a salad and I make a mean oatmeal."

"You don't want to admit you can cook," Anabelle teased. "I know that ploy."

"And I know if I spent more time in the kitchen than I already do, you'd be shooing me out."

"That's true enough." She loved cooking for her family, always had.

"How's the good doctor doing?"

"Better. I stopped to see him just before I came home. Speaking of which, I should call Kirstie and let her know what happened. She'll want to drop by to see him."

"She called earlier and so did Ainslee. Wanted to make sure we knew about the tornado. She sounded upset."

"Who, Ainslee or Kirstie?"

"Ainslee."

Anabelle set her glass down. "Did you ask her what was wrong? She was upset yesterday at our quilting meeting too. I hope she's okay."

"Just worried about the storm, I suspect."

Anabelle wasn't so sure.

When they'd finished dinner, and cleared off the table, Anabelle rinsed the dishes and put them in the dishwasher. She then tried to call her girls on her cell phone. The calls wouldn't go through. "Do you think they'll be all right? I wish they were here with us."

Cameron was sitting on the couch and patted the space beside him. "They're fine. They all have basements and know what to do if the tornado does hit."

"I suppose you're right." She sank onto the sofa and leaned back against him.

"They're adults now." He planted a kiss on her forehead. "Try not to worry."

"I do, but telling a mother not to worry is like telling a flea not to bite. Worrying is a mother's job."

He chuckled. "The Bible tells us not to be anxious."

She poked him in the stomach. "Don't be quoting Scripture to me, dear husband. I know the verse by heart. Besides, I'm not anxious. I'm concerned."

"All right then." He draped his arm around her shoulders. After a while he kissed her forehead. "It's nice to sit here and relax with my favorite girl."

"Very nice."

They snuggled on the couch for half an hour as Cameron began to doze off. Anabelle listened to the gentle rhythm of his breathing wondering if this was how nights were spent pre-electricity, before she too drifted off. Cameron eventually stirred. He yawned and gently moved her aside so he could get up. "We might as well go to bed. Doesn't look like we'll be getting the power back anytime soon."

Anabelle nodded and followed him upstairs.

Cameron set a flashlight on the bottom step and took the second one upstairs. There was no need for them to take shelter in the basement. Deerford had a top-of-the-line siren system to warn them if the tornado took a turn toward them.

Cameron seemed to have no trouble falling asleep. Anabelle lay awake listening to the pounding rain and wind as she prayed for Olga, Dr. Hamilton, Kirstie, Ainslee, and everyone else she could think of.

She finally gave up on sleep and made her way downstairs to her favorite chair. Without air-conditioning, the air felt muggy and warm. She pulled her legs up and leaned back. Like a sentinel, she stayed at the window watching the waving trees in the back-yard listening to the ferocity of the rain battering the foliage, praying that the tornado would pass them by. Before long, the rain lessened in intensity and Anabelle sighed. There'd been no tornado siren. It looked as though Deerford had escaped the storm.

Chapter Eight

BY TUESDAY MORNING, THE RAIN AND WIND HAD stopped. The electricity was back on, and a very tired Anabelle tried to gear herself up for work. Once dressed, she went into the living room and turned on the morning news broadcast. The tornado had died out and while it had hit the outskirts of Princeton, it had missed Deerford entirely.

"Thank You, Lord." Anabelle cast a gaze upward. After eating breakfast, she set her dishes in the dishwasher and turned it on.

With a cup of coffee under her belt and her devotions for the day buoying her, Anabelle headed for the hospital. On the drive, she cheered the sunshine by singing "Sunshine on My Shoulders." She loved the sun and hoped one day she and Cameron could winter in a warmer climate. But for now she was content living only minutes away from the kids.

Hope Haven was abuzz with activity and relief that the tornado had not been as bad as first predicted. Though there had been a number of injuries in Princeton from the storm, there had been no casualties; no one had to be diverted to Hope Haven.

Anabelle greeted several co-workers on her way in. In the elevator, Seri Mason, the new aide in CCU, heaved a sigh.

Anabelle took the bait. "What's wrong?"

"I can't believe he's asking us to do this." She waved a yellow paper Anabelle recognized as an official hospital memo.

"What is it?" Anabelle was surprised to hear the young aide complain to her. Seri was normally sweet and compliant, but she hadn't forgotten Winona's comments.

Seri tossed her head in a rather impudent fashion. Finally, she said, "Albert Varner, our very own CEO, is making it mandatory that all staff brush up on their emergency procedures in case a storm or disaster actually hits Deerford. He must have come unglued last night thinking we might have a bunch of injuries from the tornado."

Anabelle smiled at Seri's dramatic reaction. "Personally, I think he's made a wise decision. Can I ask why it upsets you?"

"Are you serious? He wants everyone to attend an in-service session, read a sixty-page instruction manual and watch a video. I don't have time to do all that. Like, I have a date tonight."

Anabelle sighed. "Seri, have you ever had disaster training?"

"Not exactly. Just the emergency stuff they showed me when I got hired." She gave Anabelle a sidelong glance. "Guess I need it, huh?"

"Yes you do. First of all," Anabelle said, "with the exception of reading the manual, you'll be watching the video and doing the in-service during your shift. Secondly, you can read the manual during your breaks, at lunch or at home."

Anabelle would have invited the girl into the office for a brief chat but today, with all the in-service sessions scheduled, was probably not a good time. She stepped off the elevator and made a beeline for her office where she undoubtedly had a more detailed version of the memo waiting on her desk.

The memo summoned her and the other supervisors to attend a meeting at 8:00 AM in the conference room to prepare them for the day's events. If she hurried, she'd have time to get to report; but seeing patients would have to wait until later. During the night, Dillon Blake, the patient Drew had been operating on when he'd had his heart attack, had taken a turn for the worse and required emergency surgery. He'd come through it okay and was still in recovery. Anabelle's heart felt heavy. Had it been something Drew had done—or not done—that had caused the problem?

At 7:45 AM, Anabelle started toward the stairs. The conference room was already set up with coffee, tea and pastries. Marge from ICU had already poured herself a cup and set it on the enormous dark oak table. Several of the head nurses and the director, Betty Adams, came in. A few seemed upset by the last-minute disaster plans. Most took it in stride. In-service was all part of being a quality hospital.

Anabelle snagged a custard-filled donut with chocolate frosting to go with her coffee. Once she'd set her goodies down, Anabelle picked up the folder that had been placed on the table at each chair and thumbed through it. She began jotting down a schedule for the nurses on her unit so they could stagger their times and all get the video done prior to the end of their shift.

Penny Risser, Varner's executive assistant, came in at exactly eight o'clock pushing a cart loaded with videos, booklets and the like. "Good morning." Her tone belied the statement, but then Penny wasn't known for her pleasantries. She'd been given the name Dragon Lady and was well known for guarding the CEO's office.

Anabelle doubted it had been a good morning for Penny. Having to pull all of this together must have been a big effort. But perhaps not. Knowing Penny and her propensity for being ultra organized, the job may have only taken twenty minutes.

Varner had chosen well when he'd hired Penny. She managed him as well as the office, making him look efficient, rather than the scattered disorganized man he was. While Albert Varner had charisma, Penny was often brusque and disapproving, but he didn't seem to mind. She made him look good, and he couldn't manage his job without her.

"Good morning, Penny." Anabelle stood. "Is there anything we can help you with?"

"I have it, thanks. How's that jade plant coming along?"

Anabelle returned to her seat. "Great, thanks to you." Anabelle rather liked Penny, or at least one facet of Penny. The woman loved plants and could grow anything. Anabelle had asked her about her jade plant last year, and Penny took it in as if it were a patient. Anabelle didn't know what she'd done to it, but the plant was flourishing.

Varner's office had a number of large plants and hanging baskets thanks to Penny. As far as Anabelle was concerned, anyone who could coax a dying plant back to life couldn't be all bad.

Albert didn't show up at the meeting, maybe he'd never planned to come. But it didn't matter—Penny did a superb job of making certain everyone knew their responsibilities.

Each supervisor or charge nurse would hand out the booklets along with a card to sign and hand back in when they had complied with the requirements. The folder they'd been given contained sheets listing times for the in-service and video presentations. The meeting was short and to the point. And, Anabelle thought, well done.

By the time the meeting ended and she'd returned to the unit, Dillon Blake had been brought down from recovery. While she was tempted to check on him right away, the first task on her agenda was to inform her staff as to what their schedules would be for the next twenty-four hours.

Thanks to Penny's efficiency, her scheduling took only fifteen minutes. The phone call to Kirstie, to let her know what had happened to Drew, would add another five. Before dialing the number, Anabelle slipped off her glasses, folded them and tucked them into her upper lab coat pocket.

"Mom, are you serious?" Distress registered in Kirstie's voice when Anabelle gave her the news. "Our Dr. Hamilton?"

"I'm afraid so. I wanted to call you last night, but the storm knocked out the power."

"For us too. Thanks for letting me know. I'll be there as soon as I can."

After saying their good-byes, Anabelle hung up, the word *us* lingered in her mind like a sour lemon drop. *What did she mean by us? Us, as in a couple?* Anabelle tried to clear the thought from her mind.

She posted the instructions for the in-service and told Becky so she could distribute the items to her team and explain the details to the next shift.

"I'll make sure everyone knows," Becky said. "By the way, Dr. Hamilton wants to see you when you have a minute."

"How is he?"

Becky shrugged. "He says he's ready to go home, but I think he's in denial."

When Anabelle finally made it to his room, Drew was up and sitting in the recliner, reading the paper and drinking coffee.

"I hope that's decaf."

He lowered the paper. "Good morning, Anabelle. How's my favorite nurse?" His wide grin made Anabelle think perhaps he was better than expected. He was in excellent health and his heart had been performing well since the incident. She'd have to look over his chart to see what tests he'd had and read Dr. Hildebrand's notes.

"You'll not be buttering me up, Doc." Anabelle smiled back. "How are you this morning?"

"I am doing well. I see no reason I can't go home today and finish these tests as an outpatient. I'm not an invalid. I'm a doctor, and I'm declaring myself fit for discharge."

Not that she didn't trust the good doctor, but she knew he would not allow anything to slow him down if he could help it. "Are you telling me that if you had yourself as a patient, you'd approve a discharge this soon?"

"I would."

She sighed and folded her arms. "The discharge is between you and Dr. Hildebrand. Personally, I think you need to take it easy for a while. Stay here until we're sure there's no damage to the heart."

"If there is, it's minor."

"And you know this because?"

"No pain. And the MRI and EKG didn't show any significant changes."

"I'm just saying that you're an institution here. As far as I'm concerned, you're one of the best doctors we have."

He raised an eyebrow. "That's kind of you."

"It's true. You've saved hundreds of patients. I mean, look what you did with Kirstie."

He smiled. "She did all the hard work. I just happened to be there to patch her up."

"God brought you to us at the right time." Anabelle felt her eyes unexpectedly start to water. She quickly blinked back the tears. She would never forget her own panic and fear when she got to the hospital and saw her baby lying there, after a drunk driver had hit her and left the scene. Dr. Hamilton had been in the ER that night. "You saved her life. I want you to be around a long time. That means taking your heart attack seriously."

He looked beyond Anabelle to the open door. "Hey, look who's here!"

Kirstie bounced in carrying a cartoonish get-well balloon. "Hey, Dr. Drew. Hasn't anyone told you you're on the wrong side? You're supposed to be the doctor, not the patient." She bent down to hug him and kiss his cheek. She looked lovely in her bright floral summer dress.

Drew hugged her back. "How's my favorite girl?"

"Good." She lifted her leg so he could see her new prosthesis. "It's working so much better than the straight one. The curved foot puts a spring in my step."

"That's wonderful. I see you're not trying to hide it."

She laughed. "Not anymore. I watched that film about what this prosthesis has done for people, seeing them run and walk like normal. I decided it's time to quit hiding." She stepped back and held out her arms. "This is me and this is what you get."

Anabelle hadn't heard about Kirstie's new take on life. In a way she was proud of her daughter's growth. Then again, she felt almost embarrassed that Kirstie could be so brazen about it.

Maybe embarrassed wasn't the right word. Then what? Anabelle realized that she was the one who hadn't come to terms with Kirstie's loss of a leg. Every time Anabelle saw the prosthesis, she was reminded of the horrific accident and the man who'd caused it.

George Talbot had served five years in prison—not nearly long enough. The old familiar feeling began to rise from the dark place in her heart. Anabelle hauled in a deep breath and pushed the thoughts of him from her mind. She could not, would not, let her hatred and anger consume Kirstie's joy.

"Mother?" Kirstie touched Anabelle's arm, bringing her out of her reverie.

"What? Oh, sorry. I was just thinking." Anabelle gave Kirstie a hug and leveled an I-mean-business gaze on Drew. "I'll let you two chat. I have patients to tend to—ones who actually listen to my advice."

Dr. Hamilton chuckled as she left the room.

Before heading to the cafeteria, Anabelle stopped at the chapel. Her thoughts about the man who'd nearly taken Kirstie's life lingered, and Anabelle knew it was time to have the discussion she'd been avoiding. It was time to have a talk with God.

Shortly after completing morning care on her patients in ICU, Elena sat at the nurses' desk writing her notes.

"Elena." The unit secretary handed Elena a note. "A call came in for you while you were in with a patient. I told her I'd have you call back."

"Thanks." Elena studied the number but didn't recognize it. Curious, she picked up the phone and dialed.

"Oh, Elena, I'm so glad you called."

"Who is this?" A vice gripped her stomach. She thought she recognized the voice, but desperately hoped she was wrong.

"This is Sarah."

No, no, no, no. It can't be. Panic swept over her causing an ache in the pit of her stomach.

Why is she calling?

Elena focused on steadying her voice, hoping to emulate calm. "Why are you calling me at work, Sarah? I really don't have time to talk to you."

"Please. I figured you'd hear me out more than Rafael." Her voice broke but Elena didn't care—at least she tried not to care.

Sarah Fulton was Isabel's mother. Elena seethed every time she thought of the woman who had chosen drugs over her baby, who had left Rafael to care for their newborn alone. She and Cesar had taken in Rafael and baby Isabel to live with them, and now they were a happy family. Nothing would change that if Elena had anything to say about it.

"What do you want?" Elena knew her voice had a cold edge to it, but she had nothing to say to this woman. She especially didn't want to hear anything Sarah might have to say.

"I just wanted to know how my little girl is."

"*Your* little girl?" Elena clenched her fist and held the receiver so hard she thought it might crack. "Since when?"

"I've changed, Elena. I'm clean now. And I . . . I just want to see her."

"No." Elena's heart pounded in her chest.

"Please. I'd like to give her a birthday present."

"I'm surprised you even remember when her birthday is."

"I'm her mother."

With clenched teeth, Elena quickly set the receiver back in its cradle.

Oh, Lord, not now. She can't just call and want to see Isabel. I can't let her.

A thought came unbidden from somewhere deep inside: *Sarah is her mother.*

She quickly dismissed it. *No. I am her mother. She's my child.*

Then Elena felt her shoulders slump. *She's not my child . . . she's my grandchild.*

Elena knew the voice—had always known it. Even though she'd walked away from her faith as a teenager and had only recently begun going to church again, she'd always believed in God. But how could God ask this of her?

She'd held this worry in her heart all this time, knowing that Sarah would likely come back someday. Now that day was here.

Panic gripped her. She hadn't heard a word from the woman since Isabel's birth. Elena was admittedly relieved when Sarah hadn't wanted to marry Rafael. She hadn't wanted her baby either. All she'd wanted was to return to the streets to buy drugs.

Sarah would only bring heartbreak by coming back.

I'm the only mother Isabel has ever known, and I plan to keep it that way.

Still, she couldn't help but worry. Sarah was twenty-three now, and Elena couldn't blame her for wanting to be in Isabel's life. She might even have a legal right to see Isabel.

And what about Isabel in all this? Didn't she deserve to know her mother? An image of Isabel's face flashed through her mind, and Elena saw the pain in her granddaughter's eyes, the pain she would experience if Sarah were to suddenly appear in her life only to disappear again just as quickly. No, this decision was about protecting Isabel.

Maybe you won't have anything to say about it—what if Sarah takes you to court?

Elena blinked back tears and tucked the note in her pocket. It was amazing how quickly her heart had been thrown into such turmoil. Dabbing the corners of her eyes, she left the nurses' station to answer a call light, trying to dismiss the intrusive and heartrending thoughts.

Because of the storm, the counselor Candace's mother had scheduled for her had called to postpone for Friday. Another trial bypassed, at least for the moment.

Candace managed to lose herself in babies and new mothers at work. They now had four babies in their nursery. Candace rejoiced over the new bundles of joy. She brought the twins to their mother, who, having slept through a feeding, was more than ready for them.

"Have you decided on names yet?" Candace adjusted the pillows so the new mom could feed both crying babies at once.

"Mary and Margaret, for my grandmother who was Mary-Margaret."

"That's a lovely combination."

And so her morning went. By lunchtime, Candace felt as though she'd worked several days without rest. The weariness from the code blue episode lingered and all the positive thoughts and all the babies and their mothers didn't chase it away.

Candace stopped in at the chapel before going to lunch. She found Anabelle kneeling at the altar. Candace eased into the back pew so she wouldn't disturb her friend. She wasn't surprised to see Anabelle here. In fact they met on occasion at the chapel to pray for patients or one another. Candace hadn't mentioned her resistance to counseling. Nor had she talked about her persistent grief. Maybe it was time. She could use prayer about now.

Candace watched Anabelle get to her feet and turn. Their gazes met and Anabelle smiled. "Are you all right?"

Candace didn't know what to say.

Anabelle sat down beside her. "You don't have to tell me. We can pray together, trusting that the Lord knows our needs."

"True, but I feel like I should tell you and the others what's going on. I really could use some prayers. I'm not doing so well on my own."

"None of us do. As the Bible says, a cord of three strands is not easily broken. Don't be afraid to talk with us."

"I'm not." Candace gave her friend a wan smile. "Okay, maybe I am. I went to the code blue for Dr. Hamilton yesterday and . . ." She closed her eyes. "It hit me so hard. I had a flashback of Dean and . . ." Candace paused, not sure she could continue.

"I'm so sorry." Anabelle wrapped her arms around her.

Candace leaned into her embrace. "I fell apart. I couldn't do anything but sit there."

"Oh, honey. I wish I'd known. We could have been praying for you through all of this."

"Heath was there. He walked me through it and sat with me while I processed it. Only, I can't seem to shake these feelings."

"Are you seeing a counselor?"

There was that question again. Candace shook her head.

"I didn't think so."

Candace sighed. "My mother made an appointment for me, but the counselor had to cancel because of the storm. But I shouldn't need to see anyone. I should be able to handle this with prayer. The Bible says, 'I can do all things through God who strengthens me.' I've been saying that verse over and over again."

Anabelle took hold of her hand. "Believe me, I know that feeling all too well. After Kirstie's accident, I went through a terrible depression. Nothing I did seemed to work. I was failing at home, at work and couldn't seem to hold it together. Like you, I was too proud to ask for help. My head nurse took me aside one day and made me go see a psychologist."

"You?"

"Me. Depression and grief do not necessarily go away by thinking positively, though that doesn't hurt. Sometimes, as in my case, we need something more to get us through the rougher spots, whether it's counseling or medication or a combination of both."

"I suppose. It's just. . . . I don't know how I'll be able to see a counselor. They're expensive and there's so little time with my kids as it is. And I can't ask my mom to babysit more."

"I'm sure there are answers for all your questions and concerns. Could I pray with you?"

Candace nodded. Anabelle bowed her head and squeezed her friend's hand. "Lord, we know You love Candace and we know how important she is to You. Please heal her heart and set her on the path you would want her to take. Let her find the answers she needs with regard to her children. You know her needs and we ask that You meet those needs. In Jesus' name, amen."

"Thanks, Anabelle." Candace wished she had talked to her sooner.

"You're welcome. Now let's go have lunch before our half hour is over."

They entered the cafeteria together and Candace picked up yogurt and a small salad. She usually ate a light lunch and had a fruit snack in the afternoon. At least these days she wasn't forgetting to eat altogether.

A short time later, Elena headed to the cafeteria for lunch. Seeing Anabelle, Candace and James at one of the tables by the window, Elena paid for her salad and yogurt and headed their way.

"Just the person I want to see." James glanced at her, then down at his book. "What's a four-letter word for a church recess?"

Elena shrugged and set her tray down. "I have no idea."

James frowned. "*Hmm*. One down doesn't help much. What's a Hebrew zither?"

"Sounds like an instrument." Anabelle spooned up some raspberry yogurt.

James set the crossword puzzle aside and raised his gaze to meet Elena's. His smile faded. "What's wrong, Elena? You look like you've lost . . . is it a patient?"

"No." Elena sighed. "It's a long story. I got a phone call this morning from Sarah."

"Sarah." Anabelle frowned. "Not Isabel's mother."

"That's the one."

"No wonder you're upset," Candace said. "What did she want?"

Elena looked down at her salad, her almost nonexistent appetite diminished even more by the lump in her throat. "Sarah wants to see Isabel. She wants to bring her a birthday present."

"That's a bad thing?" James asked.

"Oh my." Anabelle seemed to understand the ramifications far better than James did.

"Yes, it's a very bad thing." Elena clasped her hands together. "She can't possibly think I'll let her waltz back into Isabel's life. The woman is an addict. She walked away from my son and their baby just like that, and we haven't heard a word from her since then."

"What did you tell her?" Candace leaned forward, arms resting on the table.

"I told her she had no right to see Isabel."

Anabelle grimaced. "*Um*—actually, Elena, unless she signed papers, she may have that right."

"That thought had crossed my mind." Elena placed a hand on her stomach and released a long breath. "I can't seem to think about anything else. What if Sarah wants custody of Isabel? What if she tries to take her away from us? And what would this do to Isabel? She doesn't know about her mother. It would tear our family apart."

"I'm sorry, Elena," Candace said. "Do you think she's still on drugs?"

"She said she was clean, but I don't believe it."

James tore apart his bun and picked up a knife to butter it. "Maybe you could do some detective work. Find out where she lives and what she's doing."

Elena didn't want to.

Anabelle pursed her lips. "Or, if she calls you again, you could meet her for coffee. You'll be able to tell a lot from talking with her. It would be a good time to make an assessment."

"I don't know. I don't want to see her." Elena pushed the salad around on her plate.

"Seems to me the best way to handle the situation and save yourself a lot of grief," James said, "is to confront her and find out exactly what she intends to do."

Candace nodded. "He's right, you know. They both are."

"I suppose. It's silly to worry about something that hasn't happened." Elena didn't tell them that she suspected much of her concern had come from God of all people.

"Maybe I'll get lucky and she'll just go away."

"Somehow," Anabelle said, "I don't think that's going to happen."

"We'll be here for you." Candace reached across the table to touch Elena's arm. "And I'll be praying for the best solution for all of you."

"Thank you."

After a beat of silence, Candace cleared her throat and said, "I don't mean to change the subject, but I need prayer for something too." She told them about the flashback and her resistance to counseling.

James nodded. "Oh man. I know what you're going through. I had some flashbacks when I first got out of the service. For me they eventually subsided, but some of my buddies are disabled by them. You need to see someone."

"It's odd," she mused. "I have so often suggested counseling to my mothers with postpartum depression, but I'm having such difficulty doing what I would recommend for a patient. Maybe it's the time away from my kids and lack of a sitter. The cost. I don't know."

"The cost should be minimal," James said. "We have mental health insurance."

"I'm glad you told us this, Candace." Elena set her fork on the unfinished salad and grinned. "I can help with the babysitting. We could trade. Isabel loves to play with Brooke and Howie. I would be happy to watch them. And perhaps Isabel could go to your house sometimes."

Candace smiled as she blinked back tears. "You three are something else. You wiped out my best excuses in less than a minute."

"Glad to help." James smiled. "Keep us posted. Let us know how we can pray for you."

"I will. And for now, I think I'd better opt out of the code blue team."

Anabelle's first task for the afternoon was to check on Olga Pederson.

"You're awake. I stopped by earlier, but you were sawing logs." Anabelle stepped into the room and pushed back the curtains revealing a middle-aged woman with dark hair reclining in the chair. "Oh. I'm sorry. I didn't realize you had company."

"Anabelle, this is my daughter Carla."

Carla lowered the footrest and scrambled to her feet. "It's nice to meet you. My mother tells me you've all been taking good care of her."

"We do our best." Anabelle's gaze swept over her patient and the monitors. "You're looking better, Olga. How are you feeling?"

"Good. I told Carla she didn't have to come, but she never was one to listen to her mother."

Carla grinned as she took her mother's hand. "Don't listen to her. I was the perfect daughter. She was the stubborn one and still is."

"I'm glad you're here," Anabelle said. She felt certain Olga felt the same. "How did you get here so quickly?"

"I caught a red-eye out of Portland last night. Rented a car in Peoria." She yawned.

"I take it you've been discussing care options. Have you come to any conclusions?"

"Talking and getting nowhere." Carla sighed.

"I understand how frustrating it must be for both of you." Anabelle looked from one to the other. "I can see how difficult it would be for you to leave your home, Olga. It represents independence, and leaving might seem like you're giving that up."

"Ya—I suppose that's as good a way as any to put it."

Anabelle nodded. "Maybe I can help. You need to know that Dr. Hildebrand won't discharge you to go home unless you have someone there to care for you or until she's sure you're able to take care of yourself."

Carla sighed. "That may be a problem. I can stay for a week or two, but I'll have to go home after that. Maybe we can hire a caregiver."

"No." Olga sounded adamant. "My friend Lucille did that and the woman stole her blind."

"That's too bad," Anabelle offered, "but I don't think that sort of thing happens often, especially if you go through a reputable agency."

"She's right, Mom. Lucille should have checked her out."

"These days there are a lot of alternatives. I know you don't want to leave your home, but you might want to look at some of the senior retirement centers. You can still be independent, but you'd have a nurse available if you need one." Anabelle could almost see the brick wall forming.

"I don't want to move at all." Olga folded her arms across her chest.

"Oh, Mother." Carla rolled her eyes.

Anabelle smiled. "Why don't you both list your options and do some brainstorming?" She handed them a couple of blank pages from her clipboard. "Maybe you can come up with some ideas that will work for both of you."

"That sounds like a good idea." Carla gave Anabelle a conspiratorial smile. "We'll list the pros and cons of both sides."

"Let me know how it goes." Anabelle started to leave. "I know the facilities here in town quite well; so if you have any questions, just ask."

As she walked to her office, Anabelle prayed for the two women. She understood both sides. *Lord, please help Olga and her daughter to come to the right decision—one that will be right for both of them.*

For the rest of the day, Anabelle worked the floor taking over for each of her staff members while they went to in-service and viewed the video on dealing with disasters. Once her nurses and aides had finished, Anabelle went as well. She remembered the procedures but was glad to be going through them again.

She'd just walked out of the classroom when her cell phone vibrated.

"Hi, lass. Will you be working late again?"

"Not too late." Anabelle had decided to read through the disaster manual before heading home.

"I'll make dinner then." She could hear the smile in his voice.

"What are you planning?"

"Oh, maybe some chicken and mashed potatoes, coleslaw and rolls."

She laughed. "Hankering for some of Uncle Dan's Southern fried chicken, huh?" The fast-food restaurant made decent chicken and used real potatoes.

"What gave me away?"

Anabelle couldn't help but smile. "Just the fact that you can't make mashed potatoes."

He chuckled. "Curses, foiled again."

"Actually Uncle Dan's sounds good. I'll be home by five." She hesitated. "Would you like me to pick it up on my way home?"

"You might want to get some extra. Ainslee and Doug just pulled into the driveway."

Anabelle's mood accelerated even more. "Will do."

Though Anabelle would have preferred to head home immediately, she forced herself to stay and read the manual. She had done so several times, so it was just a matter of refreshing her memory. She signed her verification card and picked up those from all of her staff, except Seri, and took them down to Varner's office. She'd have to talk with Seri tomorrow. She hated to let people go, but Seri needed to take her job more seriously.

Penny was still there and asked her to put them in the box she had labeled. Anabelle did so, then went back to the floor. After giving the charge nurse instructions regarding the disaster drill, she stopped by Drew's room to say good night.

Dr. Hamilton wasn't there.

Chapter Nine

BACK AT THE NURSES' STATION, ANABELLE ASKED about Dr. Hamilton's whereabouts.

Heather, the charge nurse, looked surprised. "He's gone? He must have sneaked out while we were in report."

It was entirely possible. For around fifteen minutes, the nurses and aides from both shifts gathered to share pertinent information so the next shift could take over somewhat seamlessly. "I think we'd better find him."

Trying not to panic, Anabelle checked the cafeteria. No Dr. Hamilton. She peeked into the chapel. Not there. Anabelle had one more place to look. She made her way to his office, but no luck there either.

"Where could he have gone?" she muttered. "Drew Hamilton, if you walked out of this hospital, I'll . . ." She'd what? Haul him back?

Frustrated, Anabelle punched the elevator button and stepped in when it opened. As she pressed the button for the second floor, it hit her. If she knew anything about Drew, it was that concern for his patients outweighed his own health and well-being. She walked into the Cardiac Care Unit and went straight to Mr. Blake's room. Sure enough, there sat Dr. Hamilton, visiting with the patient he had been performing surgery on before his own heart attack.

Anabelle didn't interrupt them, but went back to the desk to let Heather know where their errant patient had gone.

By the time she got to Uncle Dan's, her heart rate had almost returned to normal. The lost had been found. "You certainly earned your pay today," she murmured.

She had placed her order just prior to leaving the hospital so they'd have it ready for her. The heavenly smells coming from the bags almost caused her to pull over and start eating. *You can wait a few minutes, Anabelle.* The voice in her head sounded far too much like her mother's.

Anabelle grinned when she saw Doug and Ainslee's car as well as Kirstie's red Honda parked on one side of the driveway. She pressed the garage door opener and drove into the garage.

Armed with dinner, she walked into the entry expecting a cheery greeting; but all she could hear was Ainslee sobbing. "I can't believe it. I just can't believe it."

Anabelle set the food on the counter and hurried into the living room, expecting yet another crisis. "My goodness, Ainslee, what's wrong?"

Doug, Ainslee and Kirstie were sitting on the couch. Cameron stood to one side.

Ainslee, still crying, jumped off the couch and ran to her mother, nearly knocking her down. "Oh, Mom. I'm so glad you're here. I tried to keep it a secret so I could tell you the news all at once, but these three wormed it out of me."

Cameron hugged her as well. "You might want to sit down."

"What's going on?"

Tears still streamed down Ainslee's face. "Mom, we're pregnant. We're going to have a baby!"

"You're sure?" Anabelle squealed.

Ainslee sniffed and nodded.

"What's with all the tears? I thought something terrible had happened."

"I can't help it. We've wanted this for so long. It doesn't seem possible."

"Oh, honey." Anabelle hugged Ainslee again, then reached for Doug. "I'm so happy for you—for all of us." Anabelle sat down, not sure her legs would hold her. "When did you find out?"

"I suspected I might be over the weekend, but didn't dare let myself believe it. I saw the doctor today, and she confirmed it."

Anabelle could hardly contain herself. "This calls for a celebration! I hope you are all hungry. I bought enough chicken and fixings to feed a small army."

James called Gideon during his break to set up an appointment to talk. *Odd thing that my family's so busy we can't seem to find time to talk without prearrangements,* he thought.

"Hey, son," James said when Gideon answered. "How about the two of us meet at the coffee shop after work so you can fill me in on that ROTC thing?"

"I'd like that, Dad, but I have to go to football practice, and I promised Nelson I'd drive him over to Princeton to pick up his guitar." Though he was only fifteen, they'd been able to get Gideon a driver's license due to family need. Fern could no longer drive and the kids had a lot of events, plus James had to work.

"Okay then. Maybe we can talk when you get home or in the morning after breakfast. We can go to the coffee shop before my shift starts."

"Sure. We probably won't be home for dinner. I told Mom we'd stop for burgers in Princeton."

"All right, drive carefully." James hung up. He'd forgotten about the guitar. Over the summer, his younger son had rediscovered his talent for music. He'd played violin in elementary school and decided he'd like to do guitar. They'd be doing a rent-to-own program.

Before heading back to work, he called to check on Fern. "How's my favorite girl?"

"Favorite. Does that mean you have another one stashed somewhere?"

"Oh rats," he teased. "You found me out."

She laughed, a sound James never tired of hearing. "I'm having a good day for a change."

"Wonderful. Say, I just talked to Gideon and was thinking: Since the boys won't be home for dinner, why don't you and I go out on a date?"

"*Ooh.* That sounds romantic."

"Want to go to Henri's?"

"I'd love to, but it's so expensive."

"Nothing's too good for you, my love."

"But . . ."

"We haven't been out in a while. Besides, we need some time to ourselves, and a candlelight dinner would be just the thing."

"All right. You've convinced me."

Dinner was fantastic. Henri's had an early-bird dinner special allowing them to eat for far less than they'd planned. Fern suggested they go to one of those ten-hankie chick flicks she'd wanted to see. It had been a long time since Fern had been able to go out like this, and James wanted it to be special. By the middle of the movie he'd dozed off.

Back home, a couple of hours later, as he carried his wilting wife inside, he wished someone could carry him.

That night he added Elena and Candace to his prayer list. He hadn't known about Sarah or about Candace's flashbacks. But then, he'd only been friends with the ladies for a short time. Anabelle, however, he'd known for quite some time through church and at work. He had, in fact, assisted Dr. Hamilton during Kirstie's surgery.

He smiled, thinking about the unlikely bond the four of them had developed. They were all nurses, of course, but the bond went deeper than that. They were believers and all part of God's family. Having friends to talk with and pray with was truly a gift.

Wednesday morning James awoke at five thirty. As usual, he was the first one up. When he'd showered and dressed, with everyone still asleep, he decided to grab a sausage-and-egg biscuit and orange juice on his way to work. He was sitting in report when he realized he'd forgotten about his morning appointment with Gideon.

Once report ended, James called his son and left a message on his cell. Hopefully, they could connect that evening after youth group.

That done, he began his initial rounds to see his patients. He started with his most critical patients including Tucker Blair. Tucker was only sixteen and had been a surprising and disheartening admit the previous day; Tucker and Gideon went to the same school.

He'd been at target practice with his dad and several friends. James wasn't clear on all the details, but one of the guns had accidentally discharged, and Tucker had been struck in the abdomen. Word about the accident had spread quickly as Tucker's distraught family and friends sat in the waiting room.

James spotted Dr. Hamilton and Dr. Clark leaving Tucker's room. Dr. Kathryn Clark had been taking over Dr. Hamilton's patients while he recuperated. As they approached, Dr. Hamilton was saying, "I hope you didn't mind my visit. I wasn't checking up on you."

Dr. Clark nodded. "I know. Hard to let go, isn't it?"

"A bit." He rubbed his chin. "What course of action are you pursuing?"

"Another CT, scope, blood work. Whatever I need to do to find the trouble spots and stop the infection."

"Good. When you get the results back, maybe you could let me know."

"*Um* . . . sure." She was obviously apprehensive about the senior doctor's presence when he should have been resting. "What

I don't understand is this lesion. We've gone in twice and scanned every square inch of his intestinal tract."

Dr. Clark's use of the word *we* indicated to James that Dr. Hamilton had apparently been in on the consultation process with the other surgeons about Tucker.

Dr. Hamilton sighed. "The hardest part about being a doctor, Kathryn, is that we don't have all the answers. The intestinal tract is probably the most difficult area in the body to diagnose and treat."

She nodded. "I know, with all those twists, turns and folds."

"Well, take a close look at the new scans. We may have to bring in Dr. Jeffries from St. Francis in Peoria."

"I will. Thanks." Dr. Clark headed down the hallway.

"James," Dr. Hamilton greeted. "I trust you were going in to see Tucker Blair."

"I was." James could see that Dr. Hamilton was tiring. Concern prodded James to step in. "Dr. Hamilton, no disrespect, sir, but you're supposed to be resting. The last I heard, you weren't seeing patients."

"That's all too true. But that doesn't mean I can't just visit my former patients."

"That didn't sound like 'just visiting' to me. You should be taking it easy."

Dr. Hamilton smiled. "I'll take that under advisement, James. Now that you mention it, I am feeling a bit tired. Mind if I borrow a wheelchair and an aide to take me back to CCU?"

James grabbed a wheelchair from the cubicle where they stored them and held out his hand to give Dr. Hamilton support.

The doctor refused help and sank into the chair, his face drained of color.

"Don't say it, James. If I hear the word *rest* one more time, I swear I'll go nuts."

"Sorry, sir."

"Apology accepted." Dr. Hamilton glanced at the room occupied by another of his former patients.

"Don't even think about popping in," James chided.

He wheeled the doctor to his room and waited while he got into bed. Then James doubled back to the Medical Surgical Unit, dropped the wheelchair off in its cubicle and headed for Tucker's room. Medical professionals were supposed to remain objective. Compassionate, yes, but also distant. They certainly were to avoid personal involvement. That was proving to be difficult with a patient like Tucker.

After donning a cap, mask, isolation gown and gloves, James entered the room. "Hey, Tucker."

The boy's lack of response and his closed eyes jump-started James's heart. It took a moment to realize his ears were plugged with earphones.

James reached over the bed rail and touched Tucker's shoulder.

Tucker jumped and pulled out the earpieces. "Whoa. You scared me." He caught his breath. The quick movement must have been painful.

Tucker had frightened James as well. "How're you doing this morning?"

"About the same. It hurts. The stuff I'm getting for pain helps, but I can't think."

"Don't worry about thinking. Just let your body rest."

"Did Gideon tell you that he and Nelson came by last night?"

"No. He was sleeping when I left." James checked the IV site and looked over the bags of antibiotics Tucker was getting. After his stay in ICU, he'd come to this floor.

Infection wasn't unusual with GI patients, and with gunshot cases, it was often expected. Unfortunately, Tucker's insides had been badly affected, and the bacteria had found its way into his bloodstream. Tucker wasn't responding well to treatment.

Sometimes James wished he didn't have the kind of experience needed for this kind of patient. He'd seen the worst, and Tucker's was right up there. James checked vitals and changed the abdominal dressing, praying all the while that God would heal the wounds and help them find the medications needed to kill the bacteria in his system.

"Give it to me straight, Mr. Bell. Am I gonna die?"

The question caught James off guard.

"Gideon said you were a medic in the army and that you had to take care of guys with gunshot wounds all the time. I figured you'd know."

"We're doing our best to make sure that doesn't happen, Tucker."

"But I could."

"I can't deny there's always the medical possibility, but you're in good hands."

"I never thought anything like this could happen to me." His voice broke.

James placed a gloved hand on Tucker's shoulder. "I know. And I'm sorry it did."

"Gideon wanted me to make sure I was okay with God—just in case."

James smiled. "And are you?"

"I think so. Last night we prayed for a while."

"I'm praying for you too, Tucker. And I know your family is as well."

"Thanks." He closed his eyes and sighed.

James told him he'd be back, and Tucker gave him a brief nod and inserted the earpieces again.

As he was leaving, he met Tucker's mother in the hallway outside the room.

"James, I'm glad I ran into you. The doctor said Tucker has a fifty-fifty chance of making it." She pinched her lips together, catching her tears on her fingers.

"I wish I could tell you that everything will be okay, but—"

"I know." She sighed. "How's his mood?"

"He's trying to be tough, but he's scared."

"He tells me I don't need to stay with him, but I have to."

James smiled. "Trust me. He wants you here. Don't feel like you need to carry on a conversation. Just be there."

"I will."

James discarded the contaminated clothing and washed his hands. He wasn't sure what to make of Gideon and Nelson's visit to Tucker the night before. Prayer was a good thing. That Gideon initiated it was a surprise, especially since the boys weren't that close. Gideon seldom talked about his faith, at least not to his parents.

Before heading for his break, James looked in on his other patients. They, at least, were doing better and would probably be going home in a day or two.

James made certain the proper tests had been scheduled for Tucker before leaving the floor for a quick break.

Instead of going to the cafeteria, he went to the chapel. He could pick up coffee on his way back, but right now he needed to see to his patients' spiritual needs as well as his own. Days like this could wear a man down.

Chapter Ten

NABELLE COULD HARDLY WAIT TO GET TO WORK on Wednesday. After the kids left the night before, she began calling friends and family, including cousins she hadn't seen in ten years. She got to work half an hour early and told everyone she saw.

Anabelle was about to head into CCU when she saw Elena step off the elevator. "Oh, Elena, I'm so glad I ran into you. We're having a baby! Ainslee is pregnant. I'm going to be a grandmother."

Elena squealed and grabbed her friend, whirling around in a circle. She then pulled Anabelle into the ICU. "Marge, did you hear?"

She chuckled. "I'm assuming just about everyone has by now. But you'd get more coverage if you had the operator make the announcement."

"What a great idea." Elena headed for the nurses' station.

Two minutes later the announcement came over the loudspeaker. "Anabelle Scott in CCU is expecting her first grandchild."

"Elena Rodriguez, I can't believe you just did that!"

Anabelle felt her face grow hot and she suspected it was as red as her hair had once been.

Elena shrugged. "You wanted everyone to know, right?"

Anabelle gave Elena a hug. "You are something else. I have to get back to work. See you at lunch?"

"Hopefully."

Once in her office, Anabelle stood at the window for several seconds bathed in the joy of knowing she was going to be a grandmother. Though she undoubtedly shone with delight, the opposite was true of the horizon. She watched as threatening dark clouds built in the distance. The Weather Channel was still calling for inclement weather. She couldn't say why exactly, but Anabelle felt apprehensive. Again, she was glad the CEO had thought to make certain Hope Haven would be prepared.

She sighed, determined to keep her good mood. Time to get back to work.

Anabelle stopped by Drew's room. After congratulating her on the grandchild, he told her he'd be going home tomorrow. "No sense staying around here. I'm up and around. I can probably recuperate better at home. I'll be able to sleep better, that's for sure."

"And Dr. Hildebrand agrees?" Anabelle knew the doctor thought no such thing.

"I think I can talk her into it."

"And when you get home, you'll rest?" Anabelle wore her best stern expression.

"I don't plan on running any marathons." He shook his head. "You know how Genna is. She'll keep me in line."

Anabelle didn't have a good feeling about this. Maybe her imagination was working overtime, but her intuition was usually right. "All right, I won't argue." *But I can pray.*

Anabelle stopped in to see how Olga and her daughter were coming along and was disappointed to see that they were still at an impasse.

"I keep telling her I can take care of myself," Olga insisted. "I want her to stay for as long as she can; but after that, I should be fine."

Carla sighed. "There's no reasoning with her. Did you know she's taken self-defense classes?"

Anabelle raised her eyebrows. "That's a good thing, isn't it?"

"I suppose, but she's learning how to use her cane as a weapon. She even has it hanging on her refrigerator door."

"That's so I'll remember where it is," Olga said.

Anabelle held back a laugh. She could imagine this feisty eighty-three-year-old shaking her cane at some unsuspecting burglar. Still, her situation was no laughing matter. Anabelle vowed then and there that she and Cameron would plan ahead for such a case as this.

"I see the doctor is planning to let you go home in a day or two." Anabelle tapped her pen against her clipboard. "I tell you what. Instead of listing pros and cons of the options you see right now, why don't you both write out what you'd like to see happen? If you could choose to do anything at all, what would it be?"

"Anything?" Carla asked.

"Yes. No matter how impossible or crazy. Just write down your thoughts and then talk about them." Anabelle smiled. "Carla, you could move out here. Olga, you could move to Oregon—to your own place—and see your grandchildren every day. Just do some brainstorming."

Carla shrugged. "Why not? It can't hurt."

Anabelle stepped out of the room, leaned against the wall and tipped her head back. *Lord, I know there's a perfect answer for both of them. Your perfect answer. I just pray they find it.*

The Cardiac Unit had gotten a new patient overnight, Anabelle noted, who was admitted early this morning with angina or chest pains.

Anabelle chatted with the woman first. At fifty-four, she was even more anxious about her condition than Olga had been. Karen, however, had no current symptoms; and her EKG and lab results had been negative. But she'd come in with what seemed suspiciously like those of a heart attack victim.

Dr. Hildebrand thought it was probably acid reflux but chose to do several tests to rule out a heart condition. Anabelle took time to explain each of the procedures. "Unfortunately, acid-reflux symptoms can imitate heart-attack symptoms."

"So you think that's all it is?" Karen asked. "I feel dumb, if that's the case."

"It's a good possibility since the omeprazole—the acid inhibitor we gave you—seems to be working. Your EKG looks good."

"So I shouldn't have come in?" Karen frowned.

"Yes, you should have. We'd much rather people come in when they suspect heart attack symptoms than wait and see. The symptoms can be similar, and sometimes it takes blood tests to determine whether or not a person has actually had a heart attack."

Karen sighed. "Thanks. I think the doctor told me that, but I couldn't understand all of what she said."

Anabelle grinned. "That can be a problem. If you need any of us to translate, just call."

Anabelle had only Mr. Blake to check in on before finishing her morning rounds. Then she planned on talking to Becky about a discharge plan for Dr. Hamilton. Not that they needed one. From what she'd seen so far, her favorite doctor was as headstrong as Olga. Anabelle sighed, wishing she could do something or say something to Drew that would get his attention.

When she entered Mr. Blake's room, she noted that he seemed troubled as he sat hunched over in bed weaving his fingers together.

"Mr. Blake, are you all right?"

"Yes—I mean I feel okay. I'm still having some pain, but I guess that's normal."

"Are you getting enough pain medication?"

He nodded.

"Is there something I can help you with?"

"No . . ." He looked up at her. "Maybe. I suppose I shouldn't be talking to any of you about this, but I just feel terrible."

Anabelle sat in the chair next to him. "What is it?"

"I told my son it was okay, that he shouldn't interfere, but he won't listen. He's an attorney, and . . ." Dillon paused. "He's telling me we need to sue Dr. Hamilton for malpractice."

"Oh my." Anabelle released a long breath. She wasn't surprised but hoped that James had been wrong.

"I don't know what to do." He leaned back against his pillow.

"I wish I could help you, Mr. Blake. I do know that Dr. Hamilton would never purposely put a patient in danger. He's one of our best doctors."

"That's what I said. He even came by to see me and make sure I was okay after he'd just had a heart attack himself."

Anabelle wished she could tell him not to pursue a lawsuit, but it wouldn't be right to influence him one way or the other. "If you're inclined, you could pray about your dilemma. And pray that you and your son make the right decision."

"Thanks. I'll do that."

She listened to his heart and lungs and after talking a bit more about his progress, Anabelle stepped into the hallway.

Lord, what's happening here? If they did move forward with a lawsuit, did they have a chance? Had Dr. Hamilton been negligent in operating when he wasn't feeling well? Perhaps, but Anabelle knew he'd never put a patient in danger if he could help it.

Yet he had blamed himself. *I'll add Mr. Blake and his sons to my prayers as well*, she thought as she made her way down the hall to the next room.

Elena tiptoed into Isabel's room before heading for work. "My sweet girl," she murmured. She wanted to hold her precious grandchild in her arms and shield her from all of the painful things life could bring. And one of those things was, unfortunately, the child's own mother.

Since speaking to Sarah the previous day, Elena had been in turmoil. War raged in her heart. Compassionate Elena—the nurse, the mother, the nurturer—wanted to reach out to Sarah. She knew the kind of upbringing Sarah'd had, how warmth or love had been nonexistent. No surprise then that Sarah had followed such a destructive path.

Another part of Elena wanted nothing to do with her. She tried to not see Sarah's features in little Isabel, but the resemblance was there and unmistakable. While Isabel had her daddy's dark hair and eyes, the facial features and smile were Sarah's.

Elena hadn't told Rafael or Cesar about Sarah's call. She had a feeling Rafael still pined for his daughter's mother, and she didn't want to see him become hopeful only to be heartbroken once again.

Cesar would have suggested they take Sarah in under their wing to give her another chance for Isabel's sake. Even though he worked as a police officer and witnessed the worst of the worst, he still had a compassionate heart. Elena couldn't help feeling it would be a naive heart in this situation.

Elena lightly drew Isabel's dark hair aside and planted a light kiss on her cheek. In another hour or two, Rafael would take her to preschool. Elena focused on the life they had built together, just the four of them, and tried once again to shut Sarah out of her mind.

At the hospital, she became engrossed in her work and had almost forgotten about the Sarah situation until she acknowledged the deep inner voice.

Sarah is in pain.

Elena felt her steely resolve and cynicism start to crumble. What harm could there be in just checking Sarah out over coffee?

Maybe she really was in a better place. At least she'd have made the effort God seemed to want her to make.

Elena drew in a sharp breath and retrieved her cell phone from her purse. She punched in the number the secretary had given her. Sarah answered on the fourth ring.

"Hello." She sounded sleepy. *Or drugged*, Elena thought cynically.

Before she had the chance to rethink her plan, she quickly made her offer. "Sarah, this is Elena. I have been thinking about what you said. I am not promising anything, but if you are available, I could meet you at the Cuppa Coffee at eleven thirty tomorrow morning."

Sarah's voice came out in a sob. "Thank you so much for giving me a chance, Elena. I really am clean now, and I want my life back."

Elena went cold. "I'll see you tomorrow at eleven thirty."

Sarah wanted her life back. Did she really mean she wanted Isabel back?

Chapter Eleven

AT THE END OF HIS SHIFT, JAMES KNEW HE wouldn't be going home anytime soon. Tucker had taken a turn for the worst. Dr. Clark had heeded Dr. Hamilton's advice and brought in Dr. Jeffries, a specialist from the teaching hospital in Peoria, to do a consult. She'd invited Dr. Hamilton and James to attend as well.

He felt honored being there but, at the same time, knew how much he could bring to the table. He called Fern just before the meeting and let her know he'd be late. He also called Gideon.

When his son didn't answer, James left a message. "Gideon, I'll be late tonight. Not sure when I'll get home. Make sure your mom gets something to eat. I thought you might want to know that Tucker has taken a turn for the worst. He said you came by last night. Love you, Dad."

James closed the phone, took a deep breath and stepped into the conference room.

An hour later, the four doctors and James filed out. Bottom line was that Tucker would be going into surgery again. The GI doctor from the teaching hospital would perform the surgery with Dr. Clark assisting. Since the nuclear test failed to show a specific bleeding spot, all they knew was that it was coming from somewhere in his abdomen.

Dr. Jeffries indicated that they would look for bleeders and at the same time check for pockets of infection, then start Tucker on a course of the antibiotic cocktail James had suggested. The GI doctor had used it before, and the team agreed to give it a try.

Dr. Hamilton had suggested James assist with the surgery.

James figured he'd be lucky to be home by midnight. He went back to the floor to tell Tucker the news.

"You'll be there the whole time?" Tucker asked.

"I'll make sure the doctors do everything right, buddy." James found it hard to speak. He clasped Tucker's hand. "Your parents will both be here."

"Okay." He closed his eyes.

James sucked in a deep breath and pulled himself together while he removed the gown and gloves.

Out in the waiting room, he spotted Dr. Clark and Dr. Hamilton talking with the Blairs. Mr. Blair signed the consent forms. "He's good with it." James attempted a smile. "I told him I'd be there to make sure the doctors did it right."

John Blair pinched his lips together and shook James's hand. "Thanks."

Gideon came in as James was leaving. He gave his dad a hug. "Thanks for calling me."

"I'm glad you're here." He watched with pride as Gideon took a seat beside Tucker's parents and asked if he could bring them anything.

On the way to the surgical suite James called Anabelle and asked her to put Tucker on the Good Shepherd prayer chain. Their church had people in place specifically to make phone calls when intercessory prayer was needed. To ensure confidentiality, no specific details were given, just the name. Each person called the next until the chain came back around to the first caller. In this case Anabelle was first.

"I'm sorry, James. These are the tough ones. I know. I'm praying. I'll call Candace and Elena too."

"Thanks."

James paused outside the surgical suite, then plodded to the sinks to wash up. Dr. Jeffries and Dr. Clark were already there. Once they had scrubbed and stepped into their sterile garb, the procedure began. After years of practice, James managed to shift into his objective mode. He needed to let go of his feelings and focus entirely on his task.

Dr. Jeffries used a balloon endoscopy to examine the colon and found numerous lesions and two small veins that were issuing small amounts of blood. There were several large pockets of infection that the doctor was able to drain. Dr. Jeffries felt that as long as the medications worked, he had a good chance of making it. James wasn't so sure. As a medic, he'd seen his share of abdominal wounds; Tucker's was bad.

By eight o'clock that evening, Tucker was awake and responding, his vital signs stable. James and Gideon headed home around nine. Morning would come far too soon, and James had a lot to do at home before going to bed. Having a clone would have come in handy.

Thursday morning, Anabelle sat in her favorite chair near the patio, letting her devotional for the day seep in. It had been about God's will. Did anything happen outside of God's will? Some people thought no, but Anabelle felt differently. God did not will Adam and Eve to sin. They ate of the forbidden fruit on their own. God did not choose that path for them.

God certainly did not will for people to do bad things. And oh, there were so many bad things people did to themselves and others.

As a nurse she often heard patients ask, "Why did God let this happen?" She'd asked that herself when her little girl had come so close to death. She finally realized that God had never wanted people to do evil, and He certainly never wanted harm to come to His children. God had not willed the accident that had nearly killed Kirstie. That horrid man had caused it. It had been his choice to drink, not God's.

Anabelle sighed. Such a philosopher she could be, especially when she felt maudlin like she did this morning.

Last night's meeting with the Bike Smarts committee had ended around nine. It looked as though they were all set for their school programs. The meeting had gone well but it seemed the older she got, the less stamina she had for those long evening get-togethers.

Of course, it hadn't helped to learn about Tucker. She'd read about the accident. Anabelle jotted a few notes down in her journal and prayed again for those on her list.

When Anabelle entered the hospital for her shift, she knew someone had died. It wasn't any sort of superpower—she had worked there long enough to pick up on the sorrowful tone. Though they had an excellent cure rate, death was certainly no stranger at Hope Haven. But because they counted every patient as a part of their family, they took losses hard.

She checked on her own patients, and Debbie assured her they were all doing well. "Dr. Hamilton went home last night around nine. Said he wanted to get some sleep. Did you know he was seeing patients and acting as a consultant yesterday?"

Anabelle tsked. "That man."

Debbie shook her head. "You have to admit he's dedicated."

"True." Anabelled smiled. "James called last night to tell me about Tucker's surgery. Have you heard anything?"

"Not recently. I do know he went from recovery to ICU."

Debbie hesitated and looked over Anabelle's head. "Speaking of ICU, here's Elena."

Anabelle turned.

"Hi, Debbie, Anabelle." There were no dimples in Elena's cheeks this morning, only sadness in her dark brown eyes. "I have some bad news."

"I had a feeling. Let's go into my office so Debbie can get her charting done."

"What's up?" Anabelle hitched her hip up on the corner of the desk.

Elena sat in the chair. "We lost a patient last night."

James knocked and stepped in. "Sorry to interrupt, but I wanted to talk to you." He glanced at Elena. "Did you tell her?"

"I started to."

James lowered himself into the second chair and leaned forward, elbows resting on his knees.

Anabelle touched his shoulder. "Was it Tucker?"

He lowered his head. "He died early this morning."

"James. I'm so sorry." Anabelle closed her eyes for a moment to let the news sink in.

"We thought he was doing better," James said.

Elena nodded. "He was for a while. But his immune system just couldn't fight that level of infection."

"His parents must be devastated." Anabelle wished there was something she could do for James. He seemed to be taking the boy's death especially hard.

"I can't believe it." James rubbed the back of his neck. "Maybe I should have stayed with him. I might have been able to . . ."

"Don't do this to yourself, James," Elena said. "Tucker was getting the best possible care."

"I know. Everyone did their best, including me." James got to his feet, shoulders still slumped. "Doesn't make it any easier." He hugged each of the women. "I need to get back to the unit. Thanks for listening."

Once Elena and James left, Anabelle closed her eyes for a moment to pray for Tucker's family. What a tragic loss. She reflected on the devastation she had felt when she'd learned of Kirstie's accident and knew how long the road to healing could be, how long it could take to experience joy again.

Anabelle asked for focus and the ability to tend to her own responsibilities—one of those being Seri. Becky had written another note about Seri's being a social butterfly.

After report and making her rounds, Anabelle found Seri at the nurses' station chatting. "Seri, would you mind coming into my office for a few minutes?"

"Sure. Like, now? I have to help Olga with her shower."

So what are you doing here? Anabelle held back the retort. An employer should never express disdain for an employee in front of their peers.

Anabelle smiled. "I don't think Olga will mind. I'll just need a few minutes."

"Okay." Seri eased out of the chair and walked with Anabelle to the office. Anabelle indicated for her to sit in one of the chairs in front of her desk. Rather than taking the intimidating approach of sitting with the desk between them, Anabelle took the chair beside Seri.

"How long have you been with us, Seri?"

"Um—a couple weeks." Seri twisted a silver ring around on her finger.

"Do you realize that in that time, I've had at least three complaints about your work—or I should say lack of it?"

She fingered one of her small hooped earrings. "Um, no. Well, Winona griped at me a couple of times to quit talking so much and to help the others."

"How did you feel about that? Was Winona being fair to you?"

She shrugged. "I'm not sure because I do everything on my list."

"On your list?"

"Well, yeah. Becky tells us who our patients are and what needs to be done. I figure when I'm done with that, I'm okay to do whatever. I'm pretty fast so lots of times I finish before the others."

"I see." Anabelle glanced over the memos.

"Please don't fire me, Mrs. Scott. I really need this job. Tell me what to do and I'll do it."

"I've been looking at your personnel file. You graduated at the top of your class."

She shrugged. "School is easy for me. Sometimes too easy. But my teachers put me on a fast track and into gifted programs so I wouldn't get too bored."

It was Anabelle's turn to smile. She wasn't dealing with a lazy young lady, but a bored one. "You like keeping busy?"

"Sure. Who doesn't?"

"The other day when you heard about the plan to put everyone through the disaster training course, you seemed upset and told me your date was more important."

"Oh, that." She bit her lower lip. "I was just griping."

"Did you read the manual?"

"Yes." She nodded eagerly. "During my afternoon break."

"I didn't get your signed form."

"Oh no, that's my bad. I think I left it in the book. It's in my locker." She started to get up. "Want me to get it now?"

"It can wait, Seri." Anabelle wished she'd taken time for this earlier. "I think I know what the problem is here. Would it make you too uncomfortable if I shadow you while you work this morning?"

"You mean so you can see if I'm doing stuff wrong?"

"More to see how you use your time."

"Sure." Her blue gaze met Anabelle's. "Does this mean I still have my job?"

"That depends. Do you like working here?"

"Yeah." She tipped her head to one side. "I like people, and I like helping people. In fact, I'd like to go into medicine, maybe become a nurse or a doctor."

"All right then. I think if we make a few adjustments you'll be fine."

Anabelle shadowed Seri for most of the morning and was largely impressed with the aide's work and her ability to see patients' needs and carry them through. She completed her assigned tasks thoroughly, yet quickly. She also had a wonderful bedside manner and seemed to make patients feel special.

When they'd finished baths and morning care, Anabelle suggested a break. She complimented Seri on what she'd observed.

"I think you're going to make a fine nurse or doctor."

Seri smiled. "Thanks. Like I said, I like helping people."

"I think what has happened with you is that you are able to get your work done quickly while the others are still working. I'd like you to offer to help the others. You're welcome to take your breaks and lunch, but if you see that someone is especially busy or having a rough time, come alongside them. We work as a team here. We not only look at our patients' needs, but at what we can do for our co-workers as well."

"So I should do more than what I'm scheduled to do?"

"Possibly, yes. Be available to run errands for the others or help with bed changes and patient care."

Seri nodded. "I could do that, but it doesn't seem right to punish me because I'm more efficient."

Anabelle grinned. "Rather than see it as punishment, maybe you could see helping others get their work done as an opportunity to commit random acts of kindness."

"I see what you mean." Seri's eyes brightened.

"And you'll get more experience. I really think if you become more of a team member, the others will see you for the competent worker you are."

"You got it, Mrs. Scott."

Anabelle felt good about her encounter with Seri. The girl had a great deal of potential. She was not only intelligent, she had people skills. Anabelle made a special point of observing her interaction with her peers. She also called Becky in to talk with her about Seri and explain the situation.

"I'm glad you told me," Becky said. "The more I get to know her, the more I like her."

"Me too." Anabelle laughed.

At 11:15 AM, Elena stepped into the nurses' station wishing Sarah would call to cancel. Too often throughout the previous day and this morning, she had asked God to let something happen so she wouldn't have to go. Unfortunately, she was free to take her lunch as scheduled. Elena gave in and let Marge know she would be going over to the coffee shop.

"Oh, good." Marge looked up from the computer. "Would you mind picking up a latte?"

"I'll be happy to." Elena smiled, glad for the distraction.

"Let me give you some money."

"Oh, no need. You can pay me when I get back." Elena waved and hurried off, wanting to get this unpleasantness over with as soon as possible. Truth be told, she didn't mind leaving the hospital this morning. A somberness blanketed the Intensive Care Unit, having lost Tucker. Elena hadn't personally treated him, but she had spent a part of the morning comforting the nurse who had.

At Cuppa Coffee, Elena looked around for Sarah but didn't see her.

"Can I help you?" A young, blond barista asked.

Elena glanced up at the menu board and ordered a mocha latte and nachos. She'd get Marge's drink just before she left. A few minutes later, with coffee in hand, she settled into a comfy chair in the corner where she could see everyone coming in. Elena had brought her notes for Isabel's party with her to work on if she had time.

As it turned out, she had a full half hour. Her drink and nachos were long gone. She ordered Marge's latte, decided to wait one final minute then left. She was both annoyed and relieved— annoyed Sarah had caused her so much angst and relieved she didn't have to face her. Now Elena knew everything she needed to know about where Sarah's priorities stood. Plus the time hadn't been a total loss. She'd managed to fill out and address all of the invitations for the party.

"Well, Lord, I did my part," Elena muttered as she made her way across the busy street.

But it might not be that simple.

Chapter Twelve

CANDACE, HAVING HAD A RATHER UP-AND-DOWN DAY, stopped for a latte at Cuppa Coffee. The espresso shop sat across the street from the hospital and was a favorite among hospital personnel. When she'd placed her order, she looked around for a place to sit and noticed Heath Carlson sitting at a corner table by the window.

His presence startled her. Part of her wanted to join him, but another part hesitated. The hesitation had little to do with common sense. He was a colleague and a friend. He looked up just then and put his paper down. "Hey, what a surprise." He offered a welcoming smile and stood to pull out a chair for her.

"Hey, yourself." Candace headed in his direction. "Is it okay if I join you?"

"Please do."

"Thanks." Candace set her hot hazelnut latte on the table and settled into the chair. She looked around. "I don't usually come here in the afternoon."

"I know." He chuckled. "That sounded eerie. I come in almost every day about this time and have never seen you."

"Oh." She blew across the top of the hot brew. "I usually go right home and have tea with my mother. I needed something stronger today."

"Bad day?"

"We lost a teenage boy today. I didn't know him personally, but it's sad to lose someone just the same."

"I heard. Wounds in the abdomen can be very difficult to treat. He was a really nice kid. I took the X-rays when he came in."

Candace didn't want to dwell on death, so she switched to her favorite topic: babies. "We sent the Parsons twins home today. What a sweet family. I'm going to miss those babies."

Heath smiled, the corners of his eyes crinkling. He leaned back and rested his right ankle on his left knee. A beat of silence passed between them.

"I probably shouldn't ask this, Candace, but have you decided about whether or not to see a counselor?"

"It's all right. You're not the only one who's been after me to see someone. I actually have someone lined up." Candace didn't tell him that her mother had been the one to set up the appointment.

"Good."

"I resigned from the code team." Candace wasn't sure why she told him that.

"Are you feeling okay about that?" Heath ran a hand through his hair. "It sounds like I'm cross-examining you. I'm not, really."

"It's all right. And no, I'm not okay with it." She sipped at her coffee. *I feel like a failure.*

"You can always go back to it. The most important thing is for you to get help."

"That's true." Even though his concern stirred her emotions at times, Candace enjoyed his easy, laid-back style. "So how was your day?"

He chuckled. "Busy as usual. But it's looking up. I like when I have the opportunity to spend some time with you."

A hot blush crept up her neck. She avoided his eyes and took a long sip of her coffee.

Anabelle was about to leave for the day when she got a frantic call from Genna.

"Oh, Anabelle. I'm so glad I caught you. Would you mind stopping by the house on your way home? Drew is out digging in the yard. He wants to plant some rose bushes he got just before he went into the hospital. He's afraid they will die. I told him I would do it, but he won't listen. I don't understand his reasoning. I'd much rather lose the rose bushes than lose him."

"I'll be right there."

On the way to the Hamiltons' house, Anabelle wondered what they could do to get Drew to behave himself. She knew how difficult this was for him. He wanted instant healing; and though he knew better, he refused to slow down.

She understood how he might want to be involved in the conferences with his peers to discuss his patients. A meeting where he shared his expertise with other medical staff was one thing, but what had pushed him to indulge in heavy yard work?

Had he heard about Tucker's death? Was he working off anger or disappointment? Had Mr. Blake's son approached him about a lawsuit?

Anabelle tried to put herself in his place. She'd have a hard time sitting still too. She would want to keep her fingers on the pulse of her life and the lives of those around her.

What would it take to get someone as headstrong as Drew to realize how important it was for him to rest and adequately heal? Maybe if she and Genna talked with James, Elena and Candace, they could come up with some kind of plan. Maybe if they all talked to him at once, it would help. She sighed, not sure anything or anybody could get through that thick skull of his. But they had to do something.

Anabelle pulled into the circular driveway but saw no sign of Dr. Hamilton or Genna in their expansive front yard. They lived in an older, three-story brick home that was practical, yet elegant. She parked just past the entry behind Genna's "happy car," a new red Mustang convertible, and exited her own Ford. Genna opened the door before Anabelle could knock.

"Oh, thank goodness you're here." Genna flung her arms around Anabelle in a frantic hug. "He finally gave up on the rose bushes. After planting one, he dragged himself up to the patio. He's resting for the moment and drinking some lemon water, but I don't know how long that will last."

"How many roses does he want to plant?" Anabelle asked, looking out the glass doors of the patio.

"A dozen or so."

"Oh, mercy." Anabelle pulled her cell phone out. "I'm calling Cameron. He can have those roses planted in no time."

"Perfect." Genna headed for the kitchen. "I'll pour us some iced tea, and I'll let you break the news to Drew."

Twenty minutes later Anabelle sat with Drew and Genna on their lovely deck drinking tea from a tall glass and watching Cameron plant roses.

"I suppose I should thank you." Drew sighed. "I have to admit you and Genna were right about the yard work. It's a lot more strenuous than I thought it would be."

"I can't believe you tried," Anabelle scolded. "You of all people should know better."

"Okay, I admit it wasn't my brightest idea." Drew's brows knit as he watched Cameron work, thinking no doubt about his disabilities.

"No, it wasn't." Anabelle watched her husband with admiration. He hadn't hesitated for even a second when she'd asked for his help. He wasn't bad to look at either. He'd taken his shirt off and wore cutoff jeans. Though his hair was graying, he had the physique of a much younger man.

"Just promise me you'll call Cameron if you need more yard work done. He'll be happy to do that for you."

"I appreciate that, Anabelle." He rose from his chair. "Now if you ladies don't mind, I think I'll take a short nap." He kissed Genna. "Wake me when dinner's ready."

Anabelle and Genna watched him walk inside, a bit stooped and weary. "He doesn't look good, does he?" Genna asked.

Since Anabelle's arrival his color had changed from exertion red to pale tan. "He looks better than when I came. I'm glad he had the sense to stop."

Once the plants were in, Genna invited them to stay for dinner. "It's nothing fancy, but you're welcome to join us."

"Sounds good," Cameron used a red cloth to wipe his brow. "But I need to go home and clean up."

Anabelle thanked her. "I have dinner in the Crock-Pot. And I'm not sure Drew is up to having guests. Maybe another time."

They said their good-byes and headed for their vehicles. Cameron opened the door for Anabelle and closed it after she'd settled in. Hands resting on the roof, he leaned down. "I appreciate your calling me, lass. Doc looked a bit peaked."

"I have a feeling you helped him avert a major setback. Digging is bad enough; but in this heat and humidity . . ." She glanced up at Cameron. "What was he thinking?"

"That he isn't like his patients, maybe. That he's stronger than that. It's a guy thing. He can't stand the idea of depending on other people."

Anabelle sighed. "I do understand that. I'm just afraid we'll lose him."

"I can have a talk with him if you'd like. He might be willing to listen to reason."

"You can try, my love. I'm not sure anyone can convince him, unless . . ." An idea began to form in Anabelle's head. "I think I might have an answer."

"Are you going to share?" He lowered his head to kiss her forehead.

"Not yet. I need some time to work out the details."

Anabelle watched Cameron climb into his pickup and then followed him home. She pulled into the driveway, and as the garage door opened, another car pulled in behind them.

"Looks like we have company." She stepped forward to join Cameron on the sidewalk.

"*Mmm*. I forgot to tell you. Kirstie called earlier and said she was bringing a friend over to meet us."

"Her date from the other night?"

Cameron shrugged. "She didn't say, but I'll let you do the greeting while I shower and make myself presentable."

Anabelle walked back to the car to greet their daughter and her friend. Kirstie climbed out of the passenger side and Mark, her teacher friend, unfolded himself from the driver's side.

"Hello." Anabelle smiled even though her insides were churning. Bringing her boyfriend to meet her parents? Were they getting serious?

"Hi, Mother." Kirstie hugged her and turned back to her guest. "You remember my friend Mark Holcher."

"I do." Anabelle reached out to shake his hand. "Welcome."

"Mark's been asking to see the farm, so I thought today was as good a day as any."

"Sure, though there isn't that much to see."

He chuckled. "It is to a city boy."

"Then by all means, enjoy. I trust you'll be joining us for dinner," Anabelle said, remembering her manners.

"If it isn't too much trouble, Mrs. Scott." Mark grinned. There was something warm and kind in his smile.

"Truth is, I'd be disappointed if you didn't."

When Cameron came down, he met Mark, then snagged a couple drinks from the fridge and headed outside with Kirstie's "friend." Cameron enjoyed showing people their farm. Now that he was retired, he wanted to raise goats and chickens and a horse or two.

Kirstie watched them disappear into the barn, then turned and hitched a hip onto a stool at the counter.

"Want some iced tea?" Anabelle asked as she checked the slow cooker.

"Sure. I'll get it." Kirstie walked around the island to the cupboard, took down two glasses, filled them from the ice dispenser on the fridge door and then poured in the amber liquid.

"Thanks." Anabelle took the glass and set it on the counter, then pulled a bag of salad greens from the fridge. "You're not limping as much as you used to." Anabelle spoke her thoughts out loud.

"Really?" Kirstie chuckled as she made her way back to the stool. "You know, Mother, you are the first to notice."

Smiling, Anabelle teased, "As it should be. A mother should be the first to know."

"Yeah, right. Is that a hint? You want to know more about my love life?"

Anabelle shook her head and felt a slight flush creep up her cheeks. "We were talking about the leg." She actually was very curious to know more about Mark but hesitated to ask. After a few moments of silence, she couldn't stand it anymore. "So, are you two dating regularly?"

Kirstie shrugged and turned her attention to the salad. "Don't worry, Mother. We like each other and we have a lot in common. And Mark doesn't look at me like I'm an alien when he sees my leg."

Anabelle forced a smile. "That's a plus."

Kirstie sighed. "More than you know."

Sensing that Kirstie didn't want to talk about her relationship with Mark, Anabelle asked, "Are you all ready for school?"

"Almost. I was thinking maybe you and Ainslee and I could go shopping. Like Ainslee told me the other day, I need more grown-up clothes."

"I'd love that." Anabelle lifted out the large, falling-apart chicken onto a platter, then set the potatoes, parsnips and carrots alongside. "Want to call the guys in?"

"Sure." Kirstie set the salad she'd made on the table along with service for four. She slid open the patio door and called Mark and her dad in to dinner.

Anabelle watched her; for a brief moment, she let herself imagine what it would be like if Kirstie were married and had begun a family of her own. Going back to the kitchen, she shook the thoughts away. Her baby was nowhere near being ready to settle down. Besides, with Ainslee pregnant she'd soon be a grandmother for real.

Chapter Thirteen

ON FRIDAY MORNING, ANABELLE SPOTTED DR. DREW'S car in the physicians' parking lot. "Oh no, not again." She couldn't believe that he'd come in today, especially after the rose fiasco the afternoon before.

Yes, she could believe it. One of the things that made him such a popular doctor was that he cared about his patients—too much at times. He would want to see his former patients and check on the final results of Tucker's tests. He'd check on Dillon Blake as well. And who knew how many others?

Anabelle bypassed her floor and got off on the third, making a beeline for Dr. Hamilton's office which was located just inside the Day Surgery area.

The door was closed, and no one answered. Concerned, she reached for the handle. "I wouldn't do that if I were you." Came the familiar voice behind her. "Breaking and entering is a major offense."

She turned around and met Drew's smile with one of her own. "So is working when you should be at home recovering."

"I'm not doing anything strenuous. I learned my lesson on that count yesterday."

He held up his free hand when she opened her mouth to argue. "I know what you're going to say, but I've been doing some thinking. There's no reason I can't see patients and do some paperwork. I'm fine, Anabelle."

"What happened to the one-month stress-free vacation you were going to take?"

"The only things causing me stress right now are you and Genna. Now please, go see to your patients and let me work in peace."

"Fine, but it'll be *rest* in peace if you keep pushing yourself." Anabelle backed out and closed the door. It was time to talk to the others about her ideas and do some brainstorming. There had to be a way of breaking through that stubborn veneer of his.

Anabelle closed herself in her office after report, intent on making some phone calls to James, Candace, Elena and Genna for starters.

To each she mentioned Drew's refusal to listen to reason and asked them to meet her at noon in the cafeteria.

The morning went quickly as Anabelle visited with her patients and assisted in patient care. Seri took her aside about fifteen minutes before noon.

"Can I talk to you about something, Mrs. Scott?" She seemed worried.

"Sure, let's go to my office."

Once they were seated Anabelle asked, "What's troubling you?"

She swallowed and cleared her throat. "I don't want to be ratting anybody out, but yesterday you told me to help the others when I finished my work. I won't tell you which one said it, but she told me I was working too fast and making everyone look bad."

"And she's afraid we'll give them a heavier load?"

"Yeah, she said that too."

Anabelle nodded. "Thank you for coming to me, Seri. I know what everyone on my staff is capable of doing. From now on, I'd like you to go to your charge nurse or team leader and volunteer to assist them. Let your friend work at her speed. Look around for where you can help and answer call lights. Just don't take her advice to work slower."

"Yes, ma'am."

When Seri had gone back to the floor, Anabelle grabbed the lunch she'd made that morning from her desk drawer. Upon reaching the cafeteria, she headed for the table where James was already seated.

"What's going on with Dr. Hamilton?" James asked as she sat down beside him.

"I think the heart attack has affected his common sense." She told him about the doctor's determination to plant rose bushes and how she had brought Cameron in to rescue him.

James nodded. "He was up on the Med/Surg floor this morning talking to Dr. Clark."

"I'm not surprised. I saw him at his office when I got to work." Anabelle opened her napkin. "He has me worried."

"You and me both," James said. "Though, he does have a good point. A little consulting might not be a bad thing."

Anabelle shook her head. "It doesn't work that way with Dr. Hamilton. He'd start with a little consulting; before you know it, he'd be seeing patients and work up to the kind of work schedule that most likely brought on the heart problems."

James raised his eyebrows. "You're right."

When Candace and Elena arrived, Anabelle told them that she'd invited Genna to join them. Anabelle opened her bag and pulled out a plastic container. She'd packed a chicken sandwich with meat left over from last night's dinner.

Genna approached the table and greeted each of them.

After a few minutes, Anabelle interrupted the small talk. "It would be fun to chat more, but we don't have a lot of time; I'm hoping we can develop a solid plan to get Dr. Hamilton to take it easy."

"Let's hear it." James leaned forward.

Anabelle nodded. "I'd like to share my idea and then have you add to it or make changes. Genna and I haven't been very successful in getting him to stay at home and rest. I don't know why he's so resistant. I was thinking that if Dr. Hamilton could see how many people he's helped and how much they mean to him, he might be convinced to slow down and let his heart heal. I know you'll all agree that we want him around for a very long time."

Elena opened a bottle of tomato juice. "You mean contact people and have them send cards or come by to see him?"

Anabelle nodded. "Something like that."

"That's a great idea, Anabelle." Genna jotted a note on the pad she'd brought along. "Drew has gotten hundreds of letters from grateful patients. We could start there."

"Kirstie would come in." Anabelle smiled. "And I'll bet she'd help us with our project as well."

"We could have people take turns stopping by his house," Elena suggested. "Like a parade."

"Yes," Candace exclaimed. "A Parade of Patients."

"Oh." Elena waved her hand. "I like that."

"James?" Anabelle touched his arm. "What do you think?"

"It might work; but right now, he's stressed out about losing Tucker and having the heart attack during Mr. Blake's operation. He's blaming himself. I think it's a good idea to remind him of the patients who are still alive, thanks to him. I'm just not sure he'll take it to heart."

Genna set her water glass down. "It can't hurt, and I'll try anything. I think it's a good plan. We'll have to do it soon—maybe this weekend. I can supply snacks and drinks for everyone who comes. We can set up the patio. Make a party out of it."

"Perfect, but we can all bring goodies," Anabelle added.

"I can contact the guild, Anabelle." Genna sipped her water. "I know they'll all be willing to help wherever we need them."

"Good. We'll see who wants to participate. I know several guild members who have been Doctor Drew's patients." Anabelle thought for a moment about any confidentiality issues they might run into. Since they weren't mentioning specific illnesses or personal concerns, they should be fine. Each person on their list could participate or not.

They spent several minutes writing down names of possible patients for their parade.

Anabelle counted at least a hundred. "We can split up the names between us, and we'll call everyone on the list."

When they were ready to leave, Genna gave them all hugs. "Thank you all so much. I don't think Drew realizes what he means to so many people." She sighed. "Now, if you'll excuse me, I'm going into the chapel to pray that God leads this parade and uses it to bring health and healing to my husband."

"We'll be praying too," James said.

Elena managed to leave work at her regular time. Before leaving the hospital, she stopped by CCU to see if Anabelle had a list of people for the Parade of Patients for her to call. As she entered the unit, an idea started to form. She greeted several nurses and spotted Anabelle coming out of her office.

"I'm glad I caught you." Elena grinned at her friend. "I have an idea about the phone calls. I think it would be more efficient and organized if we all met at someone's house and made a party of it. It would be fun too."

Anabelle clapped her hands. "I love it. I was thinking of asking Kirstie and Ainslee to help make the calls with me. Let's plan to meet at my house at, say, six thirty?"

"That's good for me. Cesar will be working, but Rafael should be home then to take care of Isabel." Elena frowned. "I wonder if Candace will be able to come. I know she doesn't like to leave her kids in the evening."

"You and Candace can bring the kids to my place. Cameron would love it. I'll call and make sure he doesn't have any other plans."

Elena waited until Anabelle had talked with Cameron. When she hung up Anabelle's face shone with success. "He's more than happy to take care of the kids."

"Great."

Candace came out of her unit just then. She had no plans for the evening and agreed to come. "I'll bring my mom if she's free. I'm sure she'd like to participate. Dr. Hamilton did her surgery five years ago. She's still cancer free, and I know he's one of her heroes."

Elena nodded, remembering Janet's bout with breast cancer.

"We'd love to have her join us." Anabelle glanced at her watch. "We'll need to make sure everyone brings their cell phones."

"Is there anything we can bring?" Candace asked. "Since it's close to dinner, we could do a potluck." Candace adjusted her purse strap and the three stepped into the elevator together.

"Actually that sounds good." Anabelle tucked her cell phone into her purse. "That way we won't all have to cook a big meal. I'll stop by the store to pick up some salads and maybe a couple of baked chickens. I need to run downtown to the bank and stop to see Ainslee too. Maybe she'll join us."

The elevator dinged and the doors slid open and they headed for the employee parking lot. Elena waved to the other two. "See you all at 6:30."

She headed for her dark green Jeep Liberty and, within minutes, had turned right off Cahokia on to Whittington Street. Elena sang a familiar praise song as she drove to the preschool to pick up Isabel, who was going to love visiting her Auntie *Amabelle*. Elena smiled as she imagined Isabel's excitement when she discovered what her Abuela had planned for them.

She parked in the church parking lot and went inside. First United Methodist had a wonderful preschool program, and Isabel looked forward to going. Elena hurried into the school and made a beeline for Isabel's room.

Isabel sat at her desk holding a pink backpack; but when she spotted Elena, she tore across the room. "*Buela! Buela!*"

Her teacher, Mrs. Dove, chuckled. "I think she's happy to see you."

Elena hugged her girl. "I'm happy to see her too." She paused to look at the papers Isabel handed to her. "Oh, very nice. These look like balloons."

"They are." Her dimples deepened. "I drew my party."

"Oh, I see. And lots of people."

Isabel began naming all of her stick figures until Elena said, "You can tell me the rest at home, okay? We're going to make cookies for your party, and then we get to go see Anabelle."

"Really?"

"Yes, really." Elena was beaming at her granddaughter when an unbidden thought pushed its way into her mind. Elena tried to block it out but it was too late. A vision of Sarah holding Isabel lingered.

They said their good-byes to Mrs. Dove and headed for the car. All the way home, Elena prayed that Sarah would not try to assert her parental rights. Though some of her anger toward Sarah had abated and she found herself praying for Sarah's well-being and sobriety, she just couldn't shake a certain feeling—the feeling that Sarah posed a threat.

Chapter Fourteen

ANABELLE ROLLED THE WINDOW DOWN AND LET the cool, fresh air blow into her face. She admired Deerford's wide tree-lined streets. The sun shone, and Anabelle couldn't imagine a more beautiful place in the world.

Deerford had pretty much all one could want in a town, including a bed-and-breakfast, a small park, seven schools, and even a country club with a nine-hole golf course. She entered the small downtown area, intent on finding a parking place. So many downtown areas in the smaller communities like Deerford lost business to the megastores and strip malls.

While they did have a shopping center just outside of town and a Walmart, the downtown area still had a lot of businesses. Here, they had two great restaurants, a new and used bookstore, a couple of gift stores, a drug store, jewelry store and a copy shop. And there was the decadent Chocolate Garden, located right next door to Once Upon a Time, the adorable and popular antiquities shop where Ainslee worked. Thanks to Ainslee, the hospital gift shop carried many of the items from the unique antique store.

Anabelle parked a block away from Once Upon a Time, then doubled back down the sidewalk to the store. A bell tinkled as she opened the door. Ainslee looked up from the counter where she was showing a customer some jewelry. She smiled in Anabelle's direction. Anabelle browsed, looking at the newly acquired items. She loved the store with its large pink chandelier and vintage clothing.

"I'll take this brooch," a customer said. "It'll be a perfect gift for my grandmother."

"I'm sure she'll love it." Ainslee rang up the sale, wrapped the jeweled brooch in tissue, and placed it in the shop's logo-imprinted gift bag. When the woman had gone, Ainslee came out from behind the counter. "Hi, Mother, what a surprise."

They hugged, and Anabelle's gaze went straight to Ainslee's tummy. "How's our little one?"

Ainslee laughed. "We're doing fine—except for the morning sickness. I'm glad I don't have to be here until ten every morning."

Anabelle couldn't help but admire her beautiful daughter. Was it her imagination or did she already have that special glow? The girls in the shop often wore retro clothing that went with the décor. Today Ainslee wore a long, cream and beige high-collar, laced dress that looked as if it had belonged to a debutante. "The dress is beautiful."

"Thanks. It won't be long until I'll need to shop for some maternity clothes. Maybe you and Kirstie can come to Peoria with me to pick some out. We could make a weekend of it."

"Like we used to do every year before school started." Anabelle thrilled to the idea. "Kirstie mentioned wanting some new clothes for the school year."

Ainslee smiled. "I kind of miss our shopping parties."

"I do too." Anabelle mused. "When are you thinking?"

"Not this weekend, but the next? I'll talk to Kirstie and call the hotel to book a room for us."

With that settled, Anabelle told her daughter about the Parade of Patients. "We're having a calling party and potluck at our house at six thirty. Would you like to come?"

"That's a great idea. I'll have to call Doug. Maybe we can both help."

Anabelle hugged her again and left. Before going to the car, she stopped at the Chocolate Garden to snag a small dark-chocolate bar. She ended up getting an entire box, thinking she might put them out this evening. Or maybe not.

While she'd been in the store, the air had grown more humid and clouds were doing their best to cover the sun. Anabelle had seen enough rain and stormy weather this week. She hoped the weather would behave itself at least through the weekend for the Parade of Patients. A wind gust pushed her forward a step or two as if to mock her.

Before heading home, James stopped at the chapel. He'd stopped before work as well, to pray and gather his thoughts before going to the floor.

He'd needed heavy doses of God's perspective to see him through the trauma of this past week. Dr. Hamilton's heart attack,

Gideon's desire to join ROTC, Tucker's passing and his patient load. Plus, he was letting things pile up at home.

The chaplain came in through the side door that led to his office. "Oh, James. I'm sorry. I didn't realize anyone was here."

James sighed. "I've had a rough week, and now feel like I should stop and pay my respects to Tucker's family."

He nodded. "Not an easy task." He knelt at the railing beside James. "I was there when he passed, as were both of his parents."

"So he wasn't alone?"

"Not by any means. There were moments when I felt the Lord's presence. There are times when you just know. This was one of those times. There was a certain peace. We all felt it."

Tears clouded James's vision. He brushed them away. "Thank you. I appreciate hearing that."

"I had a feeling you might. We all struggle with senseless deaths like this. Tucker was so young."

James nodded. The men prayed together, and James left with a much lightened load.

When James stopped to see the Blairs, Tucker's father thanked him for coming and invited him in. He introduced him to Tucker's grandparents and some aunts and uncles. James lost track of the names. He was surprised to find Gideon seated next to Tucker's mom on the sofa. At the hospital and now here. Gideon had always been thoughtful and caring with Fern, but to see him with others, even people he didn't know well, triggered a new understanding.

"Dad." Gideon stood. "I thought you might stop by."

He was surprised at how comfortable Gideon seemed. It occurred to him that Gideon might be more suited to nursing or ministry than soldiering. He'd make it a point to talk with Gideon about those options.

James spent several minutes talking to the Blairs and primarily listening as they spoke about Tucker and how grateful they were for the care he had received. "We know the doctors and the nursing staff—especially you, James, did everything possible for him." Tucker's father pinched the bridge of his nose. "It's all so crazy. I keep wondering if this is all a nightmare and I'll wake up. . . . It's wishful thinking, I know. Still it's hard to imagine."

"I understand. I'm still trying to process it myself." James sighed. "I'd like to stay, but I really need to get home to Fern. If there's anything you need, just call."

"Thanks. Your being here means a lot. And Gideon has been amazing. I've asked him to be a pallbearer and an usher at the funeral, if that's okay."

"Of course." He turned to Gideon. "Will you be home for dinner?"

"I'm not sure. I need to take Nelson to the music store in Princeton. He has a lesson and needs some music."

James nodded. "Just don't be too late."

His cell phone rang just as James reached his car. It was Anabelle. "Hello?"

"Hi James. Elena and I decided to have a phone party to contact Dr. Hamilton's patients. My house, six thirty. Can you come?"

James sighed. "I don't know. I haven't been home yet. And I really can't leave Fern—"

"Bring her. That is if she feels up to an outing. With all of us working it shouldn't take us very long, and we'll do a potluck."

"Okay. I'll see how she feels and call you."

Fern was in the kitchen when James came in. "There you are." She hobbled toward him, using her cane. "I thought I'd better see about dinner. Gideon told me about Tucker and asked if I'd be okay by myself for a while. I'm so proud of him."

Sapphire flicked her tail and meowed a greeting from her mat near her half empty food dish.

"So am I." James scooped his wife up in his arms and, after kissing her soundly and relishing the feel of her against him, settled her on her kitchen chair.

"I've missed you." James planted another kiss on her pixie nose. She'd been asleep when he'd come home the night before and again this morning.

"I missed you too. I tried to stay awake."

"You need your rest. But I'm home now. At least for an hour or so." He told her about Anabelle's phone party and invitation.

"I'd love to go."

He laughed. "You don't even know what it's for."

"You can tell me. But it doesn't matter. I'd love to see Anabelle and the others."

"I'm glad you're up to it. But we'll need to leave for home by at least eight thirty. I have a ton of laundry to do, and we need to have that talk about Gideon's future."

"Good."

"So how was your day?" James asked.

"Nice. I didn't do anything." She laughed.

"That's great. We could all use days like that sometimes."

She reached for him and he paused to let her hold him. "My poor James. You look so tired. I wish I could help."

"You just did." He chuckled. "And when we get home from Anabelle's you can help me even more by letting me rest my head on your lap while we talk."

"Deal."

She seemed in a better mood today than the last few days. Maybe she was going into another remission. He hoped that was the case. "Were you planning something special for dinner? Anabelle wants to do potluck."

"Just salad. I took some shrimp out to defrost and boiled a few eggs."

"*Mmm*. A shrimp salad sounds perfect. I'll pull some sourdough bread out of the freezer. Do we have olives?" James chuckled. "I guess I should ask myself that."

While he packed the food for the potluck, James told Fern about Dr. Hamilton's refusal to take it easy.

"Oh, James. I know how he feels. It's so hard to give up. I still find myself pushing to do more than I should."

"We need him to know that we want him around a long time." He double-bagged the shrimp and set it in the cooler along with the dressing and greens. "Anyway, we came up with a plan." James told her about the Parade of Patients and how they and Genna were going to call past patients and elicit the help of the Quilting Guild to put their plan into action.

"What a wonderful idea." Fern's eyes lit up. "Is there anything I can do?"

"I'm sure Anabelle will welcome the help."

James put a load of laundry in the washer, and after he took a shower, they departed for Anabelle and Cameron's home.

Chapter Fifteen

ANABELLE SAW THE LAST OF HER GUESTS LEAVE at nine, and that was Genna. The evening had been a great deal of fun. They'd eaten well and ultimately tallied 110 people who wanted to participate in the Parade of Patients. She had worn herself out playing hostess and making calls, but she relished the feeling. The night had been a success by every measure.

By 9:20 PM, she kissed Cameron and told him she was going to bed early. The entire week had been exhausting; part of it, she knew, was from worrying over Drew.

"We'll need to get things organized early tomorrow morning if we plan to implement the Parade of Patients this weekend."

Cameron hugged her. "It's a good thing you're doing, luv. I hope the doc appreciates it."

"Oh, he will." Anabelle drew in a deep breath and leaned into her husband's strong arms. She was so tired, she could have fallen asleep right there with her head against his chest.

He chuckled and, with hands on her shoulders, set her upright and turned her around. "Do you need me to carry you to bed?"

She turned back around and kissed his cheek. "I think I can make it from here."

"I'll be in shortly. There are severe thunderstorm warnings for the area, and I'd like to see what they're predicting for us."

Anabelle didn't really want to know. Just the same, the weather managed to announce its plans just shortly after she fell asleep. She awoke to lightning so bright it lit up the entire room, and then thunder that rattled the windowpanes.

"Cam?" She bolted up in bed and reached for Cameron, but he wasn't there. The red numbers on her alarm radio read 10:00 just before blinking off. Something hard slammed onto the roof. Anabelle yelped.

The terrifying noise increased with intensity. She ducked under the covers. Then she saw a flickering light from the hallway and Cameron was at her side. He set the lantern he'd brought on the bedside table. "It's all right, luv. Just a bit of hail."

"Hail? A bit? It sounds like bombs."

The large window shattered and a hailstone the size of a baseball bounced on the floor. Then came another and another.

He held her close. "We'd best go downstairs where we'll be safe. Those stones are the biggest I've ever seen."

Cameron went out to his workshop and found a plywood sheet to board up the window upstairs. Anabelle waited, her fear lessening and turning more toward worry. She prayed her children would be safe and that Hope Haven, their staff and the patients staying there would not sustain damage.

For the next half hour they huddled together on the couch in the living room. The two of them prayed for safety for their family and for the town. Anabelle offered up special prayers for the patients.

"I hate to see what our poor town will look like in the morning."

"I can tell you right now, luv, it won't be pretty."

James joined Fern and Sapphire on the couch when they arrived home from the Scotts'. It was still early, but he was too tired to do much more than put another load in the washer. He was glad he'd taken Fern to Anabelle's. The calling party had been fun and they'd accomplished the calls in short order.

He stretched out on the sofa, pillowing his head on Fern's lap. Fern had softened some toward Gideon's plan to join the ROTC but that was about it. "I don't want him in the military." She sighed. "I know it's honorable; but James, I would be so sick with worry. He's our son."

"I know." James felt a certain pride in having served his country. Did he want to deprive his son of that honor? "We need to sit down and talk with him. See if he wants to consider other options and find out what he really wants to do." He told her about Gideon's maturity in dealing with Tucker and his family.

"He's a good boy, James."

James couldn't have agreed more. They sat in silence until James eventually drifted off.

The next thing he knew, he was awakened by a loud crash and what sounded like bullets raining down on the roof.

James sat up, confused. The darkened living room came into focus as his brain gave up the remnants of a military battle.

Breaking glass and a scream from the upstairs bedroom sent James's heart to pounding even harder and his feet racing up to their bedroom. In the darkness he stumbled twice as he groped his way along the stair railing.

"*Me-o-o-ow.*" Sapphire flew down the stairs almost colliding with him.

"Honey, are you okay?" He felt his way to the bed where Fern lay huddled under the covers. James sat on the bed to comfort her as he peered into the darkness.

"What's happening?" Fern clutched at the front of his shirt.

"It's a hailstorm." As his eyes adjusted to the darkness, he could see glass covering the floor near the window and the blinds twisted as the hail pelted at them.

He reached for the bedside table and fumbled in the drawer for the flashlight he kept there. James flipped it on and walked around the bed to assess the damage. He took one look at the size of the hailstones and backed away from the window. He wouldn't attempt to do any repairing until the pounding hail stopped.

"Let's go downstairs where we'll be safe." James gently picked her up and headed for the staircase. He glanced down the hall surprised the boys weren't up. Seeing their open doors, he nearly panicked. "Where are the boys?"

"I don't know. You fell asleep and I came upstairs to read. I fell asleep too."

"They should have been home around nine." James checked his watch. It was 10:05 PM, which meant Gideon and Nelson had most likely been on their way home when the storm hit. Not wanting to frighten Fern, he said, "They must have taken shelter somewhere."

They descended the stairs, and James set Fern on the sofa and tucked a soft fleece throw around her. "Will you be okay here while I check the rest of the house?"

"I'm okay now."

"Hopefully it will end soon." With the upper floor for in-sulation, the hail sounded less intense than it had upstairs. Still, James could only imagine how much damage this storm would leave in its path.

"Be careful." Fern reached an arm toward him.

"I will." He kissed her forehead and slipped on his sandals.

James paced around the house. The eaves were protecting the windows on the lower floor, but he heard another crash upstairs. He raced up to the second floor and checked the other bedrooms. One of Nelson's windows had been smashed. James closed the bedroom doors and went back down to sit with Fern.

With the giant hailstones still bashing the house, James felt helpless. There was nothing he could do but wait for the storm to pass and hope for the best. With the entire neighborhood in darkness, James gathered up several candles and, after lighting them, placed them where they'd be needed: the kitchen, living room and bathroom.

Though only a few minutes passed as they sat huddled to-gether on the sofa, to James it seemed like hours. He remembered all too clearly holing up in bunkers with bombs falling. James tried to wipe the horror of war from his mind and focus on praying for Gideon and Nelson.

The bombardment finally lessened at 10:45 PM and then stopped altogether.

He took hold of Fern's hand. "I need to get to the hospital. I have no doubt we're looking at a serious situation."

"What about the boys?" Fern tightened her grip.

"I'll look for them on the way." James prayed they'd found shelter. "They're smart kids. I'm sure they're okay."

Before leaving, he brought her pillow downstairs and tucked her in, then brought her a glass of water and made certain she had her cell phone so she could call him if necessary—if and when the phones were working again. He doubted she'd sleep. He would try to call her parents from the hospital to check on her.

"Cam, I'll need to get to the hospital right away." Knowing Hope Haven would be getting a large number of victims from the storm, Anabelle felt the sooner she got there the better.

"I know, luv. As soon as it's safe. I'll take you over in the truck."

When the hail subsided, the two went upstairs where Anabelle shrugged into her blue scrubs and nursing shoes, then grabbed a lab jacket that bore her name badge.

Cameron put on jeans and work boots. "I'll load tools and some emergency supplies in the truck."

Anabelle took a moment to check the bedrooms for damage. Several more windows were shattered. Those would have to be dealt with later. Right now, they had to help wherever help was needed. There would be injuries to people caught out in the storm, car accidents, fallen branches and broken windows. Anabelle prayed there would be no fatalities. In Deerford, they were used to thunder and hail, but Anabelle had never seen hailstones like this.

She doused the lantern and hurried out to the garage. The hail had stopped, but the storm was far from over. Cameron maneuvered the truck out of the garage and into a deluge. With power outages, they had only headlights to guide them to the hospital. Once they reached the main road, they could see emergency vehicles already responding. They stopped at a roadblock when a police officer stopped them.

Cam rolled down his window. "I need to get my wife to the hospital."

"Is she injured?"

Anabelle leaned over to speak to him and show her badge. "I'm a nurse."

"Then you'll want to detour around to Oak Avenue. We have a big pileup on Cahokia."

"Thanks, we'll do that." Cameron rolled up the window.

At the hospital, the emergency generator had kicked in. The lights made Hope Haven a beacon, drawing people to help and safety.

Even though Anabelle had been familiar with the hospital's disaster drill, she was glad Albert had brought everyone up to date.

"I'll drop you off at the emergency entrance," Cam said, "then I'll check on the girls and Evan. There are a lot of windows to be boarded up and repairs to be made. I'll see if I can get some crews together. The men's fellowship at church will be a good place to start." Cameron seemed to be talking to himself now. "Call Al and get the lumberyard open."

While Cam went on with his list, they passed several accidents and downed power lines, a fallen tree. The chaos from the streets filled her with apprehension and Anabelle took several deep breaths to calm herself. She didn't want her husband out working in this storm. But as with her, there was really no choice.

Cameron stopped the car and leaned over to kiss her goodbye. Anabelle grasped his hand. "Be careful."

"You too." He waited until she'd reached and opened the ER door before taking off.

Though Anabelle wanted to run upstairs to check on her own unit, her first priority was to help with patients who were already streaming into the ER.

Dr. Weller, an ER doctor, had begun triaging and giving orders. He tagged each of them according to their degree of injury—with red being the highest and white being the lowest—in an effort to get to the patients with the greatest needs and point them in the direction they needed to go.

She approached him to let him know she'd arrived.

He looked frantic. "Thank God you're here. If you could take over triage, I can get to the worst cases. Right now, I'm the only doctor here."

Gurneys already lined the hallway, and people who could still get around on their own crowded the waiting room. They could have used at least a dozen more doctors and nurses. The small ER staff had been bolstered by the swing-shift staff.

Anabelle forced herself to get a grip. No point in wishing for what they didn't have. She needed to focus on what they did have and work within those boundaries. Her mother had often told her that when things looked overwhelming and she felt she was on a narrow precipice, to not look down. To just take one step at a time knowing God would be with her. Looking down only led to panic. And Anabelle was very close to the edge.

James donned a yellow rain slicker and black boots before heading into the downpour. He drove slowly through the pounding rain, sheets of water slamming across the windshield. He doubted he'd be able to recognize Gideon's car if it did pass by. He made it to the light on Whittington Street before coming across an accident. His headlights outlined two damaged vehicles, but no emergency vehicle.

He pulled over and stepped out of the car into the driving rain. Sweeping his flashlight over the area, he could see the front car had been crushed by a nearby tree branch. He surmised that the second car had rear-ended the first one. He could make out someone in the passenger seat of both cars.

James sprinted across the road. "Is everyone all right here?" James called out. "Anyone need help?"

"Over here." A man waved at James from the sidewalk next to the rear car. "My wife's legs are pinned under the dash."

James shined his flashlight into the car. The woman was sobbing. "Help me, please."

Her husband ran a hand through his sopping hair. "I tried calling 9-1-1, but we can't get a reliable cell phone signal."

"What's your name?" The cut on his hand looked superficial. James would deal with that later.

"Hank Garrett. This is Lisa."

James nodded and turned to Hank's wife. "Okay, ma'am. I'm a nurse, and I'm going to try to help you. Are you hurt anywhere else?" James shone the light into her terror-stricken eyes. Her face bore residue powder from the deflated air bags, which gave her a ghoulish look.

"N-no," she stammered. "I don't think so."

He examined her legs, which both seemed to be pinned tightly between the seat and the dash. "Do you have any feeling in your feet and legs?"

"Yes," she gasped. "It hurts so much. I can't move."

He saw no signs of heavy bleeding, but suspected one or both legs might be broken. "Okay, Lisa. Here's what I need you to do. Hold on to your husband's hand and try to relax. We'll get a rescue team here, and they'll be able to free you." James hoped that would be the case.

He turned to the husband. "Do you have a blanket— something to put over your wife to keep her warm? We want to keep her from going into shock or getting chilled."

"There's one in the backseat. I'll get it."

"All right. I'll try calling dispatch again. And I need to take a look at these folks in the other car."

The man leaned against his car looking as if he needed as much comforting as his wife. "The branch crushed the windshield."

James tried his cell, but had no service. He brushed tree limbs aside in an effort to get a closer look at the couple inside the first vehicle. The elderly driver was pressed against the headrest by the windshield. The woman lay in much the same position as the man.

James pulled away some of the broken glass on the driver's side window and reached in. He slid his fingers along the carotid artery and breathed in relief as he found a pulse.

He needed to get help, but couldn't leave these people alone.

As if hearing his plea for help, a car's headlights came toward him. James stepped out into the street and waved his arms.

The car stopped.

"Dad!" Gideon leaned out the window. "What are you doing out here?"

James ran around to the driver's side door. "I don't think I've ever been so happy to see anyone in my life. We have three serious injuries here, and I need medics out here right away. I can't call anyone."

"What can I do?"

"The hospital is only about three blocks away. Drive back that way and get help." James wiped the rain out of his face with the back of his hand. "Then I want you to go home and stay with your mother."

Gideon shook his head. "I'll take Nelson home. Then I'm coming back."

Watching Gideon drive off filled James with a sense of pride. The people in Deerford would need every able-bodied person to get them past this disaster. He made his way back to Hank. "Help is on the way. Just hang in there."

James hurried back to the first car and ripped off as many small branches as possible to get to the elderly woman. He pulled out the broken glass until he could reach in to check her pulse. He felt along her neck for a carotid pulse, but couldn't find one.

Flashing lights came toward them and James released the breath he'd been holding.

James and two police officers managed to lift the tree branch off the first car. They then began working to pull away the shattered safety glass that had once served as a windshield.

Gideon appeared at James's side. "Nelson is with Mom."

James nodded. He was too choked up to speak. Somewhere along the way, his oldest son had become a man.

Chapter Sixteen

ANDACE'S COMFORTING OF HER TWO YOUNG children didn't work so well when she was just as frightened.

They had crawled into bed with Candace when the thunder and lightning began. Hail hit with such force, Candace feared the stones would come right through the roof.

The total darkness, sounds of shattering glass, crying children and the fury of the storm were almost more than she could bear.

"Candace." Her mother opened the door letting in the blessed light of a candle. "We need to go downstairs. It isn't safe up here."

"Go with Grammy, kids. I'll be right behind you." Candace grabbed a bathrobe and hurried after them.

Her mother had already lit some candles and brought out quilts and snuggly blankets to wrap up in.

Candace lowered herself to the couch beside Janet and leaned her head against her mother's shoulder. "Thank you."

Howie drew up his knees and snuggled on Candace's lap, and Brooke squeezed between the two women.

Candace held her little guy close and kissed the top of his head.

"Don't be scared, Howie." Brooke reached for his hand. "God will take care of us."

Janet smiled. "Yes, He will."

Candace tried not to worry about the damage the storm would do. She shuddered to think of leaving her children and venturing out into the storm, but she knew a storm like this would not be without incident. "Mom, I need to get to Hope Haven."

"Of course. I'll watch the kids."

"No." Brooke clung to Candace, tears spilling onto her cheeks. "It's too dangerous. You might get hurt."

"It's okay, honey, the storm is over. I'll be back as soon as I can."

"Mommy, no." Tears brimmed in her eyes.

Candace melted. "Sweetie, you know Mommy's a nurse, and you know nurses take care of people. After this storm, there may be hurt people who need my help."

Janet took hold of Brooke's shoulders and gave Candace a look that said *go*. Candace gave Brooke a hug and kissed her cheek. "I'm going upstairs to change now."

Candace grabbed a flashlight off the coffee table and hurried upstairs. It took less than three minutes to change into her uniform and shoes. What was she thinking? She would be going into a situation that could be equally as bad as what she'd seen with Dr. Hamilton.

Candace sucked in a deep breath as she ran a brush through her hair. "You can do this," she told herself.

When she came back downstairs, Howie and Brooke ran to her with hands outstretched. "Look!" Howie and Brooke lifted up hailstones larger than any she had ever seen. "It's bigger'n a snow cone."

"No wonder they made so much noise." Candace examined both specimens.

Brooke nodded. "We're going to freeze them so people will believe they really did look like baseballs. Do you want one too, Grammy?"

Janet laughed. "No thanks. I think I'll remember this storm well enough without a memento."

Candace took the hailstones to the freezer and placed them on the shelf. She turned back around and said a hasty good-bye while the children were still in a good mood.

In the employee parking lot, Candace stepped out and opened the umbrella, facing it against the wind. About halfway there, a gust tore it out of her hand. She debated going after it, but decided she'd buy another one instead.

Candace ran the rest of the way and ducked into an ambulance bay. She'd never worked ER before, choosing instead the usually slower paced specialty of obstetrics. Even so, she was a nurse and could perform emergency procedures if necessary.

Candace hurried through the ER and into the waiting room. Her heart raced. Her stomach churned as if gearing up for panic mode. She couldn't help but remember the day she'd rushed to the hospital when she'd gotten the call about Dean. The only

storm that day had been in her heart, and it had all but done
her in.

With Isabel finally asleep in Elena and Cesar's bed, the storm
now having passed, Elena paced back and forth across the living
room floor, into the kitchen, then back again.

Frustration nipped at her. She should be at the hospital, but
with Cesar and Rafael gone, someone had to stay with Isabel.

The poor child had been absolutely terrified during the hailstorm, her head buried in Elena's shoulder during the ordeal. Of
course, Elena hadn't been all that calm herself, especially when
the windows started breaking and an exceptionally large stone
slammed through the skylight in the entryway.

Once the hail had subsided, Rafael had wiped the tears from
his little girl's face then gone up to the roof to cover the hole,
while Elena cleared the debris inside. Together they swept the
glass shards and tossed the dozen or so hailstones into the sink.
When the broken windows had been covered with boards and
tarps, Rafael headed out to help where he could.

Elena stepped outside into the damp, chilled air and examined
the yard and front of the house. As a police officer, Cesar had
been on duty the entire time, and Elena hadn't gotten any word
from him yet. Of course, neither her cell phone nor the land line
were working. She feared the possibility that he might be injured.

"No point creating trouble where there is none." It had been
one of her grandmother's favorite sayings, and it fit here. She'd
do her best to avoid nightmare scenarios from now on, given all

the anxiety she'd experienced after receiving Sarah's call. Elena wrapped her arms around herself to lessen the chill. Their single-story ranch home would need a great deal of work—they'd need a new roof and a number of windows at the very least. She hoped their home insurance would cover the damage.

Seeing the candlelight in her neighbor's front window, Elena had an idea. She made her way through the rain and knocked on the door.

"Elena?" Marion drew her inside. "Is everything all right?"

"We're as fine as we can be, given what just happened. I am hoping you can help me. Isabel is asleep, and I would like very much to go to the hospital to work. I know they probably need as many nurses and doctors as they can get."

"Say no more. I will be happy to stay with Isabel."

Marion blew out her candles, grabbed a flashlight off the entry table, shrugged on a pink fleece jacket from the coat rack and hooked an umbrella from the stand next to the door. Stepping outside she said, "The sooner you can get there the better."

"That's what I was thinking." Elena paused, flicking the light from her own flashlight over the white, uneven ground and stepped across the ice-laden walk. "Be careful. The last thing we need is for either of us to fall and break a hip."

"Been there, done that." Marion followed in Elena's wake.

Getting into her car a few minutes later, Elena wished she'd thought to ask Marion earlier. She backed down the driveway thankful that her car had been under cover of the carport, which had offered some protection.

Nothing could have prepared Elena for the chaos she passed on the way to Hope Haven. Stranded vehicles lined the road, all looking like they'd been battered by baseball bats. When she reached the hospital, she drove around to the back and was stopped by a police officer at the entrance to the employees' parking lot. Water dripped off his hat and ran in rivulets down his yellow slicker.

"We're only letting staff in here."

"I'm a nurse." Elena showed him her badge.

He smiled in recognition. "You're Cesar's wife."

"Yes." She peered up at him but didn't recognize him. "Have you seen Cesar? Is he all right?"

He nodded. "He was fine a few minutes ago."

"Thank the Lord." Elena drove on and parked as close to the building as possible, finding a place in the fifth row back. She felt sorry for the staff members who had been working during the storm. Their vehicles were a mess.

Stepping around hail that still littered the ground, Elena hurried to the staff entrance. All available wall space was taken up with stretchers that had spread out from the ER. Every seat in the large reception area was taken as were the chairs that lined the wall across from the lab.

An older woman knelt on the floor, raising her hands and praying loudly in Spanish. A middle-aged woman, probably her daughter, sat with her and acted as though this were a normal event. Elena paused to offer assistance, but the younger of the two waved her on. She was probably mourning for a family member.

The din from dozens of people all speaking at once was deafening. Somewhere nearby, a tray clattered to the floor. Someone screamed.

Elena made her way back through the ER. She had no idea who was in charge, but she was determined to find out fast and get to work.

When she reached the emergency room, Anabelle took a moment to orient herself.

Medics rushed past, wheeling a patient into the ER bays. Anabelle stepped back, brushing into the stretcher behind her. She turned and looked into the rheumy gray eyes of a woman probably in her late seventies.

The woman groaned and lifted her hand. "Help me."

Anabelle could barely hear her over the din. Her silver hair was matted with blood from a gash on her forehead. A damp washcloth lay beside her head as if someone had attempted to cover the wound.

She had been triaged as yellow, but her pallor suggested otherwise. "Can you tell me your name?" Anabelle checked her pulse. Barely palpable.

"Louise." Her eyes closed and her head lolled to one side.

"Okay, Louise. I'm going to take care of you." She took the woman's blood pressure, using the cuff already on her arm. Sixty over forty. Louise was going into shock. "We need to get to this lady right away."

Anabelle increased the volume on the IV, noting the nearly empty bag. Anabelle switched Louise out to a red tag and took her back to the ER, where she grabbed another bag of normal saline and replaced the nearly empty one.

Someone came up behind her. She turned and almost fell over them. "Dr. Hamilton, what on earth are you doing here?" He was wearing scrubs.

"Helping. What's her status?" He pulled on a pair of latex gloves.

"She's in shock and dehydrated. Looks like she's lost a lot of blood. I opened the IV, but she might need a unit. . . ."

"Are you triaging?" he asked.

"I was."

"From the looks of things, you'd better get back out there. I'll handle this one. See if you can get me a nurse."

"Dr. Hamilton, are you sure?" Anabelle looked straight into his determined gray eyes.

He frowned. "We need every able doctor."

This was neither the time nor place to argue.

"Can I help, Mrs. Scott?" Seri stepped up beside them wearing jeans and a wild rose-and-skeleton T-shirt and diamond stud in her nose.

Anabelle wanted to hug her. "Yes. Thanks so much for coming."

"I was across the street studying at the Cuppa Coffee when the storm hit. Bet it broke out every window in the place. I helped as much as I could. Brought a couple of guys over that looked like they needed stitching up."

Dr. Hamilton opened one of the cupboards and pulled out a suture set. "Well, Seri, looks like you're going to get some of that experience you wanted."

"Good thing I read up on that disaster stuff, huh?"

"Good thing." Anabelle grabbed a scrub top from the linen cart in the hallway. "Put this on over your shirt and do everything Dr. Hamilton tells you to."

"Okay." Seri shrugged into the green top and grabbed some gloves.

"Seri, get her vitals again," Dr. Hamilton ordered. "Make sure she's stable. Then you can assist while we clean her wound and stitch her up."

He began opening the suture set. "Anabelle, on your way out, tell one of the ER nurses I'm going to need a type and crossmatch. We need to hook her up to the monitors."

Anabelle left the two of them and gave the supervising ER nurse a quick report. "I know he shouldn't be here, but like he said, we need every available doctor. And Seri is new, but I think she'll be okay."

"I'll keep an eye on them. Looks like we're in for a long night."

"You think?" Anabelle couldn't believe the chaos. A couple more doctors had come in, one she recognized from family practice and another from internal medicine.

Ambulances and rescue units and police were dropping people off at the ER faster than she and the other nurses could process them. Some of the patients came in from neighboring towns saying the hospitals there were overrun as well. Ordinarily, some of the victims would have been transported by helicopter to Peoria, but the hospital was too far away and the weather had grounded all air traffic.

Dr. Weller approached the nurses' station. "Varner is trying to find a place to direct the less seriously injured. He's looking at the high school."

"I hope it works out," Anabelle said. "It'll take a lot of pressure off us."

"We just have to find people to go out there and staff the place." Dr. Weller looked around. "I'll talk to some of the staff who just came in."

Anabelle went back to triaging. She had never worked through so many victims at once. Some of the patients required little care and were moved into the lobby area or sent home. Others were taken into the ER, and many had to wait in the lobby areas and waiting rooms until someone could see them.

Though Hope Haven doctors and nurses arrived as they were able, it became clear to Anabelle that they would need another facility and more staff as soon as possible. She prayed Varner would come through.

Elena spotted Anabelle beside a stretcher and hurried to her friend's side. If anyone knew the score, Anabelle would.

"I got here a little bit ago. With both Cesar and Rafael gone, I had to find a sitter for Isabel."

Anabelle nodded as she snapped on a fresh pair of latex gloves. "I could use you here for the moment."

Elena glanced down at the man on the stretcher. His shirt had been ripped open to reveal an abdominal wound. Anabelle had covered it and was now applying pressure.

"Grab some gloves and hold this," Anabelle ordered. "We need to get him into surgery. I'll see if any of the doctors can take him."

Elena reached into the box on the wall. Empty. "No gloves here. I'll go check with the doctors and be right back."

"All right, hurry."

On the way into the ER, Elena stepped into a medical supply room and grabbed a box each of small, medium and large gloves. When she slipped back into the corridor, she nearly collided with a medic.

"Coming through!"

Elena stepped out of the way as medics pushed in another gurney. This one held a young man with a beard who had large welts and bruises on his face and chest.

"We found him out in the park, shirtless," one of the medics told her. "His buddy said he'd been drinking and thought it would be fun to dance in the hail. His vitals are stable. Looks like he might have a concussion."

"He'll need an MRI." Dr. Clark came up beside them.

One of the medics handed Elena a clipboard. "I . . ." She turned to Dr. Clark. "Anabelle needs a doctor. She has a guy with an abdominal wound."

She glanced around. "If this guy is stable, maybe one of you can take him to X-ray."

"No can do. We're piled up from here to Sunday out on the streets."

Dr. Clark sighed. "All right." She gave Elena an almost frantic look. "We need more help."

"I can take him to X-ray," Elena volunteered.

She nodded. "Show me where the guy with the abdominal wound is. Sounds like a priority."

Spotting Anabelle, Candace hurried to her friend's side.

"You made it." Anabelle glanced over at her, taking in her sopped hair and clothes. "We need someone in the waiting room. We have a lot of distraught people who need calming down."

"I'm on it."

"There's a guy from some television program called *Storm Trackers* who's been giving us a bad time. Keeps trying to get footage of the chaos in here. I'm about to have security take his camera away from him."

"Oh, joy." Candace eased out of her soaked jacket, debating whether or not she should change out of her damp scrubs.

Before she had a chance to do either, a young man carrying a small child stopped her. "I need help. We were in the car when the storm hit. The window next to my little girl shattered. She's cut up pretty bad and took some hits to the head. I stopped the car and climbed in back with her as soon as I could, to protect her, but I might have been too late."

Candace looked at the cuts, all of which seemed superficial. "Has anyone seen her yet?"

"Not exactly. I was told to wait here, but I'm worried. She keeps going in and out of consciousness."

Candace led him out of the traffic pattern. "Show me."

He took the blanket from around her. Her dark curls fell free. Candace examined the child while she lay in the young man's arms. "Her vitals are strong, but her eyes aren't as reactive as they should be. We need to get her into the back right away."

Candace led them toward the ER and immediately snagged Dr. Weller. The child's father gave her a grateful smile.

Seeing that the family was in good hands, Candace went back to her post—that of trying to calm victims and their families and make some order out of the confusion.

One woman sat in a chair sobbing. Candace knelt down in front of her. Taking the woman's shaking, blue-veined hand, she asked, "Are you injured?"

"No." She shook her head.

"What can I do for you?"

"I can't find my husband. We were here before the storm hit, but no one's come out to tell me anything since the crowds started to arrive."

"I'll try to find out what happened to him."

Twenty minutes later she had finally tracked him down to the medical unit where he was being treated for elevated blood sugar and a severe urinary tract infection. Candace hurried back to the ER waiting room and escorted the woman up to the second floor. She paused a moment to watch the happy reunion before heading back into the chaos.

Chapter Seventeen

AMES ASKED GIDEON TO WAIT WHILE HE WENT inside the hospital to find out where he'd be needed most. He jogged inside and spotted Dr. Weller.

"James thanks for coming in. We need someone with your experience out at the high school. Albert Varner has secured the school and most of the lesser-injured people are being sent over there. I'm not sure who's seeing the patients, but I know they'd appreciate your help."

James thanked him and hurried back outside. Dr. Weller's lack of information bothered him, especially the part about not knowing who the staff out there would be.

"Where are we going?" Gideon asked.

"To the high school. Apparently we're setting up a clinic there."

The rain lessened some as James drove down Cahokia Street and made a left on Rishell. He passed Anabelle's house and went on to the high school.

"Um, Dad, are you sure this is where we're supposed to be?"

James rubbed the back of his neck. The school was dark. Apparently no one had turned on the generator. Several vehicles had pulled into the parking lot and still had their lights on. Probably, like him, they were looking for the medical team they'd been told would be here.

"Stay here," he told Gideon. "I'll see what's going on." Several more cars came in behind him.

A man emerged from a white SUV. "I was told to come out here for treatment. There's no one around."

"What's going on?" Someone else asked.

"I have no idea." James pulled out his cell phone. Still no signal. He jogged up the steps of the old school and tried the doors.

"Great, just great," he muttered. Turning around, James spotted a large motor home with lights. Maybe he could use it to treat some of these people. It seemed futile to send them all back to the hospital at this point.

James jogged over to where the motor coach had parked. A bumper sticker identified the owner as a World War II veteran. An older man stood beside the trailer.

"Is this rig yours?" James asked.

"Yep. I pulled under these trees to ward off the hail. What are all these people doing out here?"

James came right to the point. "Here's the deal. Folks are being sent over here to the school for medical treatment and obviously someone got their wires crossed." James nodded toward the trailer. "I'm a nurse. Actually used to be a medic in the Gulf War. Do you suppose we could use your motor coach as a sort of base for a while—until we can fix this mess? I could look over the people who are here. See if they need treatment and what they'll need."

"Sure. Anything for a fellow vet." He grinned and shook James's hand, then opened the door to allow James entry.

James gathered everyone around him and announced the plan. "We're going to need supplies. Gideon, get the first-aid kit out of our car and see if you can round up some more." He tossed Gideon his keys.

"Once you've done that, go back to the hospital and tell them to stop sending people out here. Find out what the Red Cross is doing. They should be out here. Tell whoever is directing traffic to stop sending people out here until they get their wires uncrossed." He hesitated, then to Gideon's retreating figure said, "And, son, thank you."

Gideon nodded and took off running.

James sighed. It was going to be a long night.

To the group gathered around him he said, "If everybody stays calm, we should be able to take care of your injuries. Does anyone else here have medical experience?"

A couple of hands went up. "Okay, talk to me. We'll set up a triage unit right here in the parking lot."

James wished he could get his hands on the fool who'd sent all these people out here. The best thing to do, he decided, was to take things one step at a time and one person at a time.

An hour later, James saw the end of the people who'd driven to the high school for medical care. Most were cuts and bruises that he and his two helpers could easily take care of.

By asking everyone there to bring him any first-aid kits they might have, and using the one from his own car, they were able to make do.

James thanked the man with the RV and left with Gideon, who'd come back to help.

Once back at the hospital, James went straight to the CEO.

"I'm sorry, James." Varner said. "I understand your frustration, but that order didn't come from this office. Dr. Weller and I had talked about it, but I couldn't get hold of the superintendent. I decided to go elsewhere. Dr. Weller must have misunderstood and spread the message to go to the high school. Glad you were there to help though."

"So do we have a place to go? There's no way Hope Haven can handle everyone. Even the medical offices are overflowing." James blew out an exasperated sigh.

"We're working on it."

"What about the Church of the Good Shepherd? There's plenty of room. All we need are beds. Or the YMCA."

"Therein lies the problem. We need a place that has cots already in place, at least until the Red Cross can get some for us."

James sat on the edge of the desk. "When will that be?"

A police officer knocked on the door. "The mayor radioed in that we can use the YMCA, and the Red Cross should have cots and first-aid supplies there within the hour. The National Guard is coming as well."

Varner released a long sigh and tipped his head back. "Thank you."

When the officer left, Varner turned back to James. "I'm going to need someone over at the Y who knows what they're doing. Can you head it up?"

"Sure. Just wait until I send word that we're ready to go before you start diverting people there."

Clearly relieved, Varner shook James's hand. "We have a ham-radio operator here at the hospital who's been getting messages out. We'll try to get another one out to the Y as well; so if you need anything, get back to us."

James nodded. His father-in-law would be in his element right about now—ham-radio operators were depended on by the community.

"What do you want me to do about staff?" James asked.

"We'll make an announcement for anyone available to meet you—where?"

"At the staff entrance."

"Done. We have a number of volunteers. You can handpick a crew to work with you."

"Thanks, I will." James thought immediately of Anabelle and Elena. He'd have welcomed Candace too, but she didn't have emergency room experience.

Anabelle was still on triage when she spotted James and Gideon in the lobby. She'd just sent another patient back to the ER, so before starting in on someone else, made her way through the crowd. "James, Gideon, good to see you."

"Anabelle." James turned toward her voice. "I was looking for you. I need some good people to go to the Y with me. We're setting up a makeshift hospital there. Red Cross and a National Guard Unit are on the way with supplies."

Anabelle looked around. "I would love to go out there with you, James, but I can't leave. Check with Elena. I don't think she has a specific post as yet."

James scanned the room and spotted her back by the lab. "Thanks, I will."

"Good luck."

A moment later he had merged into the crowd.

Anabelle felt a tug on her trousers and looked down at a girl around five years old with a tear-streaked face. "My daddy is lost. Can you help me find him?"

"Oh my." Annabelle hunkered down. "What's your daddy's name, sweetheart?"

"Bill Preston." She wiped an arm across her runny nose.

Anabelle desperately needed a break. Her hip, hand and knee joints ached. She needed a strong cup of coffee and some ibuprofen; but at the moment, helping this child took precedence.

She took the little girl's hand and led her back through the ER. "What's your name?"

"Lucy Preston."

"Let's get you cleaned up, Lucy, and then we'll find your daddy, okay?"

Lucy nodded.

Stopping at a restroom, Anabelle wet a paper towel and washed the child's face. "There we go." Some of what she'd thought was dirt came away red. "What happened to your dad?"

"The car got all wrecked. Some men took him away in a ambulance and a man brought me here. He said to wait, but I got scared."

Anabelle smiled. "He left you here all by yourself?"

She sniffed and nodded.

Anabelle handed her a tissue for her nose. "Where is your mommy?"

Lucy shrugged. "I don't know. Daddy says she's a long way from here."

Anabelle enveloped the child in a hug. "Okay, Lucy, let's go and find your daddy."

Walking through the ER, Anabelle checked with the charge nurse who didn't recognize the name Bill Preston.

"Is Dr. Hamilton still here?" Anabelle asked.

"Last I knew. I haven't had time to look in on him for a while." The charge nurse turned to one of the doctors who'd come up beside her.

Anabelle, with Lucy in tow, went back to check on Dr. Hamilton.

Seri stepped around the curtain just as Anabelle was about to peek in.

"Mrs. Scott." Seri glanced down at the child.

Anabelle introduced Lucy and told her about Bill Preston. "I told her I'd help find him."

"Good luck with that." She leaned toward Anabelle and whispered, "I'm worried about Dr. Hamilton. He's not looking so good."

"Seri." Dr. Hamilton's voice sounded weak.

Seri moved back into the cubicle with Anabelle a step behind. Drew was leaning heavily against the stretcher. He lifted an arm to wipe the perspiration from his brow. His pallor prompted Anabelle to lead him to a nearby chair. "Seri, get a wheelchair and the charge nurse and page Dr. Hildebrand stat."

Anabelle whipped her stethoscope from around her neck and bent to listen to his chest. She noted erratic beats. "Are you having chest pain?"

"No." His head dropped back.

"What's going on?" Dr. Hildebrand took one look at Drew and shook her head. She listened to his chest.

"We'll have to get him up to the CCU. We have zero beds available down here." Dr. Hildie jotted some orders on a pad, ripped the page off and handed it to Anabelle. "Anabelle, can you take him up, get him into a bed and hook up the monitors? Order an EKG and get an IV started. I'll meet you up there as soon as I can." She leaned toward Anabelle. "Sooner if he codes."

Anabelle eyed the patient sitting on the gurney. "Will you be all right for a few minutes? I'll get someone else in here."

"No problem. Doc here was just giving me my discharge papers." He frowned. "Is he going to be all right?"

"I hope so." Anabelle nodded. "I'll let the charge nurse know."

"I can do that, Mrs. Scott."

"Thanks, Seri." Anabelle hesitated. "When you're finished, see if you can find James. He's going to need some help at the YMCA."

"I will."

"Lucy, honey, come with me." Anabelle took the child's hand and placed it on the wheelchair handle.

"Are we still going to look for my dad?"

"Yes. Just as soon as we take care of Dr. Hamilton."

At first, the monitor verified that Dr. Hamilton's heart was in arrhythmia. Dr. Hildebrand came in while Anabelle was working on the IV. Once it was established, they gave him medication. Her favorite doctor's heart was now beating in a normal sinus rhythm, and he'd fallen asleep.

Anabelle rested her arms on the bed rail. She should have insisted that he not try to help, but stopping Drew was as futile as trying to chase the wind. She only hoped their plan for a Parade of Patients would help him to see how important he was to them.

Genna stepped into the room and stood beside Anabelle. Someone had gone to the house to let her know about Drew, but she hadn't been there. Eventually, they discovered that she'd been at the hospital the entire time, working as a volunteer. In hushed tones she asked, "How is he?"

"Okay for now." Anabelle settled an arm around her friend. "How are you?"

"Tired." Genna glanced over at the recliner where Lucy lay stretched out and asleep.

Anabelle explained the situation. "I'll keep looking for her dad, but it's best if she sleeps. If it's all right, I'd like to leave her here with you."

"Sounds like she's been traumatized enough for one night." Genna agreed.

Anabelle nodded. "I'll get another chair."

At around midnight, Anabelle stopped at the cafeteria for coffee and a protein snack to tide her over. She'd checked every unit and looked through the entire hospital without finding a trace of Lucy's father.

Bill Preston did not appear to be at Hope Haven Hospital. Was it possible that he had been taken somewhere else and that whoever had dropped Lucy off hadn't checked to make sure the father was here?

She would try to get hold of Children's Services and let the police know so they could be on the lookout for him.

Anabelle needed to get back to work but had no idea what she would do about Lucy. The girl would be all right for now, but with so huge a mess and her father injured, it might take days to reunite them.

Elena had been working nonstop with Seri, James and a number of volunteers at the Y. The victims were coming in at a slower pace, but still coming in.

The medics hurried in with a woman on a stretcher. She was crying and apparently in pain. Elena hurried to assist. "What do we have?"

"A Jane Doe. We picked her up at a shelter. No ID. The gal running the shelter said she came in after getting knocked around by the hail. She seemed okay, then after a few minutes passed out. She came to in the ambulance but still seems out of it."

Elena glanced at the woman's face and couldn't breathe. "I—I know this woman."

"A friend?"

"No." Her reply was harsher than she'd meant it to be. Elena felt their questioning looks. "I just know who she is. Her name is Sarah Fulton."

"Where do you want her?" One of the medics asked.

Elena led them down the hall to an empty cot. "Put her here for now. I'll get someone to look at her right away." She helped transfer Sarah from the stretcher to the cot and thanked them. Setting the notes they gave her on the end of the mattress, Elena closed her eyes for a moment to organize her scattered thoughts.

Sarah grabbed her arm. The girl's dazed expression didn't appear to register it was Elena, which was just as well.

Elena tried to summon up the animosity she had for the girl. It wasn't there.

She took Sarah's vital signs. Her dilated pupils and confusion indicated either drugs or head injury.

She waved a hand to signal for an aide and saw Seri nearby removing her gloves. "Seri, do you have a minute?"

"I do now. What do you need?" Seri came toward her.

"See if you can round up a doctor. We might have another head injury."

"I can't believe how many people got caught out in that storm."

Elena nodded, then turned back to Sarah, who was trying to get out of bed. Elena rushed to her and guided her back down.

"Seri, get the doctor right away."

"I'm right here." The doctor frowned, his craggy features became more pronounced as he stepped up beside them. The tall, thin man seemed to shrink the room. "What's going on here?"

"Medics said she'd been out in the hail so we may be looking at head injury." Elena told him what she knew then lowered her voice. "But she also has a history of drug use."

"We'd better not medicate her until we do a drug screen and run some tests." The doctor muttered something under his breath, looking more solemn and forbidding than usual. "Why would the medics bring her here? She should have gone to the hospital. She'll need a scan and lab work right away."

"Maybe I can still catch the medics," Seri offered.

"Then do it," the doctor said.

Sarah's head lolled from side to side and her eyes fixated and rolled back.

Elena startled. "She's having a seizure."

By the time the seizure ended the medics had returned with a stretcher.

"Sorry about this," the female medic apologized. "She didn't seem critical when we . . ."

"Well she is now," the doctor grumbled. "Get her over to Hope Haven. I'm riding in the ambulance with you."

Elena watched them get into the ambulance and leave, lights flashing, racing toward Hope Haven. She leaned against the wall.

"Elena?" James stood in front of her. "Are you okay?"

"No, I'm not. That was Sarah—Isabel's birth mother." Elena struggled with the conflicting emotions wrapping around her like chains. As much as she tried to hold on to the anger she felt toward Sarah, all she could think to do was pray.

Though she could have done with a break, another ambulance pulled up to the entrance. *Let go, Elena. You must let go. It's time to get back to work.*

Chapter Eighteen

B Y THE FOLLOWING MORNING, THE PANDEMONIUM had settled a bit. Anabelle rode the elevator up to the third floor to the locker room. On the brief ride, she leaned against the elevator wall and closed her eyes. Normally, at this time on a Saturday morning, she'd be getting up and lazily enjoying her coffee and devotions, but there was nothing normal about this Saturday.

Her scrubs were a mess and she badly needed a shower before going into CCU.

The storm had ended. Victims were still coming in, but at a slower rate. The makeshift hospital at the YMCA had helped tremendously.

Thanks to the Red Cross, the National Guard provided volunteers from as far as Chicago, 130 miles away. Hope Haven had enough people to allow many of the hospital personnel to return to their regular jobs. Once in the staff lounge, she pulled her glasses from her pocket and hung them on a hook in the locker, then grabbed a set of hospital scrubs from the linen cart and a towel and headed for the women's showers.

Fifteen minutes later, feeling somewhat refreshed, Anabelle emerged from the staff lounge and took the elevator to the second floor. She hadn't felt this tired since her all-nighters when Kirstie was in the hospital. She took a deep breath as she stepped off the elevator. *Father, give me strength to go on.*

"Mother?"

Anabelle turned at the sound of Kirstie's voice.

"Hi, sweetie. What are you doing here?" Anabelle gave her a hug.

"I just came up to see if you were here. I've been working in the main lobby all night—trying to get paperwork on everyone coming in."

Kirstie still held on to her—or was it Anabelle holding on to her daughter? She patted Kirstie's back, gave her an extra squeeze and stepped back. "Is Mark okay?"

Kirstie nodded. "He was just dropping me off at my place when the storm hit. As soon as it was over, we headed out to see what we could do to help. Are you going home, or . . . ?"

"No, I'll stay—for a while at least. By the way, Drew was admitted again last night. He came in to help out and ended up as a patient."

"Oh no." Kirstie pinched her lips together. "How is he?"

"I haven't heard anything. I was just going in to see him." Anabelle began the trek to CCU.

"I'll go with you. Are we still going to do the Parade of Patients for him?"

Anabelle sighed and kissed Kirstie's forehead. "Apparently not this weekend. Unless we do it right here in the hospital. I'm thinking we might want to wait a few days until things calm down."

"That might be hard. There's still no phone service, so we can't get hold of all the people we called. Of course, maybe they just won't come now."

"We'll have to talk to Genna. She may already have an alternate plan."

Anabelle, with Kirstie following, meandered through the overflowing visitors' lounge into CCU, unsure of what to expect. She knew they'd gotten several new patients and had no more beds.

"Hi, Becky." Anabelle greeted her day-shift charge nurse. How's it going up here?"

"Crazy like you wouldn't believe." She looked up. "We have three people going home today. Olga Pederson, Dr. Hamilton and a man who came in last night."

"Since I missed report, maybe you can fill me in."

"So far nothing critical. Everyone is behaving themselves." She smiled. "That little girl you left in Dr. Hamilton's room woke up once, shivering. I tucked a warming blanket around her, and she's been sound asleep since."

"Good. I noticed we have a couple of patients in the hallway."

"From last night. We are seriously short staffed all over. The nursing director has been frantic. She can't get hold of anyone. She has volunteers and ham-radio operators trying to round people up. Hopefully she'll be able to pull in a few. Seri didn't show up, but then I'm not surprised."

"With good reason. Despite what you've heard, Seri is a great worker. She showed up last night right after the storm and worked in the ER. I sent her to the Y to work with James."

"Oh, I heard . . . never mind." She rolled her eyes. "I think I see what's going on. A little jealousy, maybe?"

Anabelle smiled. "We'll deal with that later. Give me a quick report, and I'll make my rounds."

Once Becky had filled Anabelle in on each of the patients, Anabelle headed to Dr. Hamilton's room to check on him. Lucy was still asleep and so, she noted, was Drew.

Genna quietly stepped out of the room with Anabelle and Kirstie and slid the door closed behind her. After giving each of them a hug, she sighed. "That poor child must be exhausted."

"Who is she?" Kirstie asked.

"Long story," Anabelle told her. "I'll explain later."

"She didn't even mention her father when she woke up earlier," Genna said. "Have you been able to locate him?"

Anabelle shook her head. "I don't think he's even in this hospital. But I don't know where else they would have taken him. The Y, maybe, but it wasn't even available when he was supposed to have come in."

"Well, don't give up." Genna squeezed Anabelle's shoulder.

"I won't." Anabelle sighed. "I can't."

"I only hope he's okay wherever he is." Genna glanced into the room.

"I know. I'm praying for the best." Anabelle made a mental note to check the morgue once she'd made her rounds.

Anabelle purposely shifted gears. "I hear Drew will be going home today."

"Dr. Hildebrand says he should be okay. He didn't have another heart attack." She folded her arms. "The bottom line is he shouldn't have come in to work last night."

"You and I know that, but convincing him . . ."

"Is next to impossible." Genna caught her gaze. "Anabelle, I'm afraid to take him home. He's going to see that mess and will start boarding up windows and cleaning up the yard. I know him."

"Maybe we can talk him into staying long enough for Cameron and Evan to take care of it. I just wish I could call him. Maybe I can get hold of a ham-radio operator."

"Good idea," Genna said. "I'm going to step out for some coffee. Can I bring you something?"

"Thanks, but not right now. I need to finish making my rounds."

"Wait." Kirstie caught Genna's arm. "What about the Parade of Patients?"

Genna sighed. "I don't know. There's no way to call people. I'll have to put a note on our door telling people he's here."

"Do you think they'd come here?" Kirstie asked. "Maybe we should set something up."

Anabelle shook her head. "We can't have dozens of people coming through the CCU. We have patients in the hall and it would be too disturbing."

"Okay, but what about the waiting room?" Kirstie suggested. "It's good sized."

"Would that work?" Genna looked to Anabelle for a go-ahead.

"I think we could manage that. If other visitors complain, we might need to move Drew down to the main lobby or the cafeteria; but you're right, we do need a plan."

"I'll go home and put out the note and get a few things. We aren't expecting anyone to come until ten, so we still have a couple of hours to get ready."

Anabelle was glad to see Genna's enthusiasm return. She gave Kirstie a smile and looked in on Dr. Hamilton and Lucy. She'd let them sleep for now and come back later. Before going on, Anabelle told Kirstie how Lucy had been separated from her father. Anabelle then had a thought. "I don't suppose you could take care of her for me today. Maybe help us find her dad?"

Kirstie's shoulders sagged. "I'd love to, but the ER supervisor asked me if I'd work as a temp secretary for the rest of today. Things are total chaos down there."

"All right. I'll keep her with me." Anabelle smiled as she gave her daughter another hug. "Thanks for coming in."

Kirstie chuckled. "What else would Anabelle and Cameron Scott's daughter do?"

Anabelle watched her walk out of the unit before checking her notes on Olga. When Anabelle walked in, Olga gave her a wide grin. Carla seemed in a good mood as well. "I see you both came through the storm okay."

Carla smiled. "Almost. Unfortunately, my rental car didn't fare so well. They're bringing over a new one—as soon as they can get one that's not too damaged to drive."

"*Hmm.*" Anabelle nodded. "I imagine this storm will give the auto industry a boost. I pity anyone whose cars were left out in this."

Carla nodded. "I've never seen anything like it. Last night mother and I dragged the bed and chair as close to the door as possible. We were afraid the window would break. I can't believe it didn't. We're almost afraid to go to the house."

Anabelle set the clipboard on the bedside table. "I hate to say it, but pretty much every house in town is going to need a new roof and windows."

"So we heard," Olga said. "My neighbor—you remember Christina—came in this morning to tell us the bad news. We have three windows to replace and the garden looks like it was trampled by a rogue elephant."

"Those kids are great," Carla said. "They offered to clean the place up for us so we can at least stay there until Mom is well enough to travel."

"That's wonderful." Anabelle removed the stethoscope from around her neck. "I'd like to listen to your heart and lungs if you don't mind."

"Go right ahead." Olga seemed in high spirits today.

Anabelle placed the stethoscope against Olga's chest. She closed her eyes to better listen and was pleased to report that her heart sounded normal. A few deep breaths later, Anabelle pulled the earpieces free. "Your lungs sound clear. Are you feeling up to going home today?"

"Oh ya." Olga's eyes shone with new light. "You'll be happy to know we decided where I should live."

"Really?" Anabelle grinned. "And what have you decided?"

"We'll stay at the house here until we can arrange to have the storm damage repaired. Then Carla and I will fly back to Portland. We looked on the Internet yesterday and found a nice little house close to Carla that looks like it might work for me. I wouldn't be living with the family, but I'd be nearby."

Carla took her mother's hand. "She can be as independent as she wants to be and have her own flower gardens."

Olga's blue eyes glistened. "If everything works out okay and I like it, we'll sell the house here."

"Sounds perfect." Anabelle offered up a silent prayer of thanks. "You might consider getting a medical alert system. You wear an alarm on your wrist or around your neck and can call for help whenever you need it. It's great for seniors who live alone." She gave them the names of a couple of companies.

Carla nodded. "I've heard about that. Thank you for telling us."

Olga sighed. "I know it's the right thing to do, but I'll miss my house—my church, my friends. Deerford is a wonderful place to live."

"Yes it is." Anabelle agreed.

"I wish Carla and her family could move out here; but like Carla says, I will make new friends. I already know some people from when I visited there before." Olga seemed to have made peace with her decision.

"I'm happy for you. I'm sure you will be missed—I know I'll miss you. I think we could have been good friends."

"Could have been?" Olga held out her arms. "I think of you as a friend already."

Anabelle agreed and promised to visit them before they moved. She gave them each a hug before looking in on the next patient.

Mr. Blake, the man whose son was considering a lawsuit against Drew, seemed much improved. "I have some good news. You'll be happy to know I told my son I'd have no part in his silly lawsuit. Like I told him, I'm just happy to be alive."

"That is good news." Anabelle checked her notes. "Looks like you'll be heading home tomorrow."

He nodded. "Dr. Hildebrand said if I kept improving she'd let me go."

Anabelle smiled. "Do you have any questions or problems at this point?"

"Nope. I feel better than I have for a long time."

Anabelle chatted with everyone on her list and was heading back to Dr. Hamilton's room when Genna and Lucy stepped into the hallway.

When Lucy saw Anabelle she ran to her and wrapped her arms around her legs. "Did you find my daddy?"

Anabelle gently freed herself and hunkered down in front of the child. "I'm still working on it. In fact, I have an idea. Why don't you and I go to the cafeteria for some breakfast." *And coffee.*

"But what about my dad?" Her face crumpled and Anabelle held her close.

"It'll be okay, sweetheart. We're going to find some people to help us, okay? Daddy might be in another hospital. But we'll find him. Until we do, you can stay with me."

Lucy hauled in a shuddering breath and nodded. "I miss him."

"I know you do." Anabelle felt close to tears herself. She stood and took Lucy's hand, thanked Genna and led Lucy to the elevators.

What was she thinking? She couldn't babysit Lucy and work at the same time. On the other hand, maybe she could. She had brought her children into the hospital to shadow her on several bring-your-kids-to-work days in the past.

Anabelle thought again about other possible family members. "Yesterday you told me your mommy lived far away. What is her name?"

"Theresa. Daddy says she went to be with Jesus after I was born."

"Oh." Anabelle thought for a moment and then asked, "Do you have grandmas or grandpas?"

"Grampa." Her face lit up.

"What is your grandpa's name?"

Lucy frowned. "Grampa."

Anabelle pinched the bridge of her nose. Back to square one.

As Anabelle saw it, she didn't have a lot of options. She had no intention of handing the child over to someone else at the moment. Lucy had been traumatized enough.

Chapter Nineteen

ANDACE LEFT THE EMERGENCY ROOM AT AROUND 9:00 AM, badly in need of a break. As much as she wanted to go home, she felt compelled to stay, at least until they had enough staff present to cover the day shift. It seemed strange having no contact with her family for so many hours.

She'd hesitated to ask a ham-radio operator to contact them when they were still working on emergency calls only. Calls to family members to let them know you were all right had to wait. Besides, she knew her mother and the kids were safe, and that's what mattered.

Before going up to the Birthing Unit, Candace ducked into the cafeteria. She smiled and waved when she saw Anabelle sitting with a little girl. Candace picked up her coffee, toast and hard-boiled eggs and joined her.

"How are you holding up, my friend?" Anabelle smiled up at her.

"Probably about as well as you are." She eyed the little girl. "Who do we have here?"

"Lucy Preston. Lucy, this is my friend, Candace." Anabelle spread some jam on a piece of toast.

Large brown eyes looked at Candace from across the table. "Do you know where my daddy is?"

Candace glanced at Anabelle for clarification.

"We're looking for her father. There was an accident."

Candace realized that Anabelle didn't want to say too much. "What's his name?"

"Bill Preston." Lucy dropped her plastic spoon into the bowl where two Cheerios still swam.

"I'm sorry, I don't remember anyone by that name."

"When we're done eating, we're going to try again." Anabelle took a sip of her coffee. She looked up, surprise lighting her features as she set her coffee down. "Cameron!"

Anabelle's husband, coffee in hand, kissed his wife, greeted Candace and Lucy, then pulled a chair up to the table.

"What brings you here?" Anabelle looked him over. "You're not hurt, are you?"

"Joints are a bit achy, but I'm fine. Just came by to tell you that Ainslee and Doug are okay. They sustained some roof damage and a couple broken windows. We got them covered, and they both went down to the store to clean up the mess there."

Once Upon a Time had a lot of breakables. "I hope it's not too bad."

"The awning might have protected the windows. I suppose we'll find out soon enough." His eyes took on a worried look. "Kirstie wasn't home, and I haven't seen her."

"She's here." Anabelle told him.

"Here? Is she all right?"

Anabelle patted his arm. "She's fine. She came in to help right after the storm, but I didn't see her until this morning. She's helping out as a secretary in ER. Mark dropped her off here and headed out to help wherever he could."

"Good for them. I'll be stopping by to see her before I go."

"She'd like that." Anabelle gripped his hand. "You look tired."

Candace felt a sudden stab of jealousy at the obvious adoration they had for each other. She and Dean had had that kind of intimacy as well.

"Shows I've been working." Cameron grinned. "I've put half a dozen teams of workers together, and we've been boarding up windows and making temporary repairs." He looked over at Candace. "We've done your place, James's and the Hamiltons'. Just finished Elena's; and since the hospital was so close, I thought I'd stop to see how you were faring."

"Thanks so much." Candace cracked her hard-boiled egg, surprised he would think of her needs and thankful he had. "I haven't had much time to think about the mess at home. Actually, I've been trying *not* to think about it."

"You've been working all night?" Anabelle asked Cameron.

"That we have. And I figure we'll be at it all day as well."

The lights flickered off and on. "If I'm not mistaken, you're getting your power back. A good thing too. I heard the hospital was running out of gas for the generator. Electricians have been hard at it to restore power—this was their first priority."

While Cameron finished his coffee, Anabelle told him about Lucy.

"I might be able to help," he said. "A couple of our guys have ham radios. I'll check around at other hospitals."

"That would be good." Anabelle reached over and gave Lucy a squeeze.

Lucy propped an elbow on the table. "My daddy's name is Bill Preston."

Cameron pulled a pen from his shirt pocket and wrote the name on a napkin then put the pen and the note in his pocket. "I'll remember. And I will be praying for you and your daddy."

"I already prayed. Jesus will find him."

A lump formed in Candace's throat. *Oh, for the faith of a child.*

She suddenly missed her own children. When she got back to the Birthing Unit, she'd try to call them.

James could think of nothing sweeter than heading home and crawling into bed. But bed and sleep would have to wait for a few hours.

Thanks to the National Guard and Red Cross, the YMCA was functioning well as an annex to the hospital. James got word that he was needed in surgery, and Elena, in ICU. Seri opted to go to the hospital as well. While Elena took her own car, James waited for Seri to finish a job so he could drive her back.

On the way into town, they spotted a deserted ambulance in the ditch along with an SUV.

"Whoa," Seri exclaimed. "That can't be good."

James pulled up alongside the scene. "Let's take a look—make sure no one got left behind." James wasn't sure why he felt the urge to stop. Chances were that everyone had been accounted for.

The two of them climbed out of James's van and walked to the side of the road to get a closer look at the accident scene.

"I don't see anybody." Seri folded her arms and winced as she took in the crumpled car.

James didn't either, but he did catch a glimpse of a plastic bag a few feet away. Seri spotted it as well. "You think that might belong to someone in the accident?"

"Let's take a look."

They found a set of keys inside the bag, but nothing else. James tried them in the SUV, but they didn't match. He checked the glove box for ID, but the registration had been taken, probably by the police.

Heading back to the car, they stopped to check the back of the ambulance. The mess inside gave James pause.

"Oh, look. A teddy bear."

James shifted his gaze to where Seri pointed. A stuffed brown bear lay crumpled in a corner.

Seri reached for it. "Do you think the victim in the ambulance was a kid?"

"It's possible."

The ambulance had been heading into town. James surmised that another ambulance or two had been sent to pick up the crew and the victim being transported. James offered up a prayer. Judging by the blood spatter, this was, as Seri had said, not a good thing.

James started walking back to his van. "Let's take this stuff to the hospital. Chances are, someone is missing them."

"I wonder what happened." Seri held the teddy bear to her chest.

James shrugged. "With things so crazy around here, I doubt we'll ever know."

"I'm going to carry the bear around with me," Seri said. "Show it to all the kids who are in the hospital. Maybe we'll get lucky."

"Good idea. That could well link us to the owner of the keys. James stopped briefly at his house and at Seri's apartment to get changes of clothes. Fortunately, Fern and the boys were doing okay. After their fiasco at the school the night before, James had brought Gideon home, telling him he was needed there.

When he got there, everyone was asleep. He kissed Fern awake and let her know what he was doing and that he'd be back, hopefully that afternoon.

When they entered the hospital through the staff entrance, Seri started for the elevators.

"Seri." James stopped her. "Thanks for helping out at the Y. You did a great job."

She smiled. "Thanks, Mr. Bell. So did you."

Seri went straight up to the lounge to change while James headed into the main lobby. He'd have to remember to write a note to Anabelle about Seri's performance for her personnel file.

James left the keys from the accident scene with the security guard along with a note as to where he found them. "You didn't by any chance hear anything about an ambulance being in an accident last night, did you?"

"No, but I'll ask around. I just got here this morning."

James nodded. "How are things, in general, around here?"

"We've got the power back on at least." He eyed the still crowded lobby. "We're still full to overflowing though."

Back in her office and thankful to at last have a working phone, Anabelle checked with everyone she could think of to locate Bill Preston. She called the Y to find out if Preston had been diverted there. He hadn't been. She even walked Lucy through the wards in case she could spot him.

They were running out of options. Practically everyone in the hospital knew about Lucy and her missing father. Anabelle felt certain he'd be found sooner or later.

Anabelle sighed. "Would you like to see patients with me, Lucy, or would you like to sit in my office and draw pictures?"

"Come with you." Her eyes widened in fear of being left alone. Anabelle held out a hand to the child. "All right, let's go."

The first item on her agenda was to look in on a new patient, who'd been admitted to the unit while she'd been in the cafeteria. She looked at the name posted next to the door and froze.

George Talbot, the name of the man who'd run Kirstie down. That had been ten years ago. Anabelle looked at the age. Fifty-eight—that would fit.

She hadn't seen George Talbot since the trial, which was fine with her. And she never imagined he'd end up here—in her unit. Painful memories flooded back and twisted themselves like angry vines around her chest.

"Are we going in there?" Lucy tugged at the hem of her top.

She looked down at the child. "Not right now."

Anabelle turned her notes on the man over and slipped them to the bottom of the pages on her clipboard. *I can't do this Lord. Please don't ask me to go in there.*

She closed her eyes for a moment and took a deep breath, then moved on. It wasn't as though she'd be shirking her responsibilities. Her job was to keep the unit running well, to make certain all of the shifts were covered, to oversee each of the nurses and aides.

Suddenly, seeing Dr. Hamilton became a priority. Drew had been her safety net after the accident. He apparently still was. How could even seeing Talbot's name bring such a powerful reaction? She had done the godly thing and forgiven George Talbot. Or had she?

Anabelle pushed thoughts and images away and paused just outside Dr. Hamilton's room to update herself on any new entries to his chart. So far there were no discharge orders, which would likely have him fussing at her.

"Good morning." Anabelle smiled, trying to set the tone.

"Aren't you going to call me an idiot for pushing myself too hard?"

She chuckled. "I think you've probably done enough of that to yourself. So how are you feeling?"

"Tired."

"I can imagine. I see Dr. Hildebrand hasn't discharged you."

"She wants me to stay another day or two. Run some more tests."

"And you're okay with that?"

"No, but she's probably right."

"Does that mean you're turning over a new leaf?" Maybe their Parade of Patients wouldn't be necessary after all.

He sighed. "I wish I could say yes. Believe it or not, I do know better; but I can't just sit around doing nothing. Taking that month off will drive me nuts. The stress will probably bring on another heart attack."

"I doubt that. During your month off, maybe you should think about taking that cruise you and Genna have talked about. You could spend time with your granddaughter."

"Maybe." Drew had a faraway look in his eyes, and Anabelle doubted he'd take her advice. Being as intelligent as he was, he just didn't seem to get it. Anabelle thought they might need more than persuasion from past patients, but it was a good place to start. "Where is Genna?"

"She headed out of here as soon as the electricity came back on. Said she had some kind of project to tend to before it was too late."

Anabelle made a mental note to check with her friend later, suspecting the project was their patient parade. She had no idea how Genna and the Quilting Guild could pull the Parade of Patients off with almost everyone in town having to deal with this disastrous storm; but if anyone could, it was Genna.

At least they would have Drew at Hope Haven for another day. Though he looked much better, Anabelle didn't trust him.

"Can I say one thing?" Anabelle asked.

"As long as you aren't going to tell me to take it easy." He pushed himself back in the bed.

"Hope Haven won't be the same without you. I know how dedicated you are to your patients; but trust me, we'd all rather have you gone for a month than gone permanently. You've had a heart attack, and you could have another one."

"I could have a heart attack whether I stay active or take it easy. There's no guarantee."

"So you want to pack as much time in as possible in case you have another heart attack?"

"Something like that."

"And I used to think you were so smart."

When she and Lucy stepped out of Drew's room, Lucy ran straight into Seri.

"Whoa." Seri flung her arms out to steady the child. The teddy bear she'd been holding dropped to the floor.

"My Bookie Bear!" Lucy squealed as she twisted away from Seri and snatched up the shaggy brown bear.

"Are you sure that's your bear?" Seri hunkered down beside Lucy.

"Yes." She tightened her grip on the stuffed animal. "It's got a *B* on the tag and it means Bookie."

"Cool name for a bear." Seri grinned.

"It's my name too. Grandpa calls me his Bookie Bear."

As Seri stood, she shot Anabelle a strange look and as an aside said, "We need to talk."

Chapter Twenty

AFTER HEARING SERI'S ACCOUNT OF THE accident involving the ambulance, Anabelle informed the police officer she'd spoken to. They were aware of the accident involving the ambulance and would try to track down everyone involved. The problem was that no one seemed to have Bill Preston listed anywhere. The medics involved in the accident were both in critical condition and as yet hadn't been able to provide any information.

Since her teddy bear, if in fact it was her bear, had been found at the scene, the victim had to have been in that ambulance.

Though Anabelle wasn't prepared to be a foster parent, the arrangement seemed for the best. She prayed they would find Lucy's father soon and that he was alive and well.

That afternoon, while Lucy took a nap with her teddy bear on a makeshift bed in her office, Anabelle stepped into the lobby area to watch as the first of Dr. Hamilton's thankful patients began to arrive. Genna had brought some goodies and balloons.

His first patient, Cora, a woman who was recovering from hip surgery, came in right after lunch. Though she was still in the hospital and using a walker, she looked ready to go home. She had even walked from Med/Surg.

Normally, they limited visitors; but today, there'd be no reprieve for Dr. Hamilton.

Genna winked at Anabelle. She'd told Anabelle earlier that she planned to stretch the visits out for three afternoons.

Anabelle laughed. "That should tell him something, but he may be discharged today."

"He won't be. I think this last episode scared him. He's willing to stay until all the tests are done."

"Good." Anabelle nodded.

"Hey, Doc," Penny, a recent cancer patient, greeted in a raspy voice. "I heard you'd had a heart attack. Came over to make sure you were okay. And to thank you."

Anabelle didn't want to eavesdrop, but she didn't want to leave either. She and Genna stood side by side near the door of the CCU unit waiting to hear Drew's response.

"Thank me?" Dr. Drew sounded surprised. "You had to have three surgeries before we finally found the source of the trouble. And even then, your prognosis isn't that good."

"Yeah, but you never gave up. James told me that you were consulting with the other doctors after you had the heart attack. I'm glad you did, but you need to take care of yourself so you can be around to help a lot more people down the road."

He chuckled. "Let me guess, my wife and Anabelle Scott put you up to this, didn't they?"

"What? I can't come visit my favorite doctor?" She laughed. "Okay, they did tell me you were being ornery and not following your doctor's advice. I happen to agree with them. You're an important part of this hospital, and your patients need you to take it easy and come back healthy."

"I'll take that into consideration," he told her. They talked awhile longer, but Anabelle didn't stay.

The Parade of Patients went on for the rest of the afternoon. Just as Anabelle was about to head home, Tucker Blair's parents came in to thank Dr. Hamilton for working so hard to save Tucker's life. Tucker hadn't made it, but the family knew Dr. Hamilton and the staff had done everything possible to save him.

One patient after another paraded through the lobby. With so many showing up, Anabelle decided to move Dr. Hamilton into the cafeteria along with all the goodies that were showing up. Previous patients were turning the event into a party, and they needed a lot more room than was available in the waiting room.

She helped Genna set up an area and put a note on the desk in the waiting room redirecting people.

By the time she returned to the floor, Anabelle was more than ready to go home, but she wasn't certain what to do with Lucy. The little girl had attached herself to Anabelle big-time. She hated calling Children's Services and yet, what choice did she have?

Anabelle called Children's Services. They were understaffed and overrun with children who had somehow been separated from their parents, and the supervisor—a woman Anabelle knew from church—told her they could make Anabelle a temporary guardian.

Once her shift had ended in ICU, Elena hurried over to the Med/Surg Unit and asked James about Sarah.

"She's asleep," James told her. "Do you know her?"

Elena sighed. "I—I was there when she came in last night, remember?"

"Oh, right. Isabel's mother." He rubbed a hand across the back of his neck. "You can tell I'm wiped out."

"So she's doing okay?" Elena asked.

"She hasn't had a seizure since that first one. Did you want to look in on her?"

"No. I was just curious."

Curious yes, but much more. Elena wanted this girl out of their lives. Ever since she'd called the other day, Elena had been in turmoil. Then, seeing her at the YMCA tore her apart. Elena rubbed at her forehead, to ease away the beginnings of a headache. *Why God? Why is she suddenly in our lives again?*

Elena told James she might come back later, then hurried to the Cardiac Care Unit in hopes of catching Anabelle. All day she'd been fighting her emotions about Sarah. She needed so desperately to talk to someone, and Anabelle always seemed to be able to see through problems and come up with solutions.

Seeing Anabelle at the nurses' station, Elena breathed a sigh of relief. "I'm so glad to have caught you."

"I'm glad you did too. Is something wrong?" Anabelle chuckled. "Besides being tired?"

"I could use some advice."

"Actually, so could I." Anabelle brightened. "Why don't we pull our little prayer group together? We'll call James and Candace to see if they can meet at Cuppa Coffee."

"That's a very good idea."

"What's a good idea?" James came up behind them.

"James," Anabelle startled. "We were just talking about you, and here you are."

"God's timing." He smiled. "What can I do for you?"

"Anabelle and I were thinking this might be a good time for us to get together to talk and pray." Elena looked down at the floor. "I have a problem, and I could really use your help."

Anabelle reached up to squeeze Elena's shoulder. "I do too, actually. In fact, I have several."

James nodded. "I hear you. I could use some advice and some prayer as well."

Elena nodded. "I will call Candace. Anabelle suggested we meet over at Cuppa Coffee."

"Sounds good to me," James said. "I came over to meet Fern. She had her sister bring her here to talk to Dr. Hamilton for the Parade of Patients."

"That's wonderful," Anabelle said, "but she isn't his patient is she?"

"No, but we both think highly of him. I'm especially thankful for the opportunity to assist him in OR." James smiled. "I need to tell him that. How about I meet you at the coffee shop in, say, fifteen minutes."

"Perfect. I'll see if I can find Candace." Elena waved at them and headed for the Birthing Unit.

The four nurses plus a very tired little girl sat in the cozy corner of the coffee shop where a sofa and two cushy chairs made a perfect spot for their meeting. Elena and Anabelle sat on the sofa while James and Candace sat in the chairs. Anabelle set Lucy up in a nearby child's corner with puzzles, books, drawing paper and a pencil.

The broken windows, which had been boarded up, served as reminders of the storm. With windows on two sides, the shop owners had been fortunate to only have lost the three on the north end. The entire front had been protected by awnings.

"I'm glad we're doing this." Elena stirred the whipped topping into her mocha cinnamon latte.

"Me too." Candace leaned back and crossed her legs. "Maybe I'm just tired, but I'm having a rough time keeping it together."

Anabelle nodded and took a sip of her amaretto latte. "Being tired and having gone through a disaster can definitely take a toll on our minds as well as our bodies." She paused to look around at each of them and then down at Lucy, who seemed content, drinking her raspberry Italian soda and drawing pictures. "Elena, why don't you start?"

James grinned. "There she goes again, taking over as group leader."

Anabelle flushed. "Sorry. It's what I do."

"We're not complaining," Elena assured her. "At least I'm not. I like having a Mama Moderator to keep us in line."

The other two agreed. "I was just teasing," James added.

Elena sighed. "I hope I can talk about this without crying. When we were at the YMCA, the medics brought Sarah in."

"Isabel's mother?" Candace leaned forward to set her drink on the large, round coffee table in front of them.

Elena nodded. "She was in bad shape. She'd been caught in the storm. She could have been under the influence."

James frowned. "She had a seizure, and Dr. Prelutski rode back here in the ambulance with her."

"I'm sorry," Candace said. "That must have been hard for you."

"It was." Elena paused. "You see, this is my problem. Remember the other day when she called? You thought it would be a good idea if I met her for coffee. I waited for her, but she didn't show up. Now she is here in our hospital. I think maybe God wants me to see her, but I don't want to. I'm afraid that—" She struggled to find the words. "Deep down I am afraid I will lose my Isabel."

"Oh, Elena." Anabelle placed a hand on her arm. "I'm sorry."

"Part of me wants to go see her and make sure she's okay, but part of me wants to walk away and never look back."

"She's in my unit," James said. "Unfortunately, I can't really disclose anything."

"Even if you could, I don't want to know." Elena bit into her lower lip.

He sighed. "I think you should go see her."

Elena lowered her head and closed her eyes. "Oh, James. I don't know. I want to do what's right, but not this."

"I'm sorry, Elena," James leaned forward, elbows on his knees. "I didn't mean to push you. If you aren't ready, you aren't ready."

"What do you think God wants you to do?" Anabelle asked. Unfortunately, she knew well what Elena was going through.

Elena tipped her head back. "I know that God is the one urging me to see her and talk to her, but I'm struggling."

"Then maybe," Candace said, "we need to pray for courage for you. Fear so often gets in the way of doing what we know is right." She gave them a wan smile. "Believe me, I know."

Anabelle agreed. "And forgiveness. I think God wants all rela-tionships healed." She stopped and looked at each of them. "And I'm thinking maybe I need to take my own advice."

"In what way?" Elena seemed eager to draw the attention away from herself.

"You all know about the accident that nearly killed my Kirstie."

They all nodded. James sat back and rested his right ankle on his left knee. "That was a terrible time for you."

"Well . . ." She sipped her coffee. "I'm reliving it all over again. I thought I'd put my anger behind me, but I haven't."

"What's happened?" Elena turned toward Anabelle.

"Kirstie got a new leg. It's wonderful for her, but she's been . . ." Anabelle smiled and shook her head. "I can't believe what I'm saying."

"What?" Elena and James asked at once.

"She's not trying to cover it up anymore." Anabelle waved her hand to stop their comments. "I know that's a good thing. But I'm not used to seeing the leg exposed so much and every time I see it, this anger roars up inside me at the guy who did it. And—and at God for letting it happen."

"That's normal, isn't it?" Candace asked. "We know anger is a part of the grieving process."

"To some extent, but it's been over ten years. I struggle with it more than Kirstie, it seems. Anyway, that's not the worst of it. The man responsible for almost getting her killed, the drunk driver who hit her is in CCU—he had a heart attack."

Elena covered her mouth. "What did you do?"

"What every good responsible, caring person does. I ran away." She released a hollow laugh. "I looked at his chart but skipped going in to see him. I don't know that I could stand there face-to-face and not want to punch his lights out."

James smiled and shook his head. "Anabelle, it's not in you to punch anyone. Besides, you are a professional. No matter what you feel about a patient on the inside, you'd keep your cool and do whatever you had to do."

"I know you're right." Anabelle shifted her gaze to him. "I just feel like I'm back to square one."

Elena nodded. "Maybe you need to bite the bullet and talk to him. I do know that when I saw Sarah last night, my bad feelings for her were gone—at least for a few minutes anyway. I saw her as a patient needing help."

"You're right." Anabelle knew full well she'd have to deal with her feelings and somehow move past them. "I can't let my emotions get in the way of patient care." Anabelle gave them each a smile. "It looks like I really needed this time with you all as well."

"Me too," Candace said. "I need another boost. The first appointment with the counselor was postponed because of the tornado warning. It was rescheduled for yesterday but I had a very good reason to cancel."

"The calling party?" Anabelle asked.

Candace gave them a sheepish grin as the rest of the group scowled.

"Now I have to work up the courage to make another appointment. I think I don't want to because I'm afraid of all the emotional pain she might dig up. I don't want to relive Dean's death all over again."

"Sometimes," James said, "a wound doesn't heal well. A scab might form over it, but under the scab there's a lot of infection. In order for healing to happen in a healthy way, the infection has to come out or it needs to be drained."

"So I let her rip off the scabs and start over?" Candace folded her arms and shivered. "Not the best image, James."

"Wise words though," Anabelle said. "I think maybe I need to confront my feelings head-on and get all that infection out of my system."

"It might not be so bad." Elena sighed. "How can it be worse than feeling as conflicted as I do now?"

"Yep. I think we all have a tendency to worry about things and let them fester." He chuckled at his pun while the others groaned.

James gulped down the rest of his coffee. "I have something to share as well. Two things actually. I've been wanting to talk to someone, but the timing never seems right; I keep thinking I should be able to handle things on my own."

Anabelle smiled. "I think we all have a tendency to do that. I also think God gave us this friendship to feel comfortable sharing with one another."

"The three of us have certainly been put through the wringer. What are you dealing with, James?" Candace asked.

James gave them a long look and rubbed the back of his neck. "Fern seems to be getting progressively worse. I'd like to do some remodeling on the house. I'd like to expand the downstairs into a master bedroom so she doesn't have to climb the stairs."

"That sounds like a good idea." Elena grinned. "What's stopping you?"

"Money. We are okay financially, but there isn't much left over for things that big."

"Have you applied for a home improvement loan?" Candace asked. She set her empty cup on the table.

"Not yet. I'm not sure I can afford the payments, and I don't want to take out a second mortgage on the house."

"Oh." Elena sat up straight. "I have an idea!"

James laughed. "When don't you?"

"No seriously. I just thought of something. The hailstorm might be a blessing in disguise."

"I think I see where you're going with this, Elena." Anabelle grinned. "The insurance money you get for the damage done on your house could help pay for the remodel."

"Help maybe, but where would the rest of the money come from?"

An idea began to form in Anabelle's head. "I think it is something we should pray about. I believe that if this is meant to be, God will bring everything together."

"I believe that too." Elena clasped her hands together.

James nodded. "All right then. Let's pray, but there's one more thing I'd like to add."

He told them about Gideon's plan to join the ROTC. "I was against it at first, but after seeing how well he handled himself with Tucker and then his performance during the aftermath of the storm, I'm leaning toward letting him do it. Unfortunately, Fern's against it. I guess we need prayer that if this is part of God's plan for my son, that we all are able to come to an agreement."

"Can we pray for my daddy too?" Lucy came over from her cozy corner spot and squeezed in between Anabelle and Elena.

"Of course, we can." Anabelle pulled her up against her. They bowed their heads and prayed for each of them and that, in the end, God's will would be done.

Lucy's resounding *amen* brought a number of questioning looks and a few smiles from other customers.

While Anabelle walked back to the hospital, the conflicting emotions she'd carried with her all day bubbled up like stew threatening to overflow its kettle. She needed to find Lucy's father. He had to be somewhere—but apparently not at Hope Haven.

She settled Lucy in her office. "I'll be back in just a couple minutes, okay?"

"Okay. If I need you, can I come out?"

"Sure." Anabelle smiled. "Just call my name."

Janet, the head nurse for evening shift, looked up from her computer. "Hi, Anabelle, I'm glad you came back. Your husband was here a few minutes ago. Said to tell you your car was in the employee parking lot."

"Oh, good." Anabelle wasn't surprised.

"You have a gem of a husband." Janet grinned.

"I know." Anabelle leaned against the counter. "I'm very blessed."

"Yeah, the good ones are always taken." Janet, at forty-two, was single. "Did you need something?" she asked.

"I wanted to check on Mr. Talbot. I never did make it into his room today." It wasn't a lie. But it sounded better than admitting how she truly felt. "How is he doing?"

"Not so good."

Anabelle frowned, taken aback by the answer. "What's going on?"

"Dr. Hildebrand says he needs bypass surgery. She wants to schedule him in tomorrow. He's pretty upset."

"Understandably. It sounds serious if she doesn't want to wait until Monday."

"It is."

Anabelle scanned his chart before heading to the room. She tried hard to separate the patient with a serious heart condition from the man who had run Kirstie down.

She paused outside his room thinking this might not be the best time for facing her nemesis. Weariness had seeped so far into her bones, Anabelle felt certain that if she closed her eyes, she'd fall asleep standing right there.

Taking a deep breath, she forced herself to walk into the room. "Mr. Talbot." Her legs were as unsteady as overcooked spaghetti.

He took one look at her and winced. "Anabelle? Anabelle Scott?"

Anabelle attempted to steady her nerves, determined to not let him see her discomfort. She was surprised that he remembered her name. She thought he would have put the accident behind him after all these years. But then, he had served time in prison.

"Hello, Mr. Talbot." Anabelle used her most professional but kind tone. "I'm the nursing supervisor here in the Cardiac Care Unit. I understand you'll be having surgery tomorrow."

He nodded and Anabelle wondered if perhaps he might be uncomfortable seeing her again. *He should be.*

Anabelle thought back to the last time she'd seen him. He had cried when the judge read the verdict and sentenced him to five years. Anabelle thought it should have been more. His gaze had locked with hers as if pleading for mercy. She'd had none to give.

He had a family who depended on him, his attorney had told the jury. They shouldn't be punished for his lapse in judgment.

He'd needed to be punished, and Anabelle remembered feeling both remorse and gratitude when the judge sentenced him. She had felt bad for his family, but that wasn't her problem.

Looking at him now brought a sense pity that seemed to override the anger. James had been right. She could contain her contempt and put on an objective front. How could she not feel compassion upon noting his labored breathing, his pallor? "Do you have any questions or concerns about the surgery or anything?"

"Yes." His gaze went down to his hands, which he'd folded and placed on his stomach. His oxygen tubing twisted to one side and he reached up to adjust it, but couldn't get the prongs to stay in his nostrils.

"All right. What can I help you with?" Anabelle slipped on a pair of gloves before adjusting the tubing for him. She then checked the IV and made certain his leads were placed correctly.

"I need you to forgive me."

She pulled back. "You what?"

"The doctor said she thought the surgery would fix me up, but it's a risky one and I might die."

"Most of our patients come through bypass just fine." Anabelle ignored his request.

"I know there's no excuse for what I did. I guess I can't blame you for not wanting to forgive me." He leaned back and closed his eyes. "Truth is, I've never forgiven myself."

"I'm sure God has forgiven you, Mr. Talbot. There's no reason you need to hear that from me." Anabelle winced inwardly. Who was she to determine such a thing? Maybe he did need to hear it. Anabelle just didn't know if she could say it with any measure of truth.

"When I was in prison, I accepted the Lord as my Savior. I felt my sins had been forgiven, but no matter how hard I tried I couldn't forget what I had done to your little girl."

"Perhaps you are not supposed to forget," Anabelle spoke more sharply than she'd intended. "I never will."

"Maybe. But I want to make things right before I die."

"My daughter lost her leg, Mr. Talbot. She almost lost her life." Anabelle felt the rest of her reserve slip away. "You will never make that right."

"Believe me, I know that better than anyone."

Anabelle clenched her jaw, barely able to speak. "I don't wish you any ill, Mr. Talbot." Anabelle stood ramrod straight. "I hope your surgery tomorrow goes well."

"Thank you."

She left, but not before seeing the sorrow in his eyes. Perhaps she wasn't as professionally objective as she'd thought.

Minutes later, when she'd gotten her emotions in hand, Anabelle headed for her office. Her hands shook as she reached for the door handle.

Anabelle opened her office door, expecting to find Lucy, but the girl wasn't in the room. She checked under the desk and in the small closet. No Lucy and no Bookie Bear.

Going out to the nurses' station, she asked the nurses if they'd seen her. No one had.

Don't panic. She has to be here somewhere.

Chapter Twenty-One

*L*UCY HAD PROBABLY GONE IN SEARCH OF HER father again. Or she might have gone to the cafeteria. Adrenaline prodded her into action. She paused briefly to order her search. She couldn't have gone far.

Anabelle would start looking for her right here in the unit. She first checked in Dr. Drew's room. He hadn't seen her. Neither had the next patient or the next. She passed by Talbot's room and made her way around. She was about to go over to ICU when she heard a giggle.

Anabelle spun around intent on following the sound. It was coming from George Talbot's room. The sight awaiting her was almost more than she could comprehend. Lucy had climbed up on the bed with George.

"Lucy! What are you doing?" Anabelle took a step forward and stopped.

The little girl beamed. "I found my Grampa."

Anabelle looked from one to the other, hardly able to take it in. This man she saw as the monster who had run down her baby was now a grandfather. "Are you really her grandfather?"

He chuckled. "This is my Bookie Bear." He hugged her close then frowned. "She was telling me about her daddy's being missing?"

Anabelle drew in a deep breath. "Bill Preston is your son?"

"My son-in-law."

Anabelle nodded. "He was injured in an auto accident. The police are trying to locate him. I've done all I can to find him."

Lucy sat up. "Anabelle said I could go home with her, but now I can stay with you, right?"

He gave Anabelle an imploring look, then smiling at Lucy said, "I'm afraid you can't stay here, Bookie. Grandpa has to have an operation tomorrow."

Anabelle stepped up beside the bed and reached for Lucy. "Is there anyone in your family I can contact? Your wife?"

He shook his head. "Lost both my wife and daughter to breast cancer just ten years apart. It's just Lucy, Bill and me."

"I'm sorry." Anabelle looked down at Lucy. "You can still stay with me, okay? We'll come back and see your grandpa tomorrow when he wakes up."

"But—what about my daddy? Somebody has to find him." Lucy frowned at Anabelle's open arms and snuggled up to her grandfather.

"I know, honey, and we will. First, we need to get some sleep." George gave her a hug. "Come on, Bookie Bear. Be a good girl for Anabelle. She'll take care of you and bring you back tomorrow."

"I wanna stay here with you."

Anabelle didn't have the energy to deal with a stubborn child, but she did have a thought. "Do you like dolls, Lucy?"

She nodded, her lower lip protruding.

Anabelle smiled and pretended enthusiasm. "My daughter has some dolls and toys you can play with. And I have a very special bedroom you can sleep in."

"Okay." Lucy released a deep sigh and scooted closer to Anabelle, allowing herself to be lifted off the bed. Before setting her on the floor, Anabelle hugged the girl and gave George a victory smile.

"Thank you, Anabelle," he said. "I can't tell you how much I appreciate your help."

Anabelle lowered Lucy to the floor and sobered when she realized she'd been talking with and even helping George Talbot. *This is not happening.* Anabelle struggled to regain her composure. "You're welcome."

Taking Lucy's hand, Anabelle stopped at her office for her bag, said good-bye to the nurses she spotted on the way out and made a beeline for the ER.

"Are we looking for my daddy again?" Lucy asked.

While searching for Bill Preston was not on her immediate agenda, Anabelle nodded. "I need to stop and see someone else too."

Anabelle spotted Kirstie sitting behind the desk, handing someone a clipboard with papers to fill out. "Hi," she said when the person left.

"Hi, yourself." Anabelle introduced Lucy to her daughter. "You must be exhausted. I hate to ask, but Lucy will be staying overnight in your room, and I was wondering if you could come by later and introduce her to your dolls and such."

"Sure. I'll be going home at around four. I'll get cleaned up and come over. You'll have to feed me though."

"You're on."

Anabelle had one more stop to make before going home. She and Lucy stopped at the cafeteria to see how the Parade of Patients was going. She was surprised to see Pricilla Nordberg, her quilting friend, with her husband and six children. Her husband Gary sat next to Drew, both involved in an animated conversation.

"Anabelle." Pricilla came toward her, with baby Olivia perched on her arm. "We heard about what you all are doing for Dr. Hamilton and had to come."

"That's so nice of you. Were you one of his patients?"

"Not me, but Gary was. Fifteen years ago, he was in an accident at work. He credits Dr. Hamilton with saving his life. I do too." She blinked back tears. "Gary's reminding him about the months of recuperation he had to go through. And what Dr. Hamilton told him."

"And what was that?" Anabelle smiled at the thought of Drew getting a taste of his own advice.

"Just that there are some things you can't rush. If you try to come back from an injury too fast, it may set you back even further. Gary used to be a very impatient man. He realized that in his rush to impress and get things done, he almost lost his life." Her gaze lingered on her husband.

Gary stood and shook Drew's hand. "I learned a lot while I was recuperating, doc. One of the most important lessons was that life isn't a race where you run as fast as you can to the finish line. It's meant to be savored, moment by moment."

"You make a good point, my friend."

"Anyway, I didn't come by to lecture you. We just wanted to thank you for giving me back my life. Without you we'd have six less kids to be thankful for."

Drew chuckled. "Glad I could help."

Gary gathered his children together and greeted Anabelle with a hug. "Thanks for giving us the opportunity to thank him."

"You're welcome. Thank you for coming."

Anabelle sat in the chair Gary had vacated. "We have more people signed up for tomorrow, you know."

He smiled. "Ever hear the line 'too much of a good thing'?"

Anabelle frowned. "Is this really too much for you?" The last thing she wanted was to cause him stress or tire him out.

"I'm so overcome. I'm just one man who was doing his job. I can't even begin to process everything I've been hearing."

"I hope you realize how much you—and your health—mean to this community." Anabelle looked around. "Where's Genna?"

"Went to get some coffee. She should be back in a few minutes."

Anabelle checked Genna's schedule. Twenty-five patients had come in this afternoon, with no one else scheduled for the day. She scribbled out a note to Genna and grasped the handles of the wheelchair. "Let's get you upstairs so you can take a nap."

"Do grown-ups have to take naps too?" Lucy laid her hand on the armrest.

Drew grinned at her. "If they're smart, they do."

CHASING THE WIND • 231

When they reached the car, Anabelle buckled Lucy in, all the while trying to sort through her conflicting thoughts. She was happy that Lucy had found her grandfather but irritated that said grandfather was George Talbot. She'd been more than willing to help Lucy find her father, but to help George find his son-in-law? She had to smile at the irony.

Anabelle had no doubt that God had somehow orchestrated this bizarre turn of events. She should not be carrying around anger toward the man regardless of what he had done. Was this God's way of saying it was time to give up her resentment?

Once she'd buckled herself in, Anabelle reached back and patted Lucy's leg. "Thank you for coming home with me. I know it's hard to have Daddy gone, but it was good to find Grandpa, right?"

She shrugged and looked out the window. "I just want my daddy."

"We'll find him. I promise." Anabelle nearly choked on the words. She just hoped it was a promise she could keep.

On the way home, Anabelle headed over to Walmart just outside of town to pick up some clothes for Lucy. She had extra personal items at home—like toothbrushes, a clean hairbrush and that sort of thing—but Lucy would need at least one change of clothes.

Once home, the hope Anabelle had for a nap fizzled when she saw what the storm had done to her home. Cameron had boarded up the broken windows and picked up the glass, but her quilting haven was a mess. Broken glass had left shards all over her fabrics. Some of the fabric was damp. Puddles of water indicated where the hailstones had come in and melted.

Fortunately Kirstie showed up about that time to care for Lucy and introduce her to her dolls and the rest of her menagerie. Lucy immediately went into play mode.

Anabelle sorted through all the soggy and damp fabrics and started a load in the washer. She vacuumed up the glass and, by 6:30 PM, was more than ready for the pizza Kirstie had ordered in.

Dinner proved entertaining as Lucy shared bits and pieces of her life. Kirstie had Lucy giggling and acting silly. Normal.

Thus far, Kirstie hadn't told them what she wanted to talk about, so Anabelle initiated the topic. "At the hospital, you said you wanted to talk."

"Right." Kirstie set the pizza slice she'd been holding on her plate. "I need some advice."

Anabelle raised her eyebrows in surprise.

Cameron chuckled. "Wonders never cease."

"C'mon, I'm not too prideful to ask for help when I need it."

Anabelle wanted her to get to the point. "So what kind of advice are you looking for?"

Kirstie sighed. "I'd like to know what you think of Mark."

Anabelle glanced at Cameron. "We really don't know him. He seems very nice, though."

Kirstie chewed on her lower lip. "I'm just not sure I'm ready for marriage."

Anabelle tossed Cameron another look. He just smiled. "Has Mark asked you?"

"No." Kirstie laughed. "But I think he'd like to."

Anabelle relaxed. "Talk to him, Kirstie. Tell him honestly how you feel. That you want to keep seeing him, but say you want to take things more slowly."

Kirstie seemed to consider this as she picked up her slice of pizza again and curled a string of cheese around the end.

Cameron looked at her for a long time. "You know there's not a man in the world good enough for my little girl. But Mark might be worth hanging on to. Seems like a good man."

Kirstie smiled. "I'm thinking if it's meant to be, he'll be willing to hang in there with me."

Anabelle nodded. "Wise decision."

Kirstie decided to stay overnight, thinking that Lucy could use a slumber party. Anabelle felt a certain joy in watching her daughter that evening. She had grown up, yes, but in a perfectly wonderful way. Maybe Kirstie's independence was a good thing.

Chapter Twenty-Two

UNDAY MORNING, CAMERON, ANABELLE, KIRSTIE and Lucy enjoyed a breakfast of cinnamon rolls, scrambled eggs and bacon before going to church. The nursing supervisor had managed to bring in enough staff to cover the shifts so Anabelle didn't have to go in.

Even so, the afternoon before, she had made follow-up calls to every agency she could think of, trying to locate Lucy's dad. She'd make more calls Monday. For the time being, Lucy seemed content being a temporary member of the Scott family.

From her closet, Anabelle chose a pair of ecru slacks and a V-neck blouse in a floral print.

"You're looking good this morning." Cameron came up behind her and nuzzled her neck.

She sighed and turned in his arms, resting her forehead on his shoulder. "Thank you."

"Tired?"

"Exhausted." Anabelle smiled as she reached up to adjust his tie. Call them old-fashioned, but the two of them had always dressed nicely for church. It seemed the right thing to do. "But I imagine you are as well."

"True enough." He chuckled. "Good thing we can at least take a bit of the morning to rest."

Anabelle agreed and hoped she wouldn't fall asleep during the sermon. She needn't have worried. Anabelle couldn't remember seeing so many people at the service since Easter.

The Church of the Good Shepherd had sustained its share of damage from the storm, but the work teams had quickly covered broken windows and patched the roof. Fortunately, the stained-glass windows, probably because they were recessed and faced away from the wind, hadn't sustained any damage.

Anabelle wasn't surprised that the church had escaped serious damage. It was one of the older churches in town, built in the late 1800s. A large stone building, it had a sharply slanted roof with a cross above the front entrance, that shone as a sign of hope at night.

Anabelle took a seat with Kirstie and Lucy while Cameron saw to his duties as an usher. A few minutes later, Ainslee and Doug arrived. As usual, the family took up most of a side pew. Their pew—or the one they'd sat in faithfully for as long as Anabelle could remember. Having been raised in the church, they were as much an institution as the church itself. Anabelle grinned. Come April there would be one more Scott—well Giffen—occupying a space there.

Anabelle greeted friends and listened as they shared horror stories about the storm. She suspected their Community Services

Committee had already initiated plans to provide help to victims of the storm. Anabelle loved being part of a church that played an active part in the community.

At 9:55 AM their seventy-eight-year-old organist sidled up to the organ and brought it to life with a series of hymns. Evan and Cameron soon joined her and the congregation rose to sing "How Great Thou Art."

Words blurred on the page as Anabelle considered God's saving grace. She thought about how much worse the storm could have been and how God had brought them through. Cameron slipped his hand into hers and gave it a squeeze.

When the service ended, Anabelle walked out with her children.

"Mother," Ainslee slipped her slender arm through the crook in Anabelle's arm. "Can I come over and sew today? I found the sweetest crib set in one of your quilting magazines and thought you might help me get started."

Mind? She was delighted. "Absolutely! You can look through my stash, but if you want something else, we can make a trip into Princeton to the big fabric store there."

Ainslee laughed. "Mother, you never cease to amaze me."

"Why's that?" Anabelle asked.

"All I have to do is mention sewing and you're like a kid in a candy factory."

"Lucy, would you like to join us?" She glanced down, remembering the little girl in their care.

"Are we going to get candy?" Lucy asked.

"We might," Kirstie chuckled and hunkered down to Lucy's level. "Would you like to go shopping with us?"

Her smile turned into a pout. "But I want to look for my dad too."

"Good idea." Anabelle smoothed her soft blonde hair. "We can all go. I'll check with the police in Princeton." She glanced at her watch. "First though, we should stop by the hospital to see how our doctor is surviving today's Parade of Patients."

"And see my gramdpa," Lucy added.

Anabelle nodded. "You bet."

At the hospital, their first stop was George Talbot's room. "We can't stay long, Lucy," Anabelle said. "He needs to rest so his heart can get better."

Lucy seemed to understand and after kissing his cheek, pulled on Anabelle's hand. "We need to let him sleep now."

Drew sat in the lobby area of the CCU. She had called Genna the day before saying she'd like him to be closer to the unit. Anabelle wanted to make certain the patients coming in to thank him didn't wear him out as they had the day before. She'd asked her CCU nurses to check on him frequently, and she'd left instructions with Genna to take him back to the unit if he exhibited any telling symptoms.

Genna took Anabelle aside. "I know it's a lot, but I really think seeing all these former patients is giving him a new outlook."

Kirstie, with Lucy in tow, reminded him again of how much he was needed.

"How many people are coming in today?" Anabelle asked.

"Thirty; a number of people canceled for yesterday because of the storm." Genna looked in Drew's direction. "He looks better, don't you think?"

Seeing the smile on his face and the color in his cheeks assured Anabelle that he was indeed looking better. He seemed to have adapted to the attention and looked to be enjoying it now.

He caught Anabelle's eye and winked. "You ladies are going to kill me with kindness."

"We'll stop when you're ready to cry uncle."

"I get the message, Anabelle. But I have to admit, I like seeing all my past and present patients."

"I'm glad." Anabelle patted his shoulder. "We should be going. We're driving into Princeton to do some serious shopping this afternoon."

Kirstie kissed his cheek. "Looking good, Dr. Hamilton."

The rest of their afternoon was anything but restful. Anabelle put a large roast in her slow cooker, seasoned it and set the temperature on low. They would all meet back at the house for Sunday dinner at four.

The girls piled into Anabelle's car, while the men headed out into disasterdom to hunt for folks in distress. When they reached Princeton, Kirstie offered to take Lucy for ice cream and to the police station, while Anabelle and Ainslee spent over an hour picking out fabric for various baby patterns they wanted to make up. Ainslee found the perfect selection of soft and cuddly fabrics in blue, pink, green, chocolate and cream that would work for a boy or a girl. Anabelle couldn't resist the softer-than-soft fleece and bought several yards for a layette.

Kirstie and Lucy came back to the store with good and bad news. They had eaten a hot-fudge sundae, but the police still had no leads on Bill Preston.

Once home, Kirstie took Lucy out to see the kittens and play on the old tire swing. Anabelle helped Ainslee clean off a space to do her cutting, then finished cleaning her studio. The crib-set pattern was adorable, and the fabric perfect for the baby. Their baby. Anabelle couldn't keep the smile off her face.

On Sunday evening, as Anabelle climbed into bed, she was still smiling, and not just about the baby. It had been a perfect day—like old times. Her family had all been together, plus Lucy. Anabelle prayed again that they would find Lucy's dad. It had been forty-eight hours since the storm. "You'd think someone would know what happened to him," Anabelle said aloud.

"I assume you're talking about Bill Preston." Cameron had just come out of the shower and must have overheard her mumbling to herself.

"*Hmm.* I am." She adjusted her covers and yawned.

"It's still quite a mess out there. The police are having a rough time sorting things out. I spoke with Cesar this afternoon—told him about the girl's dad. He'll keep an eye out as well."

"Thank you." Anabelle smiled at him as he bent down to kiss her. "I'm praying we'll find him soon. Her grandfather is in no shape to take care of her. Apparently there is no other family."

"Except us." Cameron winked at her. "I see no reason we can't keep her with us until her grandfather can work something out—or we find her father."

"Somehow I knew you'd say that." Anabelle closed her eyes as Cameron climbed into bed beside her and turned off the light. After releasing a deep breath and reminding herself that the Lord would work all things out in the best way possible, Anabelle slept.

Chapter Twenty-Three

ON MONDAY, GENNA, ANABELLE, JAMES, CANDACE AND Elena managed to eat lunch together. The sun had come out and dried up much of the moisture. Many of the flowers and shrubs that had made the courtyard a nice retreat had been crushed, but spring would no doubt bring them back. Several amber, gold and red leaves adorned the paperbark maple, letting them know beyond a doubt that summer was fading fast.

Candace glanced at Anabelle. "I see you don't have Lucy with you. Did you find her father?"

"Unfortunately, no. She's with Kirstie today. My daughter plans to do some serious detective work in hopes of finding Lucy's dad."

"You took her home with you?" James seemed surprised. Legs stretched out in front of him and crossed at the ankles, he took a drink of his coffee.

Anabelle nodded and smiled. "With permission from Children's Services, of course. Believe it or not we have a number of lost children *and* adults, and they welcomed my help."

James nodded. "I suspect it will take a few days to work through the chaos."

"At least." Candace examined her tuna fish sandwich before taking a bite.

"We'll keep praying for Lucy and her dad," James added. "And for everyone who's missing."

Elena nodded. "We have a John Doe in ICU. Very badly injured. The police took prints, but he's apparently not in the system. We'll have to wait until someone is able to identify him or he wakes up."

"How old is he?" Anabelle knew she might be grasping at straws, but her intuition—or was it wishful thinking?—had zeroed in on a load of something.

"We don't have an age listed, but I think he must be around midthirties, early forties."

"That could be about right for Lucy's dad." Why hadn't she asked George to tell her more about his son? *Because you were too caught up in the shock of George's being Lucy's grandfather.* "I hate to ask," Anabelle said, "but what's his prognosis?"

"It's touch and go." Elena's deep brown eyes reflected her sadness.

Anabelle promised herself she'd look into any details available regarding Elena's mystery patient after lunch.

"You wanted to meet with us, Genna?" Candace's question pulled Anabelle back into their original reason for meeting. "Did we need more patients to visit Dr. Hamilton?"

"Mercy no!" Genna smiled, her joy palpable. "I just wanted to touch base with my team. I thought our Parade of Patients went extremely well yesterday, even better than Saturday. I could be reading him wrong, but I believe Drew has turned a corner."

"He seemed genuinely happy to see them all." Anabelle lifted her cup to her lips. "And I must admit, he hasn't complained about staying in the hospital these extra days."

"How many patients have come through?" Elena wanted to know.

"Fifty-five so far." Genna clasped her hands. "I have another twenty-five set up for this afternoon."

"I only hope he takes all this to heart," James said.

"He will. He has to." Genna glanced at her watch and stood. "I have to get upstairs. I want to be there to greet the girls from the Quilting Guild. They're presenting Drew with a get-well quilt."

"I can't wait to see it." Anabelle knew about the quilt but hadn't been able to participate in putting it together. They all said good-bye to Genna, and she left the courtyard.

"On another note," Candace said. "You'll be happy to know that I called the counselor this morning and set up another appointment. This time it's for Thursday afternoon."

James chuckled. "Let's hope the weather behaves itself this time."

Candace shook her head. "If another storm causes us to cancel this one, I'll take it as a sign that I'm not supposed to go."

"You will not," Anabelle exclaimed.

Candace laughed at her bluntness. "Yes, Mother."

"So, James," Elena began, "did you and Fern have a chance to talk about Gideon?"

"Not yet. Gideon hasn't asked again, but I'm sure he will."

"You must really be proud of him." Elena picked a corn chip out of the small bag that came with her sandwich. "I couldn't believe how helpful he was after the storm."

James nodded. "He has totally amazed me through all of this. If Fern is okay with it, I think I'll give him a green light."

"That sounds like a good idea, James."

His gaze turned to Elena as he asked about Sarah.

Elena sighed. "Well, I decided you were right. I needed to see her. I went in to see her yesterday, but she'd been discharged." She paused. "To be honest, I'm relieved."

"So that's it?" Candace set her half-eaten sandwich down. "Aren't you going to look for her?"

"No, I don't think so. If she's serious about wanting to reconcile, she'd have come." Elena looked around at each of them. "What? God has softened my heart toward her. But I'm not going to seek her out." Elena lowered her head. "Maybe I am wrong, but that's where I stand right now."

Anabelle reached over and squeezed her hand. "We don't blame you, Elena. We're glad you at least tried to visit her again."

Anabelle told them about her attitude toward George Talbot and discovering that Lucy belonged to him. "I felt myself softening toward him and his family. Seeing Lucy on his bed and hearing him call her Bookie Bear cut right through my resentment. Now, because of Lucy, I feel a bond with him in a way. Amazing how God works, isn't it?"

They all agreed.

James stood and picked up his tray. "Speaking of work, I'd better get back to my unit."

"Me too. I still have some details to attend to regarding Isabel's party. Now that the storm is over and we're getting back to normal, I am getting all excited about it. Don't forget—you are all invited." Elena waved her arm. "I asked Dr. Hamilton and Genna to come as well. They'll be bringing their granddaughter."

Promising Elena they would all be there, they climbed the stairs to the second floor together. James headed toward Med/Surg, Candace to the Birthing Unit and Anabelle walked with Elena into ICU. "I'd like to have a look at your John Doe."

Elena nodded. "Room 200."

Anabelle watched Elena duck into the restroom, then stepped into the room. A strange sensation washed over her as she stood at his bedside. She felt strongly that God wanted her to pray for him. *Lord, I'm not sure what to say, but You know what this man needs. Please let the authorities identify him and, Lord, please heal him.*

Anabelle took hold of his hand. "Bill?" Had she felt a slight squeeze of his hand, or was it her own wishful thinking?

She tried again. "Bill, I have Lucy with me. She's safe."

He squeezed her hand again. Did that mean he heard and understood, or was it just the pressure of her hand on his? Elena said he was in an induced coma which would keep him sedated and give him a chance to heal. At this point, she wouldn't let herself believe that this man was Bill Preston, but she could hope.

Back in CCU, Anabelle headed for George's room. After reading his chart, Anabelle went to check on him and found Kirstie and Lucy snuggled in the recliner together.

Lucy was asleep so Kirstie eased out of the chair, hooked her arm through Anabelle's and tugged. "I have something to tell you. First though, thanks for telling me about Mr. Talbot last night."

"I wanted you to be prepared when you brought Lucy in today." Anabelle stepped clear of the door to allow one of the nurses to enter.

Kirstie nodded. A grin lit up her blue eyes. "I think we might be close to finding Lucy's dad."

"Really?" Anabelle didn't tell her about the man in ICU since she had only her feelings to go on.

"I talked to the police. They have Bill's wallet—and some papers they found in his car. With all the craziness going on that night, they lost track of him. The keys James found were from his car. I told them about the teddy bear Seri found in the ambulance and they made the connection."

"That's great. So is he here?"

"They think so, but they're still trying to piece things together. Someone was supposed to follow and bring Lucy's and Bill's personal items. All we know is that Bill was brought here. The new medics told a nurse in ER that his personal effects would be arriving soon." Kirstie shook her head. "But she never saw them."

"Sounds like a massive case of miscommunication. Without ID he'd be classified as a John Doe." Anabelle sighed. "If they think he's here, I may have found him. It's pure speculation and a little intuition, but I think Bill might be in ICU. Unfortunately, we really can't take Lucy in to see him."

"What should we do?" Kirstie glanced back into the room. "Her grandfather can't go see him."

"Not until we're able to get him up and around." Anabelle paused. "There's no way of really knowing for another day or two at least."

Kirstie went back in to sit with Lucy, while Anabelle returned to work. At two, Elena showed up. "Do you have time for a break?"

"Sure." Anabelle was more than ready. Afternoon drowsiness had her desperate for a cup of coffee.

A somber countenance told Anabelle things were not going well in ICU. "You seem down. What's wrong?"

"I have some good news and some bad news. Our John Doe has had a setback."

"Oh no." Anabelle settled an arm around her friend's shoulder. How was she going to tell Lucy? "You said you had some good news?"

Elena nodded. "He's not Lucy's father."

"Oh. That's good for Lucy, but how do you know?" The two of them entered the cafeteria.

"Let's get our food and sit down. It's another crazy story."

Once they were seated, Elena explained that the police had brought in a woman from Peoria whose husband had gone on a business trip and hadn't contacted her for several days. "His wife hadn't known that he'd been caught in the hail. His car was found off the road about a mile from Deerford. He wasn't in it but his ID was. He was found after the storm in a ditch and they didn't connect him to the car until the police notified her that they'd found the car. They brought her in to identify him. He is her husband."

"I'm so sorry for her. I guess we're back to square one for Lucy's dad. But we'll have to keep praying."

Kirstie was still in the room with Lucy and George when Anabelle came back. She stepped out of the room when Anabelle beckoned her and told her about Elena's patient. "Turns out that he isn't Bill Preston after all."

"I'm glad they were able to ID him though. I'm sure the police will put the pieces together sooner or later."

Kirstie reached for her cell phone when it vibrated. "It's the detective I've been talking to. I'll take it out in the lobby."

Several minutes later she came back looking thoughtful. "Detective Taylor says they have a guy down at the station they think might be Bill. They found him wandering around on the streets confused and injured."

Anabelle hugged her. "I hope we have the right guy this time."

"Me too. I'll find out and call you." Kirstie stepped back. "I'll get Lucy and head right over."

"Don't get her hopes up."

"Don't worry, I won't." Kirstie stepped into the room and told Lucy they were going out for lunch.

Kirstie called forty-five minutes later. Lucy recognized her father immediately. "He doesn't remember anything about the accident and is being transported to the hospital for evaluation."

Anabelle felt a huge burden slide from her shoulders. "Thanks for telling me."

Anabelle finished up with report, then made her way to George Talbot's room eager to tell him the good news.

Chapter Twenty-Four

OVER THE NEXT SEVERAL WEEKS, THE NURSES, Hope Haven and their little town of Deerford continued the healing process from the storm. Everyone had been accounted for as people reconnected with their families and settled into normal routines.

School had started, and fall had definitely settled in.

Anabelle had made it a point to visit several of her past patients who'd gone home around the time of the storm, including Olga Pederson and her daughter, Carla. She was surprised to see that Olga's home had already been repaired and a Realtor's sign had a sale-pending notice on it.

While the three women enjoyed tea in Olga's rose garden, Anabelle asked if they still felt good about their decision.

"Oh ya, I've never seen the powers-that-be move so fast." She chuckled. "I think God must've been pushing things along. Makes me feel like moving is the right thing to do."

"I know it's right," Carla added. "The kids are thrilled. They think Grandma is going to make them cookies every day."

Olga grinned as she snatched one of her own delicious oatmeal cookies from the plate. "They might be right."

Anabelle stayed for over an hour, getting a tour of the house and enjoying Olga and Carla's company. Before leaving, she jotted down Carla's address and phone number so they could stay in touch.

On the last sunny Saturday in September, the four friends and their families gathered at Elena and Cesar's home. This time, their only task was having fun and enjoying Isabel's fifth birthday party.

Anabelle offered up thanks for all the wonderful fall colors filling Elena's backyard. The colors were enhanced by Elena's beautiful Mexican theme and the beaming birthday girl who wore a lopsided tiara pinned to her hair. Doug and Cameron had done a beautiful job landscaping the yard.

Anabelle leaned back in the lounge chair on the patio and closed her eyes against the bright sun. She listened to the sweet sounds of children as they played together: Isabel, Howie, Brooke, Lucy, Drew and Genna's granddaughter Emma along with four of Isabel's friends from day care. Kirstie had come along to help supervise the kids and had recruited Candace's daughter Brooke to help. Anabelle still had a hard time believing that George Talbot's granddaughter had become so precious to her family.

God had certainly changed her attitude toward George. Though she would never forget what had happened to her Kirstie, she could honestly say she had forgiven him.

The delicious smells emanating from the barbeque grills on the deck tickled her nostrils and even made her stomach growl.

Cameron and Cesar manned the grills while Rafael brought out the food.

Elena lowered herself on the chair next to Anabelle. "Are you feeling all right?"

Anabelle turned toward her and shielded her eyes with her hand. "I'm better than all right." She smiled. "I was just thinking about all we've experienced these past few weeks."

Elena chuckled. "I am trying to forget."

"No, seriously. Deerford suffered a terrible disaster and the community pulled together. I'm amazed at what we've accomplished."

"You're right about that." Elena looked around. "Thanks to Cameron and his crews, we have windows and a new roof already. His idea to get the men from our churches together to help one another has worked brilliantly."

Anabelle sat up straighter. "It's like those old-fashioned barn raisings. They have done dozens of homes and businesses in the last few days. And working in teams helps them go more rapidly."

"Speaking of work," Elena said, "did you get your letter in the mail from Varner?"

"I did." Varner had sent them all letters of commendation for their outstanding service during the disaster.

James joined them and snagged a chair next to Anabelle. "Have I missed anything important?"

"We were just talking about Varner and being grateful." Anabelle smiled.

"I sure am grateful. The storm was a terrible thing; but for us, I think God is already working it for good. I've been talking to some contractors and with Cameron. With volunteers doing most of the work and using the insurance money to pay for supplies, it looks like we'll be able to do the remodeling on the house."

"That's wonderful, James," Elena said. "Fern must be ecstatic."

He put a finger to his lips. "She doesn't know about it yet. I don't want to tell her until it's all settled."

Elena glanced around. "Speaking of Fern, where is she?"

"She and her sister and mom were going to a women's retreat at the abbey." He grinned. "Us guys are hanging out and working around the house."

"That reminds me." Anabelle picked up her glass of lemonade from the small mosaic table. "What's happening with Gideon?"

James shook his head and laughed. "Fern and I agreed that we would leave the decision up to Gideon. He surprised us both. He thinks God might be calling him to be a pastor or maybe a chaplain. I think he's still opting for the military to pay for his college, but he's keeping his options open."

"Good for him." Anabelle was pleased for James.

The patio door opened and Genna and Drew stepped through.

"Hey." Anabelle waved. "I wondered when you were going to join the gang."

"We were inside talking to Rafael."

"Come, sit." Elena bustled over to them. "Can I get you something to drink? We have coffee, iced tea and punch."

They gave their orders and settled into the deck chairs.

Drew looked rested and healthy. Anabelle had received a card from him a couple days ago thanking her for her part in the

Parade of Patients. He'd said that, seeing how much people care about him and how much his health meant to them, he'd decided to stay home and enjoy it. "I understand Emma has been keeping you on the straight and narrow."

Drew nodded. "I think she inherited her bossiness from her grandma. She's been teaching me how to play games and put puzzles together." He winked. "Mostly, she's teaching me to enjoy my family."

"I'm so glad." Elena said as she returned with drinks. She looked around her own home. "We all need to be reminded of that from time to time."

Anabelle met her old friend's gaze. "Maybe our good doctor has finally learned that holding on to life as it was, or as we wish it to be, is as futile as chasing the wind."

"Well said, Anabelle." Drew reached over to take Genna's hand. "Well said."

About the Author

Patricia H. Rushford has written numerous articles and authored more than forty-eight books, including *What Kids Need Most in a Mom, Have You Hugged Your Teenager Today?* and *It Shouldn't Hurt to Be a Kid.* She also has written a number of mystery series: Helen Bradley Mysteries, Angel Delaney Mysteries, McAllister Files and Jennie McGrady Mysteries. Patricia's latest releases include The Max & Me Mysteries for children and Mystery and the Minister's Wife: *Strangers in Their Midst* published by Guideposts Books. One of her mysteries, *Silent Witness*, was nominated for an Edgar by Mystery Writers of America and won the Silver Angel for excellence in media. Patricia has a nursing degree and holds a master's degree in counseling. In addition, she conducts writers workshops for adults and children, has appeared on numerous radio and TV talk shows, and directs the Oregon Christian Writers Conference. Visit her at www.patriciarushford.com.

Read on for a sneak peek of the next exciting and
heartfelt book in *Stories from Hope Haven*.

It's available through Guideposts' direct mail program
by calling Customer Service at (800) 932–2145.

Hope FOR *Tomorrow*
by
Patti Berg

*M*ONDAY MORNING'S DEEP PURPLE CLOUDS
were skittering away by the time 6:00 AM
rolled around, leaving behind a sky tinged with
pink and orange as the first hint of sunlight peeked over the top
of Hope Haven Hospital.

What a glorious October morning.

In spite of the chill, Elena Rodriguez leaned against her forest
green Jeep Liberty, and as she did at the beginning of most every
workday, inhaled the clean fresh air.

"Father, be with me as I care for my patients today," she
whispered. A wisp of wind fluttered across her face and for
one moment wrapped her in its oddly warm embrace before
scurrying back to the maples, where it began to shake amber and
crimson leaves from their branches.

Smiling, Elena offered a quick but heartfelt *amen* and hitched up the tote bag carrying the lunch and snacks her husband Cesar had packed for her, along with a notebook full of ideas, contracts, proposals and cost estimates for the Bread of Life Harvest Festival, a charity event she was coordinating for her church and two others. Instead of heading for the staff entrance, she meandered through the hospital grounds toward the front of the hospital. It was far too beautiful a morning to shut out the outside world just yet.

The floribunda roses lining the walkway no longer bloomed with yellow, pink and scarlet blossoms. After sixteen years at Hope Haven, though, where she'd started working at the age of thirty, their sweet scent was fixed in her mind. The green grass was rapidly turning the color of wheat, storing all its energy for winter and the snow that would come all too soon—but hopefully after the Harvest Festival.

A month from now, the day after Thanksgiving, members of the hospital staff would hang twinkling lights in the trees and get ready for the live Nativity. Elena was more than ready. The holiday season was her favorite time of year.

The dried leaves crunching under Elena's baby blue clogs reminded her that she needed to head to Cavendish House one day soon to gather the biggest and best leaves for harvest decorations.

Cesar would laugh, of course. "I've been raking leaves around the house for weeks now. Couldn't you have picked some of ours?"

As she neared the front of the hospital, she was mentally compiling a few things to add to her to-do list besides gathering leaves—recruit two people willing to decorate kids' faces for free, design a maze to be built out of hay, finagle free hay from Jim Ireland—when she heard raised, angry voices coming from near the hospital's main entrance.

She heard Albert Varner's familiar baritone voice drifting toward her, and she stopped dead in her tracks to listen.

She'd recognize his voice anywhere. The chief executive officer of Hope Haven had a friendly smile and encouraging words for everyone on the staff. He also sang in the choir at Elena's church. But she'd never heard or seen him annoyed, let alone furious, until this moment; nor had she ever seen him storm across the hospital grounds, looking as if he could punch a fist through the glass doors if they hadn't slid open a moment before he disappeared inside the hospital.

Maybe this wasn't going to be such a glorious morning after all.

A moment later, Hope Haven's wealthiest, surliest board member, Frederick Innisk—whom Elena had nicknamed Scrooge—stepped into view, his face red with rage, as he fiddled with the knot in his tie and smoothed his hands through his thick silver hair. He looked around the grounds, as if searching for busybodies who might have overheard his argument with Mr. Varner. When his gaze settled on Elena, she wanted to run.

He was probably gunning for her right this moment, considering the frown she saw on his face when he stopped in front of her. She didn't need to get on his bad side today, not when she already had one big strike against her—the fact that her idea for the Wall of Hope fund-raiser was going forward despite his protestations.

A gust of wind whipped Elena's long, dark brown hair into her face, and the much-dreaded Frederick Innisk probably couldn't see the smile she offered him. Unfortunately, she could easily see his downright churlish glare.

"Be nice," she told herself.

"Good morning, Mr. Innisk. It's a beautiful day, isn't it?"

"Too windy for my liking." He looked at his watch and frowned. "Shouldn't you be at work by now? As far as I know, we don't pay you to lollygag or to stand outside listening to private conversations."

Elena hadn't been late a day in her life, and if Innisk and Varner hadn't been yelling, she wouldn't have stopped. She wasn't one to argue, but the mere fact that he was one of the hospital's board members didn't give him the right to be an uncivilized boor.

"Actually, Mr. Innisk, my shift doesn't start for another hour. Now, if you'll excuse me," she said, skirting around him, "I have a meeting to get to."

Elena pulled her scarf up close to her face to fight off the wind and Scrooge's scowl. She rushed off, feeling the heat of Mr. Innisk's glare on her back until she disappeared through the hospital's sliding doors.

"Dear Lord," she whispered, "please let that be the last encounter I have with Frederick Innisk for a good long time. Amen."

She hung a right into the administrative area, just in time to see Mr. Varner shove through his office door and slam it behind him.

What on earth was going on?

It seemed odd that the chief executive officer and one of the board members would be at the hospital at the crack of dawn, arguing and slamming doors. Unless . . .

Elena frowned. The hospital had suffered through financial woes a few months ago. Was it in dire straits again?

Elena had far too much on her plate to worry about what was going on behind the hospital's closed doors, but she had to think about her job, her future.

All the upheaval would gnaw at her nerves until she learned the truth.

Hopefully she could get to the bottom of it during her meeting with Quintessa Smith about the Harvest Festival. Quintessa was serving as the festival's financial coordinator, and—most importantly at this moment—worked as the executive assistant to the chief financial officer, Zane McGarry. She was privy to just about everything that went on behind the hospital's closed doors. Quintessa was the height of decorum and confidentiality, but if Elena worked the argument between Innisk and Varner into their conversation about donations and sponsors, Quintessa might let something slip.

Quintessa was on the phone, seated behind an antique mahogany desk, the top neat as a pin, with one corner, plus the credenza behind her, devoted to photographs of her twin brother, Dillan—a technician in Hope Haven's lab—her mom and dad, plus a host of nieces and nephews.

"I'll be another few minutes," Quintessa whispered to Elena, her hand over the phone's mouthpiece.

"No hurry," Elena whispered back, wondering if she'd hear more slamming doors or more raised voices coming from Mr. Varner's nearby office while she waited.

Elena dropped her coat, scarf and tote on one of the guest chairs, taking a load off. . . and listened, but it was only Quintessa's voice she heard.

"Let me put it this way, Mr. Welsh," Quintessa said, speaking succinctly into the phone. "If you look closely at the proposal, it's up to you to come up with a viable way to . . ."

The conversation was all Greek to Elena. Her mind wandered to her ever-growing to-do list: taking her granddaughter Isabel out for a girls' lunch, and to the zoo or the art center, as well as what she planned to fix for dinner that night.

Elena stiffened when she heard an angry voice reverberate through the wall, nearly drowning out Quintessa's conversation. There was definitely a battle going on next door.

Elena leaned against the wall, hoping she could pick out a few phrases from the conversation, but it was all rather garbled and all she could do was guess.

Had the directors finally decided to vote Mr. Innisk off the board?

Was Varner being fired?

Could there be a huge malpractice suit on the horizon?

If only she could hear more.

"It can't be helped. You know that better than anyone," board president Bernard Telford's familiar voice filtered through the wall.

What can't be helped? Elena frantically wondered.

Another door slammed.

And then, unfortunately, Quintessa hung up the phone. "Sorry to keep you waiting so long."

If only she'd been a little longer, Elena might have heard more from next door. Even though she knew Quintessa wouldn't divulge any secrets, she couldn't help but ask, "What on earth is going on? What's with all the door slamming?"

Quintessa's pretty brown eyes darted to a packet of papers on her desk that she suddenly seemed too interested in. "I haven't heard one slamming door." Quintessa was being much too coy.

And then another door slammed.

Elena's eyes widened. "Don't tell me you didn't hear that?"

Quintessa laughed lightly as if it were no big deal. "If you spent eight hours a day here, five days a week, you'd hear that a lot. It comes with the territory."

Elena wanted to dig deeper, to see if Quintessa would divulge anything, but all this crazy intrigue was pulling her away from her number one priority right now. She was the queen of multi-taskers, but she already had enough on her plate without getting completely caught up in the Hope Haven hornet's nest.

Not right this moment, anyway.

Elena pulled a file folder from her bag. "Here's the list of local businesses and those in the surrounding area that I came up with to contact about possible donations." Elena handed a copy of the list to Quintessa, plus a CD containing an electronic copy of the form.

Quintessa scanned the list quickly. "I know two women who are great at sales and love talking on the phone. I think we can crank out these calls before the end of the week."

"That would be wonderful," Elena said, tucking a wayward strand of her still wind-blown hair behind her ear. "I have a meeting with the pastors from Holy Trinity, Good Shepherd and Riverview Chapel in a couple of days. They might feel a little more reassured that the festival is going to go off without a hitch once I tell them you're handling the donations."

As Albert Varner's shouting reverberated through the wall, Elena tensed, her breath catching in her throat.

"I'm out of here. Find someone else to do your dirty work." Another door slammed in Varner's office.

Quintessa turned her head away from Elena, picked up a stack of papers, as if she had something important to get to, but Elena had seen the tears beading up in her eyes. No doubt about it, Quintessa knew exactly what was going on and hated every minute of it.

Elena put a hand on her friend's arm. "I can't possibly ignore that, Quin. You might say it's nothing, but something bad's going on. If it has to do with the hospital's finances, if there's more talk about us closing down, of me losing a job I love, I need to know what's happening." Elena dropped her file folder on Quintessa's desk and headed for the door.

"Don't go out there, Elena," Quintessa called after her. "There might be heads rolling."

"Then they might be in need of a good nurse."

Unfortunately, all Elena saw when she threw open Quintessa's office door and stepped into the hallway was Albert Varner's back as he disappeared into the hospital's main reception area, and when she turned to see if anyone was going after him, she saw the tear-stained face of Mr. Varner's executive assistant,

Penny Risser. She was known as the Dragon, the CEO's faithful, fearless and all too brusque guardian. Tears were something one never saw on Penny's face, confirming that something dreadful had happened.

"Is there anything I can do?" Elena asked.

Penny's slender shoulders drew back. Her long neck stiffened, and Elena was sure that if Penny could breathe fire, she'd do so right this very minute.

"What you can do," Penny stated, "is pretend you didn't hear a thing, that you didn't see a thing. And I strongly suggest that you keep this incident to yourself."

With that, the rather tall, gangly woman with a tight curl in her short hair, stepped back into her office and slammed the door behind her.

Mind her own business? That was impossible.

Hope Haven was Elena's home away from home, and she was like a mother hen when it came to protecting all she loved.

She was going to peck away at this situation until she got to the bottom of it.

A Note from the Editors

Guideposts, a nonprofit organization, touches millions of lives every day through products and services that inspire, encourage and uplift. Our magazines, books, prayer network and outreach programs help people connect their faith-filled values to their daily lives.

Your purchase of *Stories from Hope Haven* does make a difference! To comfort hospitalized children, Guideposts Outreach has created Comfort Kits for free distribution. A hospital can be a very scary place for sick children. With all the hustle and bustle going on around them, the strange surroundings, and the pain they're experiencing, is it any wonder kids need a little relief?

Inside each easy-to-carry Comfort Kit is a prayer card, a journal, a pack of crayons, an "I'm Special" wristband to wear alongside the hospital-issued one and a plush golden star pillow to cuddle. It's a welcome gift and has a powerful effect in helping to soothe a child's fears.

To learn more about our many nonprofit outreach programs, please visit www.guidepostsfoundation.org.

A LITTLE BIT OF
Ireland

DEDICATION
For Mum, with gratitude and love

ACKNOWLEDGEMENT
'He Wishes for the Cloths of Heaven' and
'The Lake Isle of Innisfree' by W. B. Yeats
printed by permission of A. P. Watt & Son, London
on behalf of Michael and Anne Yeats

CONTRIBUTORS
Richard Killeen pp. 18-19, 28-9, 34-5, 38-9, 46-9, 56-7, 66-7
Recipes: Nuala Cullen pp. 30-1, 40-1, 54; Helen Walsh pp. 20-1, 55
Ireland's Patron Saint: acknowledgements to Dr Lesley Whiteside
Dublin & Cork: acknowledgements to Patricia Tunison Preston
Irish Surnames & Shields: acknowledgements to John Grenham

EDITOR
Fleur Robertson

DESIGN
Triggerfish, Brighton

DESIGN MANAGER
Justina Leitão

PHOTOGRAPHY
© The Slide File, Dublin pp. 17, 23, 26-7, 34, 35, 46,
47, 52, 57, 60, 62, 63, 68, 69, 70, 71
© Don Sutton International Photo Library, Dublin pp. 10,
18 top, 24, 25, 32, 33, 36, 37, 39, 42, 48, 58-9, 61, 64-5
© Michael Diggin p. 44-5, 53
© Quadrillion Publishing pp. 9, 12-15, 18 bottom, 19,
20, 21, 22, 28, 31, 41, 43, 49, 50-1, 54-5, 67
Trinity College Library, Dublin 29

PRODUCTION
Karen Staff, Neil Randles, Graeme Proctor

5133 CLB
© 1999 Quadrillion Publishing Ltd

Published in Ireland by
Gill & Macmillan Ltd, Goldenbridge, Dublin 8
with associated companies throughout the world

ISBN 0 7171 2853 9

Printed in Spain

Previous page: Georgian Dublin doors
These pages: Recess, Co. Galway